Alistair Moffat was born and bred in t[h] a former Director of the Edinburgh Fe of Programmes at Scottish Television, a[n] Borders Book Festival. From 2011 to 2014 he was Rector of the University of St Andrews. He is the author of a number of highly acclaimed books, including *Scotland: A History from Earliest Times*, *Britain's DNA Journey*, *To the Island of Tides* and *The Hidden Ways*. *The Night Before Morning* is his first work of fiction, and TV rights were acquired by actor and producer Tom Conti prior to publication.

The Night Before Morning

Alistair Moffat

BIRLINN

First published in 2021 by
Birlinn Limited
West Newington House
10 Newington Road Edinburgh
EH9 1QS

www.birlinn.co.uk

ISBN: 978 1 78027 737 0

British Library Cataloguing-in-Publication Data
A catalogue record for this book is available from the British Library

Typeset by Initial Typesetting Services, Edinburgh

Printed and bound by Clays Ltd Elcograf S.p.A.

In memory of Jennie Erdal,
whose sparkle is sorely missed

PROLOGUE

16 June 1945

Under the canopy of the trees, it was black-dark. Through the full leaf of high summer, no light could pierce the oaks and chestnuts, and the midnight path was a matter of guesswork. The man moved very slowly. Often stopping, holding his breath, listening for the rustle of movement, sometimes stretching out a hand where he thought a tree trunk might stand in his way, he made slow, hesitant progress. And yet, about a hundred yards away, he could see where he wanted to go. High, bright and full, the moon lit the night river, glinting silver off the water. But reaching it was taking much longer than he planned and he could not risk a torch.

Edging closer to the moonlit water, groping through the darkness, his feet, not his eyes, recognised exactly where he was. The last few yards of the track were paved – a memory of its ancient purpose, harking back to the time when many walked upon it, going about their daily business. Red sandstone paving led to the river's edge because once it had been a busy ford, the Monksford. For three lazy, meandering miles the River Tweed flows through sanctity, looping around two ancient monasteries, and in the millennia before bridges, this was the place where monks had forded the great river. Now half forgotten, overgrown and used only by the occasional horse rider, the track suited his purpose perfectly.

Once the man found the wooden kayak he'd hidden earlier

that day, he dragged it to the edge of the river, making as little noise as possible. The moonlight was suddenly brilliant, almost dazzling, dancing off the water's surface as the river turned south towards his destination. Wading into the current, the man expertly steadied the kayak and sat down, rocking it slightly. Paddling quickly across to the far bank and its welcoming darkness, he allowed the current to carry him downstream and to what he hoped would be the solution to a mystery.

What John Grant had sent him was both puzzling and perplexing. At his funeral, few contemporaries gathered because the old man had outlived almost all of them. It was a sparse, quiet atmosphere in the chapel but there was one colourful emblem of the past that conjured a memory of extraordinary valour during one of the bloodiest battles in history. On the coffin lay the old soldier's regimental Glengarry cap. Navy blue with a red toorie bobble, two long black ribbons at the back, and a red, white and black dicing trim, it bore the gleaming badge of the King's Own Scottish Borderers. He had fought bravely at the Battle of the Somme in 1916, leading his men over the top again and again and rescuing two wounded comrades from the desolation of no man's land.

It was the old soldier's granddaughter who had first brought them together. At a talk on local Roman antiquities, the man had noticed her immediately, sitting in the front row: a tall, fair, classic beauty with pale, ice-blue eyes. In repose, her face seemed sad to him, etched with a memory of loss or disappointment. But when she smiled, it changed completely, and warmth flooded back. Afterwards she had made introductions, even though she did not know the man's name. Perhaps it was only politeness with a newcomer, and maybe it was his imagination, but did she do that to discover who he was? At the time he had no idea of the part she played in what was to follow.

After that first meeting, the man had joined the history society and become friendly with John Grant. The tone was mostly formal, reticent about anything remotely personal, conversation usually confined to matters historical. But behind the politeness, there glowed an immediate but unstated warmth and great respect.

A week after the funeral, a well-sealed brown envelope arrived from a firm of local solicitors. A formal letter told the man that their client had wished him to have the enclosed papers. There was a spidery, handwritten letter clipped to a sheet carrying two verses of a poem, a series of maps and a drawing.

I know that the sort of ancient history I enjoy bores you, even though over the months we have been acquainted you have listened attentively and dutifully read my papers on Roman road building and burial practices. Through our conversations, I sense that your real interest is in politics and much more recent events. I share that interest, but while I live, I dare not give voice to my thoughts, not to anyone. The Romans lie at a safe enough distance.

We have been fed an agreed narrative about this last war, its course and its outcome. Not much of it is true, and I think you know that.

But where is the first-hand evidence for a different version of history? Where are the accounts of those who witnessed it? They need to be found and made widely known before we who lived it are all dead and dust gathers over closed chapters.

I think I know where the truth can be found, but not exactly where. For the sake of a better future, will you now try to clear away the lies and discover what really happened in the recent past and how it has indelibly shaped the present?

Much taken aback at such forthright, deeply held views, the man picked up the rest of the package. The note was paper-clipped to a copy of two verses from Sir Walter Scott's poem, 'The Eve of St John'.

O fear not the priest, who sleepeth to the east!
For to Dryburgh the way he has ta'en;
And there to say mass till three days do pass,
For the soul of a knight that is slayne.

The varying light deceived thy sight,
And the wild winds drown'd the name;
For the Dryburgh bells ring, and the
   white monks do sing,
For Sir Richard of Coldinghame!

In the kayak, the man paddled along gently, quietly, keeping to the safety of the shadows of the right bank. It was long past curfew and its strict rules were policed as much by curtain-twitching watchers as by the authorities. And the moon had made the landscape graphic, like a black-and-white film.

He could soon make out stands of tall hardwood trees. They bordered the policies of a grand house, now a large hotel, and beyond that lay the ruins of Dryburgh Abbey. Pulling quickly over to the left bank, the man felt the keel of his kayak scrape the bottom. Carefully, steadying himself with the paddle, he stood up, splashed into the shallows and pulled his boat under the branches of an overhanging tree.

Having scrambled up the bank and back into the darkness of the shadows under the trees, he came to a drystane dyke and stood on the edge of the abbey precinct, what had come to seem like a giant board game, a landscape of snakes and ladders.

It was clear from the Walter Scott verses and the attached maps and drawings that the old soldier had been looking for a hiding place of some kind. Quite what it might conceal was unclear. And its precise location was even more unclear. But it was here somewhere, amongst the ruins.

In the weeks since John Grant's death and the arrival of his package, the man had come often to the abbey and begun to understand something not only of its history but also its atmosphere, a sense of otherness. He was careful always to look like a visitor and not an inquisitor. He asked no questions of the guides and carried with him none of the maps and drawings he had been sent.

But far from making progress that spring and early summer, the man's enquiry appeared to be going backwards. On his first visit, he believed he had discovered something the old soldier had missed, something that looked very like a diagrammatic map, something that could at once solve the puzzle if it could be decoded. Crudely scratched on one of the wide foundation stones of the north wall of the abbey church was a gaming board.

To amuse himself and some of his workmates on days of rain or worse, one of the medieval masons had taken his cold chisel and mel to make a board for a game known as merelles or 'Nine Men's Morris'. Very ancient, originally played by Roman builders, it is a strategy game, like chess, but played on a pattern of squares – with progressively smaller ones inside a larger, and all connected by straight lines. Each player has nine counters, usually either black or white, and they take it in turns to place them on some of the twenty-four points where the straight lines and the squares intersect. Like noughts and crosses, the goal is to set three counters in a row: what is known as a 'mill'. This allows a player to remove one of his opponent's pieces, and the ultimate goal is to remove seven of the nine so that he could no longer form a mill of three.

The man became fascinated and in a charity shop bought an old chessboard that had the grid for merelles on the back. With draughts pieces, he played out the game's strategies in an effort to make an arrangement that might look like a map. Perhaps a mill would point in a certain direction, or perhaps two would represent coordinates. The number three featured in Scott's poem and the board scratched by the masons was close to the great man's tomb. But after much frustration, countless moves, gambits and variations, the man concluded that the merelles board was of no importance, something uncovered by accident when the abbey was made ruinous by an English army in 1544. It was a curiosity, not a clue.

Over the course of his many visits, the man learned that David Erskine, the Earl of Buchan, had bought the abbey ruins in 1786. A keen antiquarian, he conserved as much as possible and planted beautiful specimen trees, rhododendra and borders of ornamental shrubs, thus converting Dryburgh into a garden. The shell of the great church and the conventual buildings became the equivalent of the follies built to fill the vistas from the drawing room windows of a grand house: a huge garden feature.

Normally a mild, well-mannered man, Walter Scott disliked Erskine intensely, writing that he was a person whose 'immense vanity obscured, or rather eclipsed, very considerable talents'. Scott was buried at Dryburgh because of rights retained by his family, but it seemed a strange decision given the visceral dislike of the owner of the abbey. Did that dissonance have any bearing on the puzzle?

More and more, the man was drawn back to the extract from 'The Eve of St John'. Walter Scott's second verse began with doubt, a sense that all was not what it appeared: 'The varying light deceived thy sight'. And so all that early summer, growing increasingly anxious that his frequent visits would be noted by the guides and the lady at the ticket office – everyone was vigilant these days – the man had varied the time of day he came to the abbey. Since he imagined that the sun's rays might reveal something, somehow, he had always come on sunny days. Perhaps at different times, when the sun threw different shadows, something would be revealed?

But his persistence shed no new light – until he realised something so blindingly obvious, it annoyed him. A schoolboy could have worked it out. Light does not come only from the sun. Scott wrote of deceit and 'a varying light'; perhaps a clear night with a full moon would answer all questions – if he was not seen and caught breaking curfew. The man decided that, after a month of frustration, the risk of one last effort to solve the old soldier's puzzle was worthwhile. And so he had waited for the night of the next full moon. Tonight.

Having looked over at the façade of the hotel to reassure himself that all was quiet, and no one had dared to venture out, even for a breath of night air at the grand entrance, the man scrambled over the drystone dyke and into the abbey precinct.

It was close to midnight and the moon was climbing to its zenith. The man could see that the nave of the abbey was brightly lit, its pink sandstone almost glowing. His plan was to enter through the west door and face east towards the presbytery and the high altar to see if moonlight showed him something sunlight could not. But when he passed under the rounded arch and stood about halfway down the length of the great church, he could see nothing that looked different.

As he stood looking about him, the quiet of the still night was suddenly shattered.

Very close by and coming quickly closer, sirens screamed

and the man saw headlights swing across the parkland beyond the ruins. He froze, exposed in the bright moonlight, the nearest cover thirty yards away. Willing himself not to run or make any sudden movement, he slowly sank to his knees and crawled behind the low stump of a pillar. Three cars raced into the hotel car park, ripping and spraying the gravel as they turned and stopped.

Peering over the pillar, the man saw six officers in black uniforms slam doors and run towards the main entrance of the hotel. He exhaled with relief, blowing out his cheeks. He could not stay in the open. Bending almost double, he scuttled back through the west door and hid in the shadows of a huge wellingtonia. Looking across at the hotel, he watched lights go on in the public rooms of the ground floor and then in corridors and rooms.

Moments later, four of the officers re-appeared at the entrance. Two dragged a handcuffed man, still in his pyjamas, and behind them, two more pinioned the arms of a woman in a nightdress. She yelped and stumbled as the gravel cut into her bare feet. One of the officers grabbed her hair, dragged her and almost threw her into the back of a car. Gunning their engines, sirens flashing and howling, two of the cars sped off into the night.

Soon afterwards, two more uniformed men appeared on the steps of the main entrance and shook hands with a civilian in a suit. Watching from the shadows, the man recognised an all too familiar pattern. Officers from the Department of Public Safety preferred to make arrests, usually on the basis of information received, in the middle of the night without any warning. That was when suspects were most vulnerable, most likely to confess to crimes or misdemeanours. Those who supported or reluctantly understood the necessity for this sort of policing called the officers 'the Vigilantes'. The name came from their motto,

Semper Vigilans, 'Always Watchful', and their style, which was redolent of those trigger-happy cowboys who sometimes took it upon themselves to act beyond the law in Westerns.

Winded by the brutality he had just witnessed, the man considered abandoning his search. He did not even know what he was looking for. This quest had become an obsession, a very dangerous preoccupation that could see him bundled into the back of a car and beaten by a bunch of Vigilantes. And yet cold logic told him that the local thugs were busy. And they had two captives to amuse themselves with.

The windows of the hotel were still lit and frightened guests would be whispering to each other, wondering what had just happened. The last thing any of them would do is venture outside after curfew. If the man was to make one last effort to find what the old soldier had been looking for, then this was probably the safest time to do it. And once nothing had been found, no hiding place uncovered, well, then he could forget about the whole thing. He had done his best, taken very considerable risks, and would have nothing to reproach himself for.

Nevertheless, it seemed prudent to put the ruins of the abbey between himself and the hotel. The Vigilantes might extract information from the terrified couple that would bring them back – and quickly. The man skirted the low wall that bordered the nave, turned right down a flight of steps through an arch and came to the entrance to the chapter house. It had survived almost intact from the depredations of the sixteenth century and there were stone seats around its edges. Leaning back against the cold stone wall and stretching out his legs, the man tried to gather his thoughts. Patting his pockets, he found a bar of chocolate and munched a few squares for a shot of energy.

His watch told him that the moon would reach its culmination in about fifteen minutes. If its rays were to show up anything then that would likely be the time. Staying close

15

to the pillars of the chapter house doorway, the man looked around the cloister to be sure that he was alone and could not be seen from the upper storeys of the hotel. At the foot of a stair and through another arch, a path led to the gatehouse and the bridge over the water channel. Beyond it were the policies of Abbey House. It stood about three hundred yards to the south-east and was once the stately home of the antiquarian, David Erskine. Its windows were dark. In the stillness, the man could hear no movement.

And then at that moment, the heavens shifted and the world stopped still. It was as though stage machinery began to grind to produce a fleeting illusion, something that observers knew was incredible but saw clearly. A thick cloud passed over the moon and the land plunged abruptly into darkness. Such was the shock of it that the man stopped, had to steady himself and then look up at the sky. And then the wheels ground again, the heavens shifted once more, the moon was revealed, the land brilliantly lit and the old soldier's puzzle was suddenly solved.

No more than a hundred yards away, hidden by trees until that moment, stood a small circular building with a conical roof. And on the point of the cone there shone a tiny moon, an earthly reflection of the astronomical body above. It seemed to radiate a light of its own. But as the man moved closer, magnetically attracted, as if he saw that it was a steel ball of some kind. Burnished to a brilliant sheen, it absorbed the milky light of the moon and appeared to have its own aura.

There was a low wooden door on the far side of the building, hidden from the big house. Captivated and made bold by the otherworldly moment, the man did not hesitate, or trouble to look around or care about the noise when he shouldered the door open. In the musty blackness, he put on his head torch and looked inside. There was nothing. The little building was empty, completely empty; there were no chests or containers of any sort on the paved floor. Not rounded like the outside, the walls were squared, making a box-like interior. There was nothing at all to be seen.

The man raked his torch beam up and down the walls. They were not flush but covered with square stone boxes about a foot across. He had broken into an old dovecote and these were nesting boxes for pigeons, although no pigeons nested and nothing seemed to have been left or hidden anywhere. Nonetheless, the man felt sure that Walter Scott's 'varying light' had led him to the right place. He stood in the middle of the paved floor staring at the stone squares and, very slowly, almost without thinking, he realised that they were not only nesting boxes. They were also something else.

He was staring at a giant merelles board.

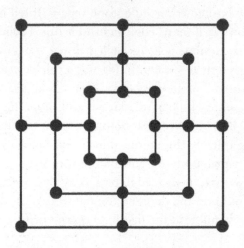

On one wall, twenty-four boxes imitated the twenty-four points on a board, and he could see two mills. Three small round stones had been placed in one row of boxes that were horizontal, and in another three was a mill of three more round stones that ran vertically. He could see that they were arranged as coordinates. The mills almost met in the middle of the wall of boxes. Almost. Both pointed at a nesting box that had been closed, made blank. A stone square had been fitted over the box.

The man could reach up and touch it but he was not tall enough to shift the square piece of stone. Climbing, using the lower boxes as footholds, he managed to squeeze his fingers into a tiny gap on one side. But the piece of stone would not shift. Tearing his fingernails, he could not pull it out. His chest heaving, sweat running down his face, he tugged and scraped at the edges, but there was not even the slightest movement. The cover seemed to be fitted flush. Tiring, and grunting with effort, the man tried to climb up a little higher to get more purchase, but he lost his footing, grabbed at anything – and accidentally pushed at the little stone square. It fell inwards.

The man lifted up its edge and slid it out. Feeling with his hands in the nesting box, he pulled down a package, something wrapped in an oilskin. Inside was a thick, weathered and battered leather-bound notebook. That was all there was. The man managed to climb a little higher and shone his torch into the nesting box but there was nothing else to be found.

Riffling quickly through its thin pages, he saw that he had found not a printed book but hundreds of pages of small but clear handwriting. It seemed to be a diary or a journal of some kind. Brushing off the dust and the cobwebs, the man opened the notebook and read the first lines on the first page.

This journal is the property of Captain David Erskine of the 1st Battalion, King's Own Scottish Borderers. If you have retrived it, that means he is a dead man.

I

What you have in your hands is, for the most part, an account of history in the old sense. For the Greeks who invented it – Herodotus, Thucydides and the others – the word *histor* meant 'witness'; what witnesses saw with their own eyes and reported that was history. Much of what you will read, I saw and was witness to.

Too disorganised and episodic for a diary, what follows is more like a journal, a record of what I remembered and wrote down, sometimes at the time, sometimes later. I have also occasionally added material about events that took place elsewhere and I did not witness, as they help explain how and why things occurred as they did. Especially when events began to accelerate, running far beyond my ability to record them directly, I have had to rely on my imagination. But I have invented nothing. Instead, I have used my knowledge and understanding of how our enemies thought and acted to give context to the awful incidents I did witness. And I have included my own versions of what others – particularly one who is very dear to me – told me of their experiences at the time.

Everything I did, I did for the best as I understood it, and of course I made terrible mistakes and calamitous misjudgements. My actions sometimes caused heart-breaking sadness and I will carry the guilt and regret for those to my grave. But I tried to act in the best interests of my country, more particularly in the interests of the best of my country. God knows, others behaved wickedly and brought down shame on all our heads.

What you have here is a true record of a most momentous time, a period when the world was changed utterly.

Through bright and dark times, I kept in mind lines from Walter Scott. He is buried with my kinsmen in our ancestral place and even though he wrote spitefully about my people, he captured the wellspring of why I did all that I did as the world hurtled towards the edge of an abyss.

> Breathes there the man, with soul so dead,
> Who never to himself hath said,
> This is my own, my native land!

Addendum – 28 March 1945

You are about to read a copy of the original journal. It was made soon after the events it describes, when memories were fresh. The copyist has included their own accounts of events the primary writer knew very little of. In particular, the copyist made a journey into the Cheviot Hills to discover the fate of someone whose role was pivotal to all that happened and to listen to a remarkable story.

II

6 June 1944

Rum, vomit and fear, all soaked by salt spray. As the flat-bottomed landing craft whumped down on the choppy seas of the Channel, sometimes yawing from side to side, men retched, soiling their clothes, smearing sick over the packs of those in front of them. Some, even though their throats were raw from dry heaving, took a swig of fiery, sickly sweet rum as the canteen was passed around. Some men vomited into their helmets and let the continuous spray rinse them.

Holding tight onto a bow rail, I forced myself to look ahead fixedly, determined not to throw up. This was bad enough, but God knows what we would face when the landing craft finally stopped throwing us around and the ramp went down at 07.25.

Fear makes a mockery of us all, voiding our bowels as well as our stomachs, making our hands shake and our hearts race. But the truth is that fear keeps us alive. It makes us react, incites us to retaliate, to lash out, to be violent and to kill.

Earlier, when the sergeants assembled the three platoons on the deck of the transport ship, waiting for the order to embark on the landing craft, I shouted for the men to gather round for some brief words I had rehearsed many times in the previous twenty-four hours. A senior officer had firmly advised me to keep it brief and not to try to rouse emotions. The Borderers were all regular soldiers, and some had been under intense fire on French beaches before, at Dunkirk. Nevertheless, I sensed that they looked to me, of all people, for reassurance – of any sort. What I said was banal. On the page, it even looks dull, uninspired, not fitting for the moment. But on that night before that morning, nothing could be banal, all was heightened.

'Borderers!' I said, fighting to keep my voice steady. 'In a short time the ramp will go down and we'll face the enemy. Reconnaissance tells us that we'll see a beach at low tide, a sea-wall, a road behind it and a row of houses on the other side. At all costs, we must get off the beach as soon as we can. Go forward. Do not stop. Take the fight to the enemy. God speed, and God protect the Borderers!'

The truth was that I believed in neither God nor my ability to lead these soldiers to victory, safety or even survival. I had been given my commission not for any military merit but because I could speak German fluently and had been in the officer training corps at my university. And also, I suspect, on account of my family and its history. Titles carry obligations as well as privileges, as well as the baseless assumption of an inherited ability to lead men.

As the ceaseless spray washed over the landing craft and men retched as it slapped down on the sea after each swell, my hands were shaking and my head spinning. God knows what we were about to face. I prayed that such courage as I had would not fail me, my legs would move and I would not dishonour my name.

*

Nothing, I suspect, had prepared even the most experienced regular soldiers and officers for the sights that greeted them on embarkation at Southampton the night before. The 1st Battalion, King's Own Scottish Borderers boarded one of more than five thousand ships about to set sail from the Channel ports to rendezvous in a sector south of the Isle of Wight. It was an astonishing armada, but one travelling in the opposite direction from the Spanish. On every side the sea was studded with dark, looming shapes: huge battleships, the *Warspite*, *Ramillies* and others; many cruisers; even more destroyers, minesweepers, transport ships and craft I could not identify. Armed, waiting, hoping against hope, more than one hundred and fifty thousand men were being carried by this armada to attack the Normandy coast. Surely it was enough? Surely sheer numbers and firepower would overwhelm the German defences. As we steamed southwards, the edging light on the eastern horizon picked out smoking funnels, masts and the spiky outline of batteries of great guns. It was a belly-hollowing sight.

But most of all on that night voyage, I remember the pipes. Cutting through the hum of the engines of the ships and the wash of the choppy sea, I could distinctly hear bagpipes playing and immediately recognised 'The Road to the Isles'. Its familiar lines – 'the far Cuillin are putting love on me', or 'by Tummel and Loch Rannoch' and 'the tangle o' the Isles' – rang round and round my head. The Borderers cheered, glad to have something to distract them. It was not a war rant, but a march of sorts, one that crossed another sea, and its jaunty melody somehow sent us into battle in better spirits. Later, I learned that Simon Fraser, Lord Lovat, had asked his piper, Bill Millin, to play, telling him that the Scots ought to lead the invasion of Hitler's Europe. Other ships heard the skirl of the pipes and captains ordered more music to be played over the tannoys as the armada steamed through the fateful night.

When their commando landing craft reached its beach, Lovat apparently asked Millin to play 'Highland Laddie' and 'All the Blue Bonnets Are Over the Border'. Crazy, but somehow the music seemed to dissipate the terror around the men. A German prisoner of war taken that day said they did not take aim at Millin as he marched up and down the beach, his drones and their tartan trim an easy target, because they thought him a madman. An extraordinary image as war raged around the lone piper.

From the transport ship I had seen a pale dawn rising, no sun but streaks of light blue on the eastern horizon. Above us, squadrons of Lancasters and other planes I did not recognise droned towards the French coast and in moments we saw flashes as their bombs burst over the land. It was encouraging. Perhaps we would find the German defences pulverised, soldiers emerging from the rubble with their hands in the air, ready to surrender. From that moment, time began to accelerate so quickly that I did everything without thinking, relying only on instinct.

The ship's tannoy crackled: 'Prepare to man your boats.' There was no turning back now.

My three platoons had to climb down the sides of the ships using scramble nets in the subdued morning light. The sea was so rough that the landing craft bobbed up and down alarmingly, and despite the efforts of the crew, the swell opened up gaps between it and the transport ship, or the two clanked as they collided. It was very dangerous. Some men carried more equipment than others and my radio operator, Mallen, had great trouble. But enough of us had made the descent to be able to pull the scramble net tight against the landing craft. We bundled Mallen down, although he yelped when he cracked his elbows on the metal deck.

Twenty-four hours before, the briefing had identified our objective as Queen Beach, near the small seaside town of Ouistreham, not far from Caen. Air reconnaissance had shown defences, pillboxes and artillery batteries behind a long sea wall. It would be vital to reach it, get over it, get across the road and get behind the defensive line. The plan was for amphibious tanks to land first, attack and attract fire, and before that bombers would attempt to make craters for infantry cover. But the two hundred yards of the beach below the wall looked to me like the perfect killing field. To say nothing of wading agonisingly slowly through the sea before it was reached.

Three regiments each supplied a battalion in the first wave: the Borderers, the Royal Ulster Rifles and the Lincolnshire Regiment. Scotland, Ireland and England. For completeness, we should have been joined by the Royal Welch Fusiliers.

Despite the choppy sea, the crews of the landing craft managed to get us all in formation so that we would reach the beach at approximately the same time, 07.25. A staggered series of landings would have been disastrous, allowing the defenders to concentrate their fire on each craft in turn. But before we could move forward together, thunder boomed and fire rent the sky. The naval bombardment began. It was deafening, as though the heavens were exploding. Behind us, the *Warspite* and the *Ramillies* fired their huge guns and the shells shot over our heads like express trains racing out of a tunnel.

My chest seemed to tighten and the pressure waves pushed hard on our landing craft as salvoes from the battleships, cruisers and destroyers made the great ships recoil. The roar and the flashes should have made us cheer, but in truth the overwhelming instinct was to cower and flinch and hope none of the shells dropped short.

When the guns were finally silenced, it was like a signal. Now it was our turn. The formation of landing craft moved forward like a monstrous metal tide. We were carried into the eye of a gathering storm, one that would burst on us in moments.

*

I looked over the edge of the forward ramp and it seemed in the eerie, grey stillness that the winds of the world swirled around us. When we reached the shallow water of the foreshore, the ramp would be let down and I would lead my men into the killing field. In all my life, I had never felt such hollow loneliness.

I was jolted back into the moment by Sergeant Taylor shouting in my ear, 'Thirty minutes to landing, sir!'

I turned and nodded.

'You'll be all right, sir,' he added with a tight, grim smile.

That flash of kindness told me we would fight for our country and against a manifest evil, certainly, but most of all, we would fight for each other. We were a band of Borderers, and perhaps brothers too.

Maddened by fear, by finding themselves in the jaws of hell, skeins of sea birds flew low and very fast just above the surface, like tracer fire. God knows what carnage was happening on the farms inland, with animals running in blind panic as shells exploded and bombs tore craters out of the fields.

As we moved closer, I could see that the Ulsters on our left were holding formation. And then a moment later I felt the shock of finding we were in range, as a rattle of metallic pings tinged off the sides of the landing craft. A hail of what must have been machine guns bullets hit us. I could hear them whipping through the air. In an instant reflex, we all cowered down below the hull. The moment we let down the ramp, we would be fired on. We were in their sights.

'Be ready,' I roared to Sergeant Taylor, 'to give the order to disembark!'

My watch had 07.25 precisely. I risked looking to my right to the line of Borderers' landing craft and then left to the Ulsters'. They had all halted or were slowing but none had let down their ramps. Why the moment of hesitation? A sense of 'you first'? Were they waiting for one craft to charge the beach and attract fire before giving the order to disembark? Surely not.

We were not now under fire. Now was the time to go,

whatever any other commander decided. On the beach I saw two disabled and abandoned amphibious tanks. Had there been a successful landing? Had some broken through? Where?

The Ulsters' ramp inched forward, and I shouted, 'Now!'

Grinding, cranking down through what sounded like rusty gears, the ramp splashed into the water. Grabbing the handrail, losing my slippery footing, almost falling as the craft suddenly shifted, I scrambled down. The shock of the water sharpened my senses even more. Up to my waist, it made me pump my legs and move. The Borderers followed.

I turned to Sergeant Taylor and, as he opened his mouth to speak, he was hit in the face. He toppled forward, instantly dead, knocked me down and saved my life. Others pulled at the straps of my pack and I spluttered upright and waded ashore, soaked, breathless with shock.

Enemy fire was sporadic. Thoughts flickered. Perhaps they were too few to direct their guns at every landing craft at once. But they clearly had snipers, perhaps in the tall houses I could see, picking off the first down the ramps, those men moving so, so slowly through the water. And one of them had missed me and killed my sergeant.

Now on wet sand, I ran, half falling as it gave way under my boots, and made for the sanctuary of an abandoned tank. Taking cover behind it were half a dozen other Borderers. At that moment, a landing craft behind us was hit by a shell, killing and maiming many, buckling the hull. Clearly the Germans had wheeled artillery into their defensive line, and the tank was a big target; we had to move, get off the beach. Ahead of us, out in the open, a young recruit, clearly terrified, was digging feverishly with his entrenching tool. He made me move. Roaring for them to gather round me, I ran out with my men from behind the tank, a spray of machine gun fire throwing up sand in front of me, and I grabbed at the boy's pack and dragged him behind me. We were forty yards from the sea wall and safety.

'Run! Run! Now!' Screaming at my men, we sprinted, pushing at the loose sand with our boots.

The young soldier scurried like a crab behind me. And was shot dead, by the snap of a single report. Another sniper kill. I began to think myself lucky. Or next.

We hunkered down behind the sea wall, chests heaving, safe for the moment. The respite gave me the chance to turn and see what was happening behind us. Many had not been lucky. A tide of blood streaked the white foam of the foreshore. Wounded men called out pitifully. Some were still behind the abandoned tanks; they needed to get off the beach. But below the sea wall, I could see most of my men. Maybe thirty had made it. They crouched, holding fast to their rifles, looking at me.

About a hundred yards to my left was a gap in the wall where a concrete ramp led down to the beach. If the amphibious tanks had advanced, that was the only way they could have gone. If. If they had trundled up the ramp, we should follow because they might have used their 75mm guns to clear a path through the pillboxes and trenches strung out along the road. My watch said 08.00. We had been on the beach long enough. I decided to take Corporal Lauder, to act as a runner. He had played rugby in the Border League, was agile and quick, and he could take back orders to the waiting men.

Still roaring over our heads, the naval bombardment was directed further inland, or so I hoped. When Lauder and I reached the concrete ramp, we crawled on our bellies up to the level of the road. In each direction, we could clearly see fire spitting from gun emplacements, pillboxes and the upper floors of the tall seaside houses. For some reason, I remember the brightly painted shutters folded back on each side of the windows.

Further along, I saw the smoke of artillery fire. Wherever the Lancasters had dropped their bombs, it was not here. But directly in front of us, between two houses that had been badly damaged by shelling, there was a trail of destruction, where tanks had flattened fences and struck inland.

Don't stop and think. Think when you have stopped. Without realising that I had learned it, that was the visceral lesson of an extraordinary morning on Queen Beach. Moving targets are harder to hit and if I could only keep my men moving forward, the picture would change constantly, forcing the Germans to turn, to look for us, to throw up barriers, move back from prepared positions. So long as we could keep moving, I felt sure confusion would be our friend as well as our enemy. We were in a strange land and the Germans knew it well. But we were running with the tide of history. Surely we were.

With two other units of Borderers joining us, we moved inland, the map telling me we were about half a mile west of Ouistreham. We exchanged fire with retreating defenders who knew and used the landscape to make their escape. Having set up a perimeter around a battered, badly shelled and deserted farm steading, we needed to contact brigade headquarters, wherever they were, for fresh orders. Now what? Our mission was to push on and take the city of Caen, about eight miles to the south. But we needed more than infantry: tanks, more firepower, greater numbers and clear leadership amidst the confusion were all essential.

The radio crackled into life and Private Mallen pressed his fingertips on the earphones, trying to find the right wavelength amongst all the deafening noise and the static. 'That's brigade, sir,' said Mallen, handing me the headphones.

I could hear only part of what Colonel Murray said but gathered enough to know that we were to rendezvous at 18.00, north of the village of Hermanville.

'Must mean the Germans have it.' Mallen smiled. 'The Hermans.'

Not very funny, but a break, a jolt, a different train of thought.

We pressed on. The naval bombardment had been pitiless. We saw many dead cows and horses, but it was the awful, elemental bellowing of those that had been savagely wounded that haunted our steps. I shall never forget catching sight of a horse with most of its hindquarters blown away, an awful mess of blood and bone. Shrieking in agony, it was pulling itself forward with its forelegs, trying to run away from the pain. Corporal Lauder reprimanded men who spent bullets ending the suffering of wounded animals, but I told him to leave it.

Before death had come screaming out of the skies, this had been dairying country. Small, lush fields were enclosed by ancient, high hedging and their peace had been shattered as bombs blew open ragged craters and dense blackthorn and juniper were smashed down by advancing tanks. Idyllic though this place must once have been, it was also dangerous. Known as *bocage*, it was perfect for ambush.

I have no memory of falling. Only of coming round, dizzy and choking.

The back rim of my helmet had hit the ground so hard after I somersaulted that the chinstrap was choking me, only freeing when I rolled on my side. I had no idea if I had been hit, no pain, no feeling in my limbs or torso except a floppy disarticulation.

Lauder's face loomed over me. 'Mortars, sir,' he shouted, inches from my ear, his voice echoing down a long tunnel. 'We need to get off the road.'

I realised I was lying on my revolver, and I was glad I could feel it jabbing into my side. My rifle lay a few feet away and I tried to roll onto all fours but collapsed slowly sideways. Lauder dragged me into a ditch choked with briar and willowherb. From a long, long way away, I heard, 'You're not hit, sir,' and darkness closed over me.

Very badly concussed, or worse, the pain in my neck excruciating and overwhelmed with nausea, I came to at the sound of engines. No more than a few feet from where I lay, I saw the wheels of vehicles passing slowly. Time seemed to collapse on itself and light at first faded and then brightened. When Lauder broke into my nightmares, arriving with stretcher-bearers, I realised that many had had marched past me thinking I was a goner, another casualty of a *bocage* ambush.

*

Like church spires rising above the fog, my recollections of the following few days are sparse, seen fleetingly, only sharp impressions. My left side was at first numb and I pissed myself more than once. But once feeling returned, I could stand, unsteadily at first, rocking on the balls of my feet, and then I could walk.

I was desperate to return to my unit. Such was the intensity of my new-found sense of responsibility that I felt I had let them down. I wanted to know who amongst my band of Borderers had survived the mortar attack, where they had been deployed and who commanded them.

'What's happening?' I asked a sergeant from the Royal Ulster Rifles who lay on the bed next to me at the field hospital.

'Panzers,' he said. 'Probably SS. They broke through, between us and the Canadians.'

Perhaps this would all go wrong, I thought, perhaps we would be driven back into the sea. 'What about Caen?' I said. 'Surely to God we've taken it. It's only a few miles away.' I felt myself lurching into despair, on the edge of tears and also, I'm ashamed to say, of fear.

'Didn't have the bloody kit, did they,' said the Ulsterman.

31

'Not enough armour. That's why the Panzers broke through, how they kept us out of Caen.'

Dear God in Heaven, was this all beginning to unravel? The sergeant was panting, grimacing with the effort of talking. I saw that his right leg was splinted and bandaged, and after blowing out his cheeks and a long sigh, he turned away. But I couldn't. My men were still out there and I was lying here without a mark on me.

The orderlies were overwhelmed by casualties – real casualties, not confused malingerers like me – and I had no difficulty persuading them that I was fit and should not take up room.

'The Jocks are up ahead, sir,' said a sergeant from the Royal Signals as I left. 'Heavy fighting at Hermanville, and beyond.'

Stiff, limping and constantly thirsty, I made my way forward to where my unit might have been. 'March towards the sound of distant guns' was a standing order given by Napoleon to his marshals, and even though it was probably apocryphal, it was what I was doing.

Waving green wheat beginning to turn biscuit-ripe is an image that has stayed with me, and sends a shiver of fear up my spine. It was dusk at the edge of a wide field, not typical of the hedged enclosures but just as deadly: an open killing field, like the beach. The Ulsters had advanced across it, taking very heavy casualties from hidden machine gun nests at the edge of the village on the other side. But they took it, showing immense determination, and the Borderers came behind to reinforce and consolidate.

I remember seeing one of the Paddies carrying a sten gun as though it was a toy and opening up at a target I could not see. Showing extraordinary physical courage, he charged a sandbagged emplacement, constantly firing, shouting at the top of his voice, '*Hände hoch! Hände hoch!*' Maybe too many of his mates had died. When he kept coming, they surrendered.

Astonishingly, attacked by only one man, the Germans stood up with their hands held high. But two made a fatal mistake when they suddenly turned away from the Ulsterman. He mowed them down instantly.

9 July 1944

The night before the attack on Caen, Colonel Murray ordered me to leave my unit and stay by his side throughout the operation. As a fluent German speaker, I was to interrogate prisoners. Intelligence about the strength of enemy resistance had been very poor and two Panzer divisions supported by grenadiers and other units had held up our advance for a month. The positioning, supply and robustness of artillery and machine gun emplacements had also hampered us greatly. I frankly doubted that prisoners of war would give up any information but Murray insisted we try to extract what we could. I suspected he thought I was still not fit enough to lead my Borderers.

Clearly, I had suffered a severe head injury but showed no outward signs of having been wounded. That spurred me to protest that I should be allowed to return to my unit, but the colonel was adamant. He had another reason for keeping a German speaker on his staff: to find any information about the massacres of Allied prisoners. Waffen SS Panzer grenadiers had killed seventeen captured Canadians, and other atrocities had been discovered as the Germans retreated. On both sides, I suspected.

Our startline lay to the east of Caen, on the farther side of the River Orne, which flows through the middle of the city. In the centre were the Royal Ulster Rifles, and from the west, having broken through from Juno Beach, the Canadians and their armour would attack.

At 09.00 we moved off, at first under heavy shellfire. It was misty and the very badly damaged buildings of the outskirts of

Caen loomed up like ghostly ruins. And when ghosts emerged, civilians who had been sheltering amidst this chaos, we almost fired on them. One old lady carried a bottle of cognac in one hand and in the other two crystal balloon glasses; she was like a figure from another world. Suddenly there was a rattle of machine gun fire and, as we scrambled for cover, she walked over to us as though it was a mere irritation. '*Là-haut! Là-haut!*' She pointed to a church tower. 'Up there!'

To keep the Germans' heads down, the Borderers maintained a steady volley of fire until a bazooka could be assembled. A direct hit just below the topmost window silenced the machine gun, and moments later five Germans ran out of the doorway quickly enough to disappear into the narrow streets of the old town. There was no time for cognac.

Advancing slowly, darting from doorways to street corners, covering each move with rifle fire, the Borderers slowly cleared the town, despite snipers downing several men. French civilians pointed out German positions, and through bomb craters and around tremendous piles of debris strewn across the streets, our men made their way down to the river. I was certain many local people had died in the bombardment. Near a railway bridge, a young boy pointed out *Boches* and a well-defended battery. But after a sustained and merciless series of mortar volleys, the defenders lost heart. When five of them surrendered, I recognised the uniforms and insignia of the Waffen SS.

The SS colonel was defiant. 'Your bombers destroyed our cities, murdering thousands of our people, mothers and children, and we seek revenge!' To my astonishment, he admitted to killing Canadian prisoners but would tell us nothing about the strength of German forces in Normandy. 'If you defeat us, you will soon be fighting the Russians alone!'

Colonel Murray was unequivocal, despite the fact that I wanted to question the prisoners further: I should march the

Germans to the rear of the HQ, where they would be shot by firing squad. And, if possible, the other POWs captured when Caen had been surrounded should watch the execution.

Even though I had seen nothing but death for a month, the Colonel's orders took me aback. His summary judgment was certainly justified. Seventeen Canadians had been massacred. But something niggled at me. Were we not better than them? Should we not send them back across the Channel and then follow the processes of the law? But then, in the chaos of war, witnesses die, facts become forgotten or twisted. For now, there was no doubt. These men, these black-uniformed Nazis, these fanatics, had admitted murder, and they were about to suffer the ultimate field punishment.

'*Götterdämmerung!*' shouted the SS colonel, still defiant. 'That is what will descend on you from the skies if you dare to put one foot in the Reich.'

The five prisoners were lined up against the half-ruined gable of a farmhouse. Behind the five soldiers selected to perform the execution, hundreds of German POWs watched, sitting on the ground, their guards with their guns cocked and ready.

'The Führer will call down the wrath of the Gods and the whole world will burn – and he will renew it in the flames. Ruin waits for you.'

They refused blindfolds. I noticed that one of the younger soldiers, little more than a boy, had pissed himself and was shaking. Just before I gave the order to fire, they all saluted and called out, *Heil Hitler*. The force of the close-range volley slammed them all back against the gable wall, and the SS colonel spun and fell on his side.

Gritting my teeth, I walked over to the crumpled tangle of bodies to put a bullet through each head. When I came to the colonel, I crouched lower, fired into the ground beyond him and whispered, 'Stay there and do not move.'

III

Disobedience of a direct order from a superior officer had only one consequence. Any court martial verdict would be a foregone conclusion. I would be convicted and at best sent to the Glasshouse, to a military prison. As much of a punishment would be the sense of shame, of failure, and even betrayal. I would have let down my band of Borderers and brought ill repute on an old Border family. But I still thought it right to stage the execution of the Waffen SS colonel. My promise to the men in the firing squad that I would finish him off myself after more interrogation, his tongue loosened by near-death and the sight of his comrades dying beside him, seemed to satisfy. In the chaos north of Caen, as armour rumbled towards the smoking, disintegrating city, an odd incident like that stood every chance of being forgotten.

Before the march back to the rear of the HQ, I had ensured the SS prisoners' hands were bound, in order to minimise the escort needed. While two Borderers had led the four grenadiers in front, I had walked beside the SS colonel. Tall, erect, despite an exhausting battle for the city, and with fair hair, he looked like a specimen, the sort that Hitler, Goebbels, Himmler and the others had in mind when they ranted from platforms about *das Herrenvolk*, the master race. More than once, I had mused on the contradiction: none of the Nazi leadership looked anything like the Nordic ideal they worshipped. Hitler was dark and had black circles under his eyes; even in his pomp, Himmler was chinless, bespectacled and balding; Goebbels was emaciated and limping; and Goering fat and jowly. But the man beside me, walking to his death, appeared to be the embodiment all of their poison, of *Rassenkunde,* the crazy nonsense of race-science.

Nazism had long struck me as an ideology of narcissism and immense male vanity. The look of everything mattered. The uniforms, the jackboots, the insignia, the decorations, the Wagnerian names of regiments and units, the universal use of the swastika and the elaborate staginess of ceremonies all added up to the worship of the heroic soldier. When the Pathé newsreels played snatches of Hitler's speeches, I could understand the harsh and pounding oratory, and the use of the first person plural was constant throughout: 'We, the German people. We, the soldiers of destiny. We, the children of the Fatherland.' But when the crescendo came, 'we' became 'me': *Ein Volk, Ein Reich, Ein Führer!* On the wide cinema screen, the theatre of the rallies was spine-tingling, brilliantly performed as thousands of flags fluttered, stormtroopers marched, searchlights played across the *Sieg Heil!* chants and the raised right arm of the Nazi salute. Germany seemed intoxicated with itself.

'Your German is excellent, completely without accent,' the colonel had said suddenly. 'Do you have German relatives?'

In thirty minutes or so, this man would be dead, bullets having shattered his chest at close range, and yet he was making conversation. Perhaps he might be persuaded to say something useful. Ignoring his question, I wanted to know why the resistance in Normandy had been so fierce, even fanatical. 'You're a soldier. You understand history,' I said. 'Fighting on two fronts, being driven back by the Russians: you can't win. The war's lost. Our bombers will pulverise your cities. Why not surrender and save lives?'

He turned and smiled, indulgently. 'You have no honour. You cannot hope to understand.' A shell suddenly burst behind us, but while everyone else flinched, this man did not so much as break his stride. 'We swore an oath to the Führer, a sacred oath to defend the Fatherland, the holy soil of the Reich.' With no hint of irony, his voice was even, resolved and not raised.

When I said that it was only a matter of time before there was a breakthrough in Normandy, he cut in.

'We also fight for time. When Germany launches weapons the like of which have never been seen before, it is the Allies and the Soviets who will beg for peace. We have *Götterdämmerung*. When the Führer calls down the Twilight of the Gods, the roar of their thunder will silence your guns and stop your tanks in their tracks.'

This was more than bombast or the repetition of propaganda about *Vergeltungswaffen*, commonly known as 'Wonder Weapons' – although the literal translation is 'Vengeance Weapons', a label that intrigued me. We had heard reports that rockets had hit London, but their impact had apparently been negligible. It struck me that this man was talking about something much more powerful, and from personal knowledge of some sort.

'It will be the Führer who demands unconditional surrender,' he said emphatically. 'And I will die knowing that the Fatherland and National Socialism will be triumphant.'

Somehow, it seemed to me, vanity had broken down the colonel's resolve to remain silent, to give away nothing. To face his death with the necessary dignity, perhaps he needed the comfort of a boast, the certainty of ultimate victory, something to give his death purpose. But *Götterdämmerung* puzzled me. It sounded less like a glorious Wagnerian reference, and more like a project or a codeword.

*

After the execution, once the watching POWs had been marched back to their barbed wire pens and I had dismissed the firing squad, I found myself more or less alone. Jeeps and trucks bounced up the east road into Caen and units of infantry marched past, but no one even cast so much as a glance at a tangle of dead Germans and a British captain.

I found a deserted stable yard nearby and somehow its tack room had survived more or less intact. 'Sit on the floor in that corner,' I hissed at the SS colonel. Using my revolver to point where I wanted the German to go, I slid down the opposite wall.

The faint smell of oiled leather, the wood-panelled walls studded with saddle racks and hooks for harnesses, and the fact that the only light came from a small window above the feed bins made this place seem closed, somewhere apart from the clangour of war and the roar of battles that raged only a few miles away.

'What is your name, rank and number?' I said.

The German merely smiled at the formula.

With my revolver in my lap and the likelihood that we would not be disturbed, I could wait, take my time. No one was going anywhere.

'If you could untie my hands', said the colonel, 'I could offer you a cigarette. French, I am afraid.'

He held his arms out straight, and once I had cut his bonds, he sank back against the wood panelling. Opening a silver cigarette case, he took one and slid the case across the floor. When the sharp, almost acrid blue smoke filled the space between us, the German began to talk.

'I am Oberführer Manfred von Klige, formerly of the 1st SS Panzer Division Leibstandarte Adolf Hitler, recently seconded to the 21st Panzer Division and now, it seems, your prisoner. May I know your name?'

His even tone and good manners prompted me to tell him. I wanted him to talk as much as possible, and an exchange rather than a one-sided interrogation might be a better tactic. After I gave him my name, rank and regiment, he seemed to relax.

'Each Christmas, without fail, the Führer sends boxes to each man in our division. There are bottles of schnapps and excellent chocolate but, alas, no cigarettes.' Von Klige looked away and smiled at the recollection. 'He thinks cigarettes bad for our health, and so Reichsführer Himmler has to add a carton. He simply wants us to have a happy Christmas.' Von Klige rolled the Gauloises between his finger and thumb. 'The Reichsführer knows that even more than food or drink, soldiers need cigarettes.'

Without much prompting or reciprocation, the German began to reminisce a little more, talking of his sunlit childhood on a family estate east of Berlin. 'We had ponies and horses, and a room like this one where we all used to gather after supper. When I was a boy, I had always to groom my pony myself, clean my own tack and not leave these tasks to others. My father was insistent. I had a personal duty, a responsibility to do everything for my little horse.'

I looked around at the saddles on their racks with the long stirrups hanging below them.

'That saddle above your head is English, I think,' he said, 'perhaps used for hunting.'

I turned my head to look up directly above where I sat, and in an instant von Klige lunged across the floor, caught the stirrup iron, pulled the saddle off its rack down on my head and snatched my revolver from me.

Standing over me, still smiling, he backed away, to where he had been sitting a moment before. 'Did you ever hunt?' he asked as he sat down, pointing the gun at my chest. 'Well, did you?' When I nodded, he went on, 'So, we share a love of horses, no? And you chose to come to a place like this because you are comfortable amongst all of the bridles, halters and saddles?'

Like a cloud passing over a warm summer sun, the German's expression abruptly changed, hardened, and he stared directly at me for a long moment. 'But we are not alike, you and I.' Shaking his head, von Klige continued, 'No. You are clearly intelligent, and you have guessed that I have knowledge of something of great importance. I said too much when we marched from Caen. I should have said nothing of *Götterdämmerung*.' Flicking his thumb to check that the safety catch was off, he aimed the Webley straight at me. 'I am a man of honour, and that is a certainty that shall stay with me forever. But now, I think,' the German said, 'your guessing game has to stop.'

I felt every muscle clench, tried not to close my eyes and then von Klige put the gun barrel to his temple and pulled the trigger.

21 July 1944

The night wind blew rain in off the Atlantic. Back with the 1st Battalion, bivouacked in an orchard not far from Caumont, south-west of Caen, I blessed the rain and the break in the weather. Since we advanced southwards into Calvados, it had been oppressively hot and mosquitoes were a constant torment. Battle fatigues are not designed for comfort in warm weather and I authorised shirt-sleeve order for the men. Waiting is what most soldiers do most of the time and the regulars used it well; washing clothes, cleaning equipment, scrounging and foraging for food, writing letters home but mostly sleeping.

In the previous days, as we moved through the farms and fields behind the front line, we found the landscape almost deserted. Any civilians we saw were invariably old people, often in forlorn groups, walking the sunken lanes behind the high hedges, trying to get out of the way. They seemed pleased to see us, though, and happy to see the back of the Germans. But

I feared that the civilians caught in the battle zone had paid a terrible price for liberation: their towns and villages were often shelled to rubble and the farms looted and destroyed.

Once we camped down in the orchard, the first letters from home began to arrive, something that much cheered the men. Knowing that their families back home were safe was a great comfort in the face of the present danger. After all, what were they fighting for if not hearth and home?

Never one to 'bang on', my father wrote something more like a report or an inventory. Although he did not explicitly state it, all seemed to be well at Abbey House. The lambing and calving had passed without incident despite there being little help on the farms, the hayfields needed rain and the locality had settled down for the summer with the merciful departure of the Polish Armoured Brigade. (There was a good deal of muttering amongst the Borderers when the popularity of the heel-clicking, polite and even exotic Polish officers had been hinted at in the letters from their loved ones.)

What pleased me most about my father's letter was not what he wrote but the image of him writing it. Drumming his fingers on his desk, sighing, chewing the stem of his pipe, often staring out of the bay window over the grass parks that led the eye down to the lazy bend of the Tweed, he would have taken an age to write the two pages of the tissue-thin airmail paper he had sent. But I was glad to have it, and for a moment I could feel the breeze off the river on my face.

I wondered about another estate and another father a thousand miles to the east of Dryburgh, not far from Berlin. When von Klige killed himself, I am ashamed to say that I left his body and the ruin of his head in the tack room, only retrieving and cleaning my pistol. Several SS officers had committed suicide to avoid the humiliation of capture and here was another one. No one would remark on it. For days, I had tried to imagine what had gone on in his brain in the moments before he put a bullet through it. I suspect that he did not trust himself to remain silent under interrogation. The Germans tortured prisoners and perhaps he assumed the Allies would not hesitate either, especially if I had passed on my suspicions about the importance of *Götterdämmerung*. That was what he meant by honour. To keep it, to bring no shame to his family, he killed himself.

At midday, a jeep bounced down the narrow lane by the orchard. 'You are to come with me to Brigade HQ immediately, sir.' I sat down next to the driver, a private in the Royal Scots Fusiliers.

At the HQ, under an awning rigged up to keep the rain off, a field radio was crackling and around a broad table several senior officers pored over a map.

'Erskine' – Colonel Murray walked over to shake hands – 'there's a good deal of German radio traffic, much of it uncoded, and we want you to listen.' He gestured towards a chair beside the operator, who slid me a notebook and pencil. 'Gist of it is,' said Murray, 'there has been an attempt on Hitler's life. On German radio this morning, he himself apparently gave details. Sounds like he was bloody lucky to survive.'

5 August 1944

In the morning air after rain, you could smell the earth and its rising goodness. Amongst the apple trees of Calvados, the soldiers had churned the grass to mud, but the musty sweetness was still there. Robotically checking over my equipment, making sure everything was in place and in working order, my mind drifted back to the fields at Dryburgh and the soft, distant bleat of lambs from the high pasture beyond the river. The red earth of Berwickshire will be forever grained into my hands.

The waiting was over. Orders had come down from Brigade HQ for a general advance. Morning mist clung to the orchard and did not lift until the afternoon. It muffled the gathering rumble of battle. Now supplied through the port of Cherbourg, General Bradley's 1st US Army had been massing for days for an attack on German defensive formations. There was talk of a decisive breakthrough, a dash for the Seine and the great prize of Paris. British infantry and armour was to protect the Americans' flank and prevent the enemy from mounting a controlled fighting retreat and an ability to regroup. Intelligence reports believed that at least two SS Panzer divisions opposed us, as well as artillery and infantry regiments. In the wake of the attempt on Hitler's life, I feared the fighting would be fierce.

Supported by infantry, the Guards' tank division passed through our lines on its way to attack the village of Estry, astride a strategically important crossroads in the maze of lanes and tracks of the Normandy landscape.

And then it was our turn.

That day I was certain we would take casualties. Even though we had armoured support, an infantry assault against a defensive line that had repulsed the Guards' tanks for three days would mean some of my men dying or being wounded. Having spoken to my band of Borderers, I had to find my own courage so that I could lead them into battle, lead from the front, something commanders had done for millennia.

An hour before the assault was due to begin, we waited behind a blackthorn hedge for the order that would take us to the startline. We had been promised support from the Grenadiers' tanks and their vicious flame-throwers, but in the pauses in the artillery barrage whistling over our heads, I could not hear any engine noise. Word came up the line that our armour was held up in the narrow, sunken lanes and could not break out of them by mounting the high, steep banks and

44

hedges on either side. When I was told that they could not even get close enough to bring their guns within range of the village, I realised that we would be very exposed if we attacked without the armour.

But we did. Our startline was a stream north-west of Estry and as the order to advance came, the defenders saw us, found our range and the barrage began. As mortars and shells exploded around us, the air filled with flying debris, clods of earth, limbs torn from shattered apple trees and their bizarre shrapnel of tiny, hard cider apples. But we took no direct hits and moved forward with great caution, knowing we could soon be close enough to take machine gun fire.

At the north end of the village, the SS had Panzers dug into protective emplacements, their turrets constantly traversing, searching for targets. There were 88mm guns, mortars and machine gun nests firing from the upper floors of houses. The area around the church, whose spire had been decapitated, was heavily fortified as a strongpoint. And hidden in the hedges, copses and trees, there were snipers.

All of them were waiting for us.

From the edges of Estry, I heard the creak and grinding of tanks turning. Had the Grenadiers reached the battlefield by another route? But then, swinging into the orchard rolled a Panzer with grenadiers running crouched behind it. Such was their determination, the defenders were counter-attacking. We withdrew quickly, but still found ourselves under mortar fire.

It was clear to me that the SS simply refused to abandon this strategically pivotal village and, if they could, would in all likelihood fight to the last man, do what their Führer demanded. We were still in Normandy; it would be a long, hard fight to reach the frontiers of Germany.

Orders at last came to withdraw all of our forces and the Grenadiers were sent to find a way to block the roads south in case the SS did try to escape. My men were exhausted, sleepless because of the mortar bombardments through the night and sickened by the ever-present stink of the dead cows rotting in the fields around the village. Estry was a charnel house.

Two days later, the guns and mortars fell silent. Under cover of darkness, the Germans had withdrawn, almost certainly because they had run out of ammunition, food and probably, crucially, cigarettes. Slipping past the Grenadiers, moving south, looking for supply dumps, linking up with the SS Panzer-Division 21 and others, regrouping, they were clearly determined to fight on.

To the west, however, Bradley's 1st US Army were beginning to break out of Normandy. German forces were too stretched and too sparse to contain such a sustained and powerful thrust.

South of Estry, we made our way through the farmland, carefully clearing the area of snipers and stragglers. Many of the men were much moved by the terrible suffering we saw in the fields. Cows stood stock-still, lowing in agony. No one had milked them and any movement of their bloated udders caused even more pain. Several of my Borderers had come from farm places and I allowed them to relieve the animals' agony by milking them by hand, the milk splashing in warm jets on the grass. What reduced me to unashamed tears was the sight of a bay mare and its foal. In one of the small fields, the mare lay motionless, bleeding on the ground, probably killed in a crossfire coming from the surrounding hedges. In a hopeless circuit of loss and puzzlement, the foal was walking round and round its mother. So often had this orphan done this that there was a path worn in the grass. One of my men spoke softly to the young horse, stroking its withers, trying to tempt it away with handfuls of torn up grass, but the bewildered foal would not leave its mother.

31 August 1944

More than anything it was the music that lulled me. It drained the tension, washed like a warm and welcome tide over the images of slaughter. I sat in the corner of a vast, mirrored restaurant on the Rue de Rivoli in Paris, not far from the Louvre, enjoying coffee and cake, listening to a young woman singing softly at the piano. She wore a flower in her dark hair. It sounded as though the song was in English, but the sort learned phonetically, with the words blurred together, something about waiting for a train to come in.

After the breakout from Normandy, Bradley's 1st US Army, General Patton's forces, the Canadians' and ours raced across central France to the Seine. Having learned the art of armed retreat on the Eastern Front, the Germans had pulled back in good order northwards, seeking the sanctuary of the Westwall, the much-strengthened Siegfried Line. On August 25th, Paris was taken without a destructive fight. The city of Napoleon III and Baron Haussmann, of the Place de l'Etoile and the Champs Élysées, the Left Bank, Notre-Dame and the Eiffel Tower had not been bombed to rubble.

As a German speaker, I had been seconded to No. 30 Commando and the staff of Squadron Leader Godwin. In one of the few flashpoints, we were attacked when we captured a very grand château on the edge of the Bois de Boulogne. It had been the HQ of Admiral Dönitz, the commander-in-chief of the German navy, and we discovered many tons of abandoned documents, a huge cache that had somehow not been destroyed. My team and I were ordered to sort and catalogue them. I had also to help with negotiations. The German garrison had absolutely refused to surrender to the French Resistance and insisted that, as soldiers, they could only make a formal agreement with opposing officers, either the Free French Army, ourselves or, preferably, the Americans. For good reason, they were also terrified that they would be lynched by the crowds of Parisians who had flooded into the streets. My own view was that the formalities did not matter much but the heated arguments I witnessed told me that post-war politics was already crackling around the Paris streets like electricity.

I have never been kissed so often and by so many different women as I was in Paris. '*Vive l'Écosse!*' shouted one woman who embraced me – and with more than a peck on the cheek. After all that had happened on Queen Beach and in Normandy, I was proud to wear the regimental Glengarry that marked me out as a Scottish soldier. Paris exhaled with relief at the departure of *Les Boches*, the Gestapo, the strutting SS, and exulted in what seemed like a true liberation from years of oppression.

And I exulted in clean clothes, a shave each morning, a bath each week and a billet in the Château de la Muette, Dönitz's former headquarters. From the windows of a bedroom that could have slept twenty, I looked out over the Bois de Boulogne, its lush green grass, mature trees, broad walkways and not a hedge in sight. It was a very far cry from the bunks of the barracks at the regimental depot in Berwick-upon-Tweed. Autumn would tint the leaves soon but it was good to be alive in late summer in Paris.

Our work was straightforward. With characteristic efficiency, the German clerks had filed incoming and outgoing correspondence into daybooks. With Squadron Leader Godwin's agreement, I decided we would begin with the most recent correspondence and work backwards. Old files dealing with anything earlier than June 6th 1944 were not likely to be of much use in informing us about current German strategic thinking, the state of their resources or the swirl of politics within the Nazi Party hierarchy.

But I discovered one cache of earlier documents that I will never forget.

Beginning in March 1944, with the German invasion of Hungary, a series of memoranda had been circulated to several high-ranking government ministers and military leaders, including Admiral Dönitz. They came from SS Lieutenant Colonel Adolf Eichmann and concerned a programme of mass deportation of Jews from Hungary. Many thousands, it seemed, had been taken by train to a place called Auschwitz in southern Poland. There were several lists and a proliferation of numbers. But the language was vague, talking of following 'the Wannsee Protocols' and 'the Jewish question', and the tone was sinister. We had heard stories of labour camps and atrocities committed in ghettos and on the Eastern Front by the SS, but this seemed altogether different. The phrase used by Eichmann that leapt off the page for me was 'the fate of the Jews is an internal matter for the SS'.

I showed what I had found to Squadron Leader Godwin, translating for him as I turned the pages from Dönitz's files. He too knew the stories, and the treatment of the Jews in Germany before the war was well documented. While Godwin agreed that the memos did indeed sound sinister, what they contained was not an intelligence priority. I should put that material to one side and carry on with the analysis of much more recent documents.

In the cafés and bars, and even in our mess at the château, I overheard a good deal of jaunty talk about a swift end to the war. The Germans had retreated behind the Westwall but in the process had lost many men as casualties or prisoners of war, and been forced to abandon weapons and supplies that would be impossible to replace. The RAF's Bomber Command was pounding their cities and factories, and in the east the Russians were in the outskirts of Warsaw, only three hundred miles from Berlin. The Allies would squeeze and starve the Germans into surrender.

The military correspondence told a different story. The

pivotal date was July 20th, the day of the failed assassination attempt on Hitler. At that moment everything changed.

In the days that followed, the Nazi leadership of Goebbels, Himmler and Speer had declared a state of *Totaler Krieg*, total war. Every sinew of the German economy would be stretched to the utmost, a Replacement Army would be recruited, citizens in the *Volkssturm* would be armed and trained and every last drop of blood would be wrung out of the army. That was where the plotters had found support. The army owed the German people a debt of honour, and of blood.

It seemed to me that the Allies' insistence on unconditional surrender was a propaganda gift to Goebbels. He had been able to convince millions of Germans to fight on regardless of loss, to the last man if necessary, to buy time for the development of Wonder Weapons, the *Wunderwaffen*. My own assessment was that the war would continue through the winter and into the spring of 1945, perhaps even longer.

Amidst the chaos of conflicting reports and views, I kept my own counsel amongst my contemporaries. Only in conversation with Squadron Leader Godwin was I completely candid.

3 October 1944

Only ten days after Paris had fallen to the Allies, the front line had advanced dramatically and, on September 4th, the great port of Antwerp was captured.

Supply lines across northern France had become so extended that an emergency one-way system known as the Red Ball Express operated from the Channel ports to keep tanks and other vehicles supplied with petrol and troops supplied with food and ammunition. The distances were so great that it cost four gallons of fuel to deliver one to the front. That made Antwerp vital. Only a few miles from the German border, it was a deep-water port where tankers could dock. The difficulty was that the Germans still held the shores of the Scheldt estuary and could easily prevent the passage of sea traffic to the port. The 1st Canadian Army had been handed the task of clearing the estuary and two battalions of Borderers would fight alongside them. I found myself in Antwerp to liaise with the Canadians and compile a situation report for my regimental commanders.

The jagged litter of war lay everywhere. In contrast to the miraculously preserved glories of Paris, the ancient merchant city had been bombed to smithereens. I had to weave my jeep between mounds of rubble at the foot of gaunt ruins, many of them gable ends that stood like tombstones. On one of them were the sad remains of three homes: three fireplaces that had warmed families were now exposed, somehow obscenely, one with tattered wallpaper flapping in the late afternoon breeze.

But even though the price of freedom had been the destruction of their city, the people of Antwerp thanked us for it. When a military policeman stopped me at a crossroads, a group of men working with wheelbarrows to shift the scatter of rubble stopped and waved, one of them managing a passable version of Winston Churchill's V-sign.

When I reached the Canadians' headquarters at the port, where the Albert Canal meets the Scheldt, and reported to the adjutant's office of Lieutenant General Simonds, I was told that a massive bombing raid had begun on German positions at the mouth of the estuary.

'Your Lancasters are coming across the North Sea in waves,' said Captain Charet of the Royal Hamilton Light Infantry. 'Pounding the dykes to pieces. I guess they want to breach them to let the sea in, put Walcheren island under water. Flooding will hamper the Germans. Us too. But they'll be marooned, easy targets for the bombers.'

'Is there a vantage point where I can look westwards down the Scheldt?' I asked.

'There's no high ground around here,' Charet said, 'but you can get a good idea of the lay of the land from the harbour cranes.'

Helpful, cheerful and generous (giving me a pack of the excellent American cigarettes, Lucky Strikes), Charet offered to come with me. 'The Belgian resistance did a great job, really brave,' he said. 'Before they evacuated, the Germans set explosives on all the cranes but these guys defused every one.' As we climbed up the iron ladders and crossed the landings to the operator's box, the Canadian chattered about how, pretty soon, the tankers would begin to arrive with fuel and supplies, and we would not be looking west but east, to Germany, its borders only a few miles away. 'Once our guys clear the estuary, the war is as good as over.' We wound down the windows and focused our binoculars.

At the same time as Charet and I clanked up the crane at Antwerp, the Americans were launching a long-awaited attack on the Westwall at Aachen. An ancient city at the centre of the empire of Charlemagne, what the Nazis called the First Reich, it was freighted with great symbolic significance. Vastly outnumbered and pounded by bombers and artillery, its defenders fought fanatically to prevent the Allies defiling the holy soil of Germany. With only eighteen thousand soldiers, many of them *Volkssturm*, and eleven tanks, they held a force five times larger at bay.

Throughout the four months since our landing on Queen Beach, I had been continually in awe of the fighting spirit of the German army. Most of our soldiers, British, American and Canadian, were conscripted civilians who would fight against what they saw as a manifest evil, but they also wanted to survive. By contrast, under the Nazis, German soldiers knew that savage punishment, often summary execution, awaited those who disobeyed orders, deserted or even showed something less than total disregard for their own safety.

And added to this unbending regime was a visceral wish for vengeance. Many German soldiers had lost family, often children, to the terror bombing of their cities, fuelling their rage. For many, four years of fighting on the Eastern Front had also forged them into highly professional fighting units, able to improvise and surprise their enemies again and again. I had seen the iron resolve of the Germans at Estry and the Americans saw it at Aachen.

But on October 3rd 1944, the Westwall was finally pierced, north of the city, US units crossed the River Wurm and, despite ferocious and repeated counter-attacks, they established the first bridgehead inside Germany, breaching the borders of the Reich.

Although Walcheren island was more than forty miles west of Antwerp, Charet and I fancied we could hear the drone of the bombers' engines as the Lancaster pilots over-flew their targets and began to turn for home. From our dizzyingly high vantage point we looked directly west over the Scheldt estuary and the billiard-table flat landscape to the north and south.

Like most of their equipment, the Canadians' binoculars were more powerful and of better quality than ours. Sharing them meant that one of us could have all-round vision while the other tried to make out detail in the far distance.

But when it came, neither of us understood what we saw.

Like sheet lightning in daytime, a sudden and dazzling flash lit up the western horizon. We exchanged open-mouthed glances.

When Charet looked again through his binoculars, adjusting the focus with his thumbs, I heard him whisper, 'My God. My God in Heaven. What in hell is that?' He handed them to me.

A great distance away, far across the North Sea, it seemed, a giant cloud was rising, forming itself into the shape of a mushroom.

'What in God's name is that?' said Charet.

'*Götterdämmerung*,' I said. 'It is *Götterdämmerung*.'

IV

22 December 1944

A slow, pink dawn crept over the snow-covered landscape, the sort of dawn when few would venture out who did not have to. On the eastern horizon, a sliver of the sun's disc began to turn the gun-metal grey of the sky a pale blue; the wind beat down from the north, whistling through the stones of the old tower. High on a crag, it was both visible for miles around and offered views for miles: south to the dark heads of the Cheviot Hills and north to where the foothills of the Lammermuirs shelved up to their watershed ridges; to the east, looking down between the arms of its sheltering hills, were the white fields and farms of the great river valley, my native place, the valley of the River Tweed.

Believing that all of the bridges would be watched and probably manned by sentries, I had decided to keep to the north bank. Travelling only at night and resting by day, though not often sleeping, I had reached the foot of the tower in four nights and three shivering days, moving slowly in the black darkness along empty country lanes, listening for movement, watching for watchers, imagining shapes in the gaunt, leafless hedges, remembering the dangers of the *bocage*. I often zig-zagged inland but always kept the river on my left. Even though I knew this country well, it would be easy to get lost in the formless fields or stumble into a drain or down the steep banks of an unseen stream and injure myself.

For most of the previous day, I had lain hidden amongst the dense rhododendra at the side of the long driveway up to Floors Castle, near Kelso. An ugly pile, its pepperpot turrets making it look like a rectangular wedding cake, I did not want to get too close but the evergreen shrubs supplied the only cover I could be sure of in a leafless December when the snow made the land graphic and even the smallest movement noticeable. I had only a duffel coat and a thick pullover over my army fatigues to keep out the chill as I curled up on the ground amongst the debris of a dozen dead summers. And keeping still did not mean keeping warm. But the day was short and when gloaming came and I could pull aside the branches and look up the drive to the castle; I watched its lights twinkle but saw no movement outside in the courtyard. Staying in the shadows, I passed by to the north, following the river westwards.

A peel tower built as a refuge from the incessant English raiding of the fifteenth and sixteenth centuries, it had long been abandoned in favour of a much more comfortable mansion by the Tweed. But the old fortification had survived the snows, ice and rain of five hundred winters more or less intact, its roof of stone slabs keeping out the weather and the pigeons. Its glowering mass had prompted the father of one of my friends to describe it as 'sod off in stone'.

Having shouldered aside a wooden door tied to the iron bolts in the walls, something to discourage curious sheep but not a cold traveller, I climbed the steep spiral staircase to the roofwalk. It was something I had done often as an adventuresome boy in another world, one that had fled and would never return. Next to the blackened stones of the old chimney stack with a recess above it for a lantern was the watchman's seat. Slipping my rucksack off my shoulders, I looked out as the day lit the land and sat down to wait.

*

I had been an unwilling witness to a moment when history shifted. On the way back to their East Anglian bases, the crews of the Lancasters had seen it seconds before Captain Charet and I watched the mushroom cloud rising many miles into the evening sky.

In what we were told was an airburst, there was a gigantic explosion over central London. Through a ring of fire, the white mushroom cloud climbed to a height of perhaps twenty miles while at the same time a circular black cloud formed and in seconds it spread over the city like a tidal wave rolling up everything in its path. Those who were within a mile of the blast zone were burned to carbon in moments, some simply evaporating in the thermal flash. The black shockwave killed even more people, blistering and tearing at their flesh, leaving it to dangle from their skeletons like ragged clothing.

This was what von Klige had known something of. It was an atomic bomb, *Götterdämmerung*, the Twilight of the Gods, the instant that plunged the world into darkness.

Once the borders of the Reich had been breached at Aachen, Hitler had given orders that a rocket, carrying what the Germans called a warhead, be launched from an airfield near The Hague, not far from Antwerp. According to what we were told, it was the ultimate *Vergeltungswaffe*, the Weapon of Vengeance.

When Charet and I climbed down the crane by the dockside and reached Canadian HQ, there was chaos. The Lancaster crews had sent back radio messages and some of their photographer flight-recorders had taken pictures. These were passed to the Allied Commander-in-Chief, General Eisenhower, and his staff scrambled to find information. How bad was it? How many killed? Where was the king, the prime minister? What had happened? What had been dropped on London?

Just after midnight on October 4th 1944, the Germans answered all questions.

In a radio broadcast of chilling simplicity and brevity that could be heard all over Britain and by Allied forces in Europe, they explained what had happened. 'The Allies are defeated. The war is over,' crackled a triumphant voice. 'The centre of London has been obliterated. Half a million people have died. The king is dead. The prime minister is dead. German weapons have changed the course of history. The Führer has led Germany to total victory.'

The broadcast ended with a clear ultimatum: unless the Allies immediately halted their offensive and agreed to an unconditional surrender, the Führer would authorise the launch of more warheads in the coming days to attack British cities. The Allied air forces were to remain grounded and all naval ships were to return to port.

It seemed that in those hours and days that followed, the stunned world had ceased to turn, history had been turned upside down.

*

The winter wind soughed around the roofwalk of the tower and I longed for the moment when I could seek the sanctuary of the chamber behind me. The reason I had come there was its high vantage point and that the crag around it was open ground. There were no woods or cover of any kind for at least half a mile on every side. If anyone approached, I would see them long before they saw me. I had asked my friend to meet me an hour after first light, at approximately 09.00, and to come on the eastern track. And to make sure no one was following.

Four nights earlier, I had become a fugitive, running for my life. If apprehended, I would be summarily shot.

When photographs of the destruction of London and leaflets listing the appalling numbers of casualties were dropped all over the Western Front on October 4th, and the death of

King George, his family, Winston Churchill and the entire war cabinet had been confirmed, General Eisenhower issued orders for an immediate ceasefire. In the absence of a civilian government of any sort, the British Commander-in-Chief, Field Marshal Montgomery, acted on his own initiative and sought a parley with his German counterpart, Field Marshal Model. His overtures were ignored and almost four thousand miles to the west and sixteen hundred miles to the north-east, actions spoke much louder than words.

As the autumn sun climbed, clearing the morning mist over the Hudson River, and the city of New York began to rumble into life, Captain Horst Schellenberg looked through his periscope.

His orders were unequivocal. At 08.00 he was to stay submerged and manoeuvre his U-boat as close as possible to the shores of the Battery on the tip of Manhattan Island and then surface at 08.30. Once the conning tower was clear of the water, a red, white and black swastika flag was to be flown so that no one who saw the U-boat could be in any doubt where it had come from.

At the same time a telegram was received at the White House. Having passed through several agencies, it was addressed to Harry Hopkins, for his eyes only. He was a key and trusted aide to President Franklin Roosevelt. The terms were stark:

```
Unless you immediately direct General
Eisenhower to surrender all of the Allied
armies in Europe under his command, and
unless the war against our allies in
the Pacific ceases at once, the city of
New York will suffer the same fate as
London. Be in no doubt that hundreds
of thousands of civilians will die
instantly and the city will be destroyed.
For the Fatherland, our brave sailors
have brought an atomic bomb even more
```

```
powerful than that dropped on London. If
you do not immediately comply with our
directive, the bomb will be detonated.
If the U-boat is attacked, it will be
detonated. Await further instructions.
```

Later the same day, another, more detailed communication arrived on Hopkins' desk. It demanded that a team of US government physicists should cease their work at their laboratory and be flown to Europe within forty-eight hours. All of their data, all of their research workings and such materials as could be uplifted were to travel with them. Their immediate families would also accompany them – with no exceptions.

Meanwhile, sixteen hundred miles north-east of Antwerp, in the Gulf of Finland, between the port of Kronshtadt and the port at Leningrad, another U-boat waited in the darkness of the deeps for its orders.

It became quickly clear in the following weeks that the precision and coordination of the terrible events of October 3rd and 4th had not been linked to any coherent plan of action. It was as though the Germans were taken as much by surprise as the Allies. Von Klige had talked of the need to fight desperately, fanatically, in order to buy time and it seemed that the use of these devastating weapons had only become a possibility a short time before one of them was unleashed on London. In no condition to convert their retreating and depleted armies into guards able to control hundreds of thousands of Allied prisoners of war, the Germans relied on frequent reminders of the ever-present threat of detonating more atomic bombs to induce compliance. Instead of making any attempt to deal with the impossibly vast logistics of detaining, feeding and supplying hundreds of thousands of captives, their major focus seemed to be to expel Allied soldiers from Europe as soon as possible, back to the USA, to Canada and to Britain.

This extraordinary reversal resulted in a stunned silence all along the front. No more guns roared, no more machine guns rattled, and nothing moved on the roads.

Appalled at the flow of fearful statistics and photographs of twisted, incinerated bodies and the rubble of London – only recognisable by the stubborn survival of the southern façade of Westminster Abbey – almost all Allied units complied with the German demands. On their part, the Nazis insisted on complete disarmament and encouraged Allied soldiers to think that their war was over and they would be home soon. All of the vast supply dumps were commandeered, and any hesitation to cooperate was met with a brutal and instant response. It was later said that when General George Patten refused to hand over his ivory-handled pistols, an SS colonel shot him in the chest at point-blank range.

The Germans could also call on the loyalty of an army of ghosts. Since D-Day, almost two hundred and fifty thousand of their best front-line soldiers had been held in prisoner-of-war camps on the British mainland and, on their release, they immediately assumed the role of an occupying army. Transport ships began to shuttle British soldiers from Antwerp back to Harwich, Felixstowe and Ipswich – where they were met by motorised military escorts and told they would be marching back to their regimental depots around the country.

With little in the way of supplies, no wet weather clothing, only the fatigues they wore at the moment of surrender and bivouacking in the open as the October weather grew colder and damper, the 1st Battalion of the King's Own Scottish Borderers began a long march home. We had to make our way up the length of England to its most northerly town, to our depot at Berwick-upon-Tweed. On disembarkation at Harwich, all of our senior officers had been detained. Some of the more cynical reckoned they would not be bashing the roads like us but on their way north by train. We had no idea where they had been taken, however, and as we made our way through the flat Suffolk landscapes, I feared that they might have been executed. A leaderless army is half beaten before it begins to fight.

Having not let on that my German comprehension was excellent, I overheard a great deal as we marched north. It became brutally clear that our escorts – former prisoners of war from the huge camp at Devizes, thugs rather than soldiers – were bent on vengeance. It seemed not to occur to any of these former POWs that any of their captives might understand what they were saying to each other, and their boasting was uninhibited.

'We should bomb them again,' said one SS sergeant. 'We have won the war by a stroke of the Führer's genius, but we need revenge for Hamburg, Dresden and for the destruction of Berlin.'

But since none of them were in a position to order the detonation of more atomic bombs, they took it out on us. When we at last stopped, at the end of a long first day, we were formed up into ranks and addressed by an SS officer who had somewhere acquired a swastika armband.

'You know the Romans? Yes?' In somewhat halting English, but with evident relish, this little man strutted back and forth, wagging a finger in the air. 'Not obey orders, we de-ci-mate you.' His smirk chilled me, convinced me he would not hesitate. 'Kill one man in ten. No question.' He held up both hands, spreading his fingers and counted them off. 'One out ten, we kill. You all obey. Or you die. Simple.'

In the course of what I began to realise was a hunger march, I heard several comments about stragglers, about shooting them anyway, not waiting for exhausted men to fall behind or drop. And always, push them harder!

More Borderers died in those terrible October days than in the battle for Normandy and France. When we finally came to the southern bank of the Tweed and crossed to Berwick, only about a hundred men had survived the journey. I found that I was the most senior officer. All of the familiar burdens returned, but without any power to ease them. In desperate circumstances like these, the Borderers needed leadership of some kind, however ineffectual in the face of such inhumanity and gratuitous cruelty.

When we drew ourselves up into ranks on the parade ground between Berwick Barracks and the Elizabethan town walls, calling on every shred of regimental pride to make our backs straight and keep our eyes front in this, the home place of the Borderers, we came to attention. The officer who had threatened decimation all those weeks ago, and had carried it out more than once for the slightest offence, asked who the senior officer was. I stepped out of the ranks, saluted and identified myself.

Smiling at me, this man said, 'You are responsible for the conduct of your men. Completely responsible.'

Perhaps only five foot six but straining to stand as tall as he could, clutching a black swagger stick behind his back, he had to look up at me, and I could see that irked him. He struck me as someone who relished any opportunity to exert dominance but lacked the height to do it physically. As though he was weighing me up, the officer walked around behind me. I stared straight ahead, standing to attention. At any moment, I sensed he might strike me with the stick but instead he faced me and poked my chest with it.

'You are now a defeated people. To survive, you must be loyal to the Reich and our Führer. Well?'

'Yes, sir,' I replied.

He barked back at me, 'Disobedience or disrespect will mean de-ci-ma-tion. You understand?'

'Yes, sir, I do. Thank you, sir.'

This pleased him and, it being late in the evening, we were dismissed. My men were out on their feet, but at least that night we would have a roof over our heads, what was once our own roof. Permitted to sleep in our old barracks – not through kindness but in an attempt at incarceration – and supplied with basic rations, we began a life of what turned out to be the daily attrition of slave labour.

The Germans used the small harbour at Berwick to land supplies and equipment from across the North Sea. In the icy winds, we manhandled cargoes onto the quayside beyond the old walls. It was there, witnessing a moment of casual cruelty, that something snapped in my head. After a wet tea-box container had slipped out of his hands, one of the Borderers had fallen at the very edge of the quay. But before he could get up, a German guard ran forward and booted him off balance so that he toppled into the freezing waters of the harbour. Unable to swim, thrashing the water, he called frantically for help, but the guards turned their guns on us, daring anyone to move to rescue their comrade.

That night, I passed around the word. If one of us, or a small group, tried to escape, they might well succeed, but those left behind would all be shot in reprisal. We needed to mount a mass breakout. All or nothing. And once we had broken out, we had to split up into ones or twos to make it more difficult for those who would pursue us. Some might be caught but surely some would also get away. There was no future in this death camp. We would all die anyway.

'There's supposed to be a tunnel,' whispered Private John Campbell. 'That's the way out.' For reasons of safety, the powder magazine had been built outside the barracks, beside the Elizabethan walls, and Campbell was sure that a tunnel led to it: 'The magazine is barred and bolted from the inside and there's only one door, for safety and security.'

'But where is the entrance?' I asked.

'Must be through the officers' mess,' he replied.

'Damn! That's used by the Germans. What we need is a diversion.'

The next day, after darkness had fallen, I positioned myself in the corner shadows of the cobbled parade ground, surrounded on three sides by high barrack blocks that made my voice echo.

'*Achtung! Achtung! Jetzt auf Parade! Schnell! Schnell! Achtung an alle!*' I bellowed. 'Colonel Stauffel's adjutant has telephoned. He will be here in minutes. Out now! On parade now!'

On the north side of the quadrangle, two sentries were hurriedly fiddling with the padlock and chains on the main gate. Others were clattering downstairs, buckling on their kit and streaming into the open.

I slipped back into the barracks and, with all of my men behind me, ran along the corridor and smashed open the door to the officers' mess. Our impetus overwhelmed two Germans who had been slow to react to my theatricals. A farrier in a previous life, Corporal Angus Wilson used his tremendous strength to snap the neck of one and the other was simply overrun and kicked senseless. In seconds, Private Campbell had sounded the wood panelling, found a snubbed catch next to the fireplace and we were in.

And plunged into total darkness. Without any torches or even matches, we stumbled and scrambled down a narrow stair, feeling for the damp walls, moving as fast as possible. I had pulled the panelling door shut, hoping it would stay flush and that we would not be pursued by guards who did have torches and could see where they were going. After a frantic few minutes, punctuated by much swearing and many scraped elbows and knees, Campbell led us up another stair and into the powder magazine. At the far end was a massive wooden door. Bolts

65

were felt for and slid back. The door pushed open to reveal an astonishing promise of freedom: the vast and dark horizon of the North Sea greeted us. No one hesitated as we dropped down the face of the Elizabethan walls and onto a dangerously open and wide expanse of grassland, what had been a golf course before the war. For our lives, we ran north, scattering in all directions in ones or twos, putting as much distance as possible between us and the guards before they realised that no colonel was about to arrive in his staff car.

Knowing the town and the ground around the barracks, I made rapid progress at first, running north through the sleeping streets past some grand houses and then making for Halidon Hill. From that vantage point, I could see back to Berwick and the sea beyond. Lingering only to look for the headlights of pursuing vehicles coming in my direction – and thank God there were none – I turned inland, up the Tweed Valley, towards home.

'Will you accept the charges?' There was an agonising pause. I looked around the telephone box I had come across in the village but could see no lights on and no one about. 'Please go ahead, you are now connected.'

'Hello. Katie? It's me. Yes. David. I need your help. Desperately.'

*

As much as the cold, it was the wind that kept me awake, the long soughs of it around the tower. I could see that some warmth might come, watching the slanting winter sun wash down the flanks of the distant hills; and along the rigs, the ridges of the valley unfolding below, long shadows began to shorten.

Although I was very cold, constantly pulling my coat tighter, all of the everyday glories of the great valley touched my heart once more. It had been a long time. Camouflaged against the snow, I watched a flock of ewes moving slowly in the field on the far side of the track.

Katie was late. I had an uninterrupted view along the eastern track for about half a mile before it turned behind a crag, but there was no sign. Perhaps she had been stopped, questioned, arrested? All varieties of jeopardy spooled through my imagination, mixed with guilt for asking her to come, and self-justification. What choice did I have?

There was no one else I trusted. And there had been no one else I loved.

Before the chasm of the war opened and swallowed the world we once knew, Katie and I had met as undergraduates at St Andrews University: 'Bejant' and 'Bejantine', in the odd and slightly arch terms for first-year students. Both of us Borderers, both of us unsure of ourselves, we fell back on the familiar at first. Just as Katie did, I felt myself in the company of scores of bright people, all cleverer and more confident. But we quickly grew out of that and by the time we boarded a train at Leuchars station bound for home and Christmas, we could not wait for the following term, when we would resume what neither of us understood had become a love affair.

Something flickered on the edge of my field of vision, like a crow lifting into the air.

And then I heard the drone of its engine. Flying low over Brotherstone Hill to the west, the iron cross insignia of the Luftwaffe visible on the underside of its wings, a spotter plane was approaching fast. Clearly, the Germans were scouting the countryside for the Borderers who had broken out of Berwick Barracks. I pulled the hood of my duffel coat over my head and, to avoid attracting attention, turned very slowly to face the tower wall. I prayed that Katie was not on the road, and if she was, that she had seen the plane and hidden. Once I heard the engine begin to fade, I watched it moving eastwards towards the sea. I imagined they were methodical – quartering the Ordnance Survey grid – and would soon turn and come back in this direction.

And then I saw her, as if by magic, appearing from nowhere. Cycling quickly up the track, her body bent low and forward to push down hard on the pedals, her fair hair tucked under a black beret, she quickly reached the wrought-iron gate at the foot of the crag. I rushed down the spiral staircase to shove open the wooden door – and there she was. There she was.

I could say nothing. I felt my heart surge. I had no words. Katie cocked her head to one side, and smiled. Like she always did. I felt tears running down my face, the prickle of warm tears on my cheeks.

'Oh, David. There's nothing of you.' She leaned her bicycle against the doorway and took my arm, gently pushing me inside. 'I think we should get all of this and ourselves out of sight. Don't you?'

Still I could say nothing, only smile and shake my head.

Katie turned to me. 'Come here.' She held me for a long time in the doorway of that old tower, and my tears would not stop.

After a time, some words came. 'I've never forgotten how beautiful you are. But I did forget how your smile could swell my heart.'

Taking off her beret, she shook her hair loose and looked up at me. She held my hand.

'I must look a sight,' I apologised.

She laughed. 'Yes, and around you there is an interesting aroma.'

I started to laugh, too, recalling many withering rebukes about my student dishevelment. By contrast, Katie sparkled. Her fair hair kept back off her face with an Alice band, her looks were classical, as someone I glared at once said. Classical beauty could be cold, an icy, wintry perfection, but it was the kindness that glowed from her eyes that melted my heart. And the hearts of many others at St Andrews.

We had sometimes walked out to the end of the pier, a long, wave-worn finger of stone that reaches into the North Sea. With the ruined cathedral and the university behind us, we found ourselves in our own private world. Sitting as close as we could, folded into each other, it was enough for me to look at Katie, to gaze into her welcoming eyes. No words needed. I could find a peace in that, and sometimes to shut out even more of the outside, I would hold up my hands on either side of our faces to blinker us. Sometimes my gaze disconcerted Katie and she would laugh and shake her head. But she never looked away.

'Aren't you going to invite me into your castle?'

We had been standing at the foot of the spiral staircase for long moments and I did not want to move, to make ordinary time restart. The tears had come, I understood later, because no one had touched me with any tenderness for a very long time, and no one had smiled at me with such warmth.

With a gun slip slung over one shoulder, a knapsack over the other and the basket from her bicycle full, I realised that Katie had remembered everything I asked for, and more.

'Now, let's see what we have,' she said.

We sat in an embrasure in the tower wall by one of its few windows. I had not eaten anything for three days, only drinking from burns and a horse trough I passed. She lifted a linen napkin off the basket to reveal wonders, the like of which I had not seen for a long time. Katie had baked bread, there was cheese, four boiled eggs and a twist of salt-cured ham, some wrinkled apples, a comb of honey and a half-bottle of whisky.

'Slowly, now,' she said as I tore off a hunk of bread and some cheese. 'Your stomach will be the size of a golf ball.'

As I ate, Katie undid the buckles of the gun slip. She had brought from her father's cabinet an old, beautifully kept Dickson shotgun, its barrels well oiled, the wooden stock polished and the metal action engraved with the maker's name. A thing of great beauty. There was a box of twenty-five twelve-bore cartridges, an oiled cloth, an old army bayonet and a penknife. From her knapsack, she brought out two packets of Player's Navy Cut, two boxes of matches, a torch, two candles, six pencils held together with a rubber band and the thick, leather-bound notebook I had asked for. 'And this is my mother's cashmere wrap to keep you warm. Light as a feather. Made in Hawick. I shall want it back.'

On some musty, dust-covered old hay I found in the basement store, shaken and taken up to the top chamber, I lay down and slept for the whole day, filled with food and wrapped in cashmere. When Katie came back at gloaming, certain she had not been seen, we opened the whisky and exchanged fiery sips. What would have made the moment even warmer was a fire in the vast old grate, but we were taking enough risks.

'What will you do, David?' she said, concern etched on her brow.

'Well, I can't stay here. And I can't keep putting you in danger.' I paused, not knowing what else to say. What *was* my plan now? But I was still too tired to think straight. For now, all I really wanted was to listen to Katie's voice. 'Tell me everything,' I said. 'What's been happening since the bomb went off in London?'

'It's been awful, the confusion and rumour almost as bad as those terrible pictures we all saw,' Katie said. 'It's thought people in the south-east are still dying, although no one knows for certain. Apparently something called atomic bomb disease is killing them. They can't stop being sick.'

She paused, shaking her head, brow furrowed.

'We don't get much from the radio except rules and regulations. Obviously, the Germans control everything that's said, and we're not allowed to go anywhere that's not essential, so we don't see many people.'

I attempted to interrupt.

'Don't worry, darling,' she said, 'I've been careful.'

All I heard was the word 'darling'.

'The farm's not far and I got here okay. But they've also set a strict curfew and there's even less food available than there was during the war.' She smiled as she watched me eat a little more, slowly as instructed. 'But we have our sources. It's handy being farmers.' But then her smile faded. 'All the big cities – Birmingham, Manchester, Leeds, Newcastle and Glasgow – they call them hostage cities, targets. If there was any resistance, of any sort, they say they'll do to them what they did to London. Every night they recite the list and they don't allow anyone to forget that they'll drop more atomic bombs if we don't do exactly as we're told.'

All those MPs who had not been in London on October 3rd had been summoned to Leeds Town Hall, where they were invited to support a motion, unanimously, that Sir Oswald Mosley should be appointed prime minister by 'King' Edward VIII, recently returned from the Bahama Islands. Aneurin Bevan, a Welsh MP, had attempted to object but was removed, beaten and apparently imprisoned. This rump parliament had then voted itself out of existence, granting Mosley dictatorial powers. 'All the Germans wanted,' said Katie, 'was someone to sign an armistice. As you know, they like the paperwork to be in order. I'm perfectly sure Mosley takes his instructions directly from Berlin.'

That was the gist of what she knew, almost all of it from German broadcasts. No newspapers at all had been published. But there was one more thing.

'You remember my Aunt Jenny from St Andrews?'

Married to a professor of physics, she lived in a wonderful house in Hepburn Gardens and was very convivial. More than once, Katie and I had been invited for drinks and sat in the MacDonalds' sheltered garden, Jenny bringing trays of gin cocktails and food through the French windows from the kitchen. Barely out of school, raw undergraduates, we were made to feel like sophisticated adults.

'She told my dad on the phone that odd things were going on in St Andrews. Hundreds of SS soldiers had suddenly arrived in trucks, freed from the prisoner-of-war camp over at Comrie. They immediately began fortifying the town, digging trenches right across the first and eighteenth fairways of the Old Course, for goodness' sake. Uncomfortable, not knowing who might be listening, my dad shushed Jenny and changed the subject. But I did think that was odd.'

More warming whisky passed between us in the candlelight. We talked of sunlit days as students in St Andrews. Katie had lived in a very grand bedsit in North Castle Street, directly opposite the ruins of the bishop's castle and close to steps that led down to the narrow beach below it. I had borrowed money from my father to buy tickets for the Union Ball, and to look the part I had also borrowed his dinner jacket and bow tie. 'My God,' Katie had snorted, 'you could get two of you in that!' In a red silk ballgown, her mother's pearls and scarlet, film-star lipstick, Katie looked the part. In fact, she looked even better: a real woman, not someone on celluloid. She was glorious – tall, willowy, elegant – and mine.

'Close your mouth, you'll catch flies,' she'd said.

Before walking along the Scores to the Younger Hall and all the buzz and racket of the ball, I asked if she would come down the steps to the beach with me. 'We won't go onto the sand, I promise. Just as far as the bottom step.' We looked out over the

North Sea, shivered a little in the evening breeze, and that was when I first told her I loved her.

'What's that?' I stood up. 'I can hear something outside!' It could have been sheep snuffling around the wooden door at the foot of the spiral staircase, but it was sharper than that. 'Where did you leave your bicycle?' I whispered.

'Outside the door, I'm afraid.'

As quietly as possible, I pulled the shotgun out of its slip, flipped the top lever to break it and pushed in two cartridges. Now we could both definitely hear movement, and it definitely wasn't sheep. I snuffed out the candle. We heard the scuff of footsteps on the spiral staircase. 'Stay behind me,' I whispered.

Clicking the shotgun closed and thumbing off the safety catch, I knelt down to present a smaller target and aimed at the dark rectangle of the doorway.

V

'Christ-All-Bloody-Mighty, Wilson!'

Just as I began to exert pressure on the shotgun's delicate trigger, the familiar, unique, agricultural bulk of Corporal Angus Wilson filled the doorway. In the darkness, I could not see his face but those coat-hanger shoulders were unmistakable.

'Who's that behind you?' I barked, momentarily fearing that it was someone with a pistol jabbed into Wilson's back.

'Campbell, sir. Private Campbell!' he said quickly and, from behind this monument to oatmeal, I heard the voice of the man who found the tunnel out of Berwick Barracks. 'Sorry, sir. Sorry about that.'

Once Katie had relit the candle, the two men sat gratefully in the window embrasure. 'I expect you've had nothing to eat for a while,' she said, putting the remains of our collation on the napkin. Having been on the run for five days, they almost wept with thanks. And, as with me, Katie was kind enough to remind them to go slowly. She gave them the last of the cheese and I gave them what was left of the whisky. The fire of the dram made them smack their lips, visibly reviving the two exhausted soldiers. They talked of their escape from Berwick, taking much the same route as I had. Between mouthfuls of food, it was good to hear the soft-spoken accent of the Borders after all the harshness we had listened to in recent weeks. I thought how it was a pleasure to be home, even though a bleak world lay beyond the walls of the tower.

'You should sit here, miss,' said Wilson, after they had eaten every last crumb. 'Campbell and me will be happy on the floor.'

Both slid down the wall, blew out their cheeks, stretched out their aching legs and smiled their thanks. 'Sorry for bursting in on you, sir.' Wilson made it sound like he had caught Katie and I *in flagrante*. 'But we knew the tower was empty. Or we thought it was. How many made it? Any idea, sir?'

I shook my head.

They had both seen the spotter plane and, like me, had kept themselves out of sight during the day and travelled only at night. 'I just hope that some of them were not daft enough to go home,' Campbell added.

'None of us can go home now,' I said.

On the march north, the thugs who tormented us had no interest at all in who we were; no one ever asked for our papers, and even at Berwick they only counted us each morning. We were no more than numbers. But I had given my name, and I knew the little commandant would have remembered it. He would have had to report the breakout to his superiors, and no doubt suffered them coming down on him like a ton of bricks. For any soldier they recaptured, the Germans would be unhesitatingly brutal in extracting information. And out of a hundred men, some would have been much less careful than Wilson, Campbell and me. Somehow, I needed to get a message to Abbey House, to my father. Until my two comrades appeared, that had not occurred to me, to my shame. I had been too concerned with my own survival to think of my father, all alone, rattling around that big house. Since my mother died, he had talked not about adjusting, about making changes, but the opposite, about continuity. 'I shall be going nowhere until Father Doran gives me my last rites and the casket is carried across to the abbey,' he had said. Perhaps Katie could call him to warn him, but that felt like an evasion.

'So, what are we going to do now, sir? Maybe we should talk about it?' said Campbell. A highly intelligent man, an electrician before he joined the regiment, he also turned out to be resourceful. 'But we might need a wee bit of help.' Smiling at us all, he pulled his knapsack onto his lap, undid the buckles and brought out a bottle of whisky.

In the circle of candlelight, our faces bright against the black darkness behind, we were, I think, at that moment, simply glad to be alive. Stolen from a store behind a grocer's shop in St Boswells where he once worked as a delivery boy, Campbell's whisky warmed us.

Straightening his back, looming large in the light, looking up from under his bushy eyebrows, Wilson repeated the question that continued to hover over us: 'What should we do, sir?'

The two soldiers turned and looked at me as though they were waiting for orders. Katie was quiet.

'What can we do? The Germans are holding a gun, or rather a bomb, to everyone's head,' I replied.

Silence settled on us as we stared at the flicker of the candle flame.

After a time, very quietly, Katie started talking, not to anyone in particular, more as though she was thinking aloud. 'You are all Borderers. You should remember your history, remember why places like this tower were built. What's happening now is not really anything new. For centuries English and Scottish armies burned and killed their way across this landscape. What Borderers did then is what you should do now. They endured. You need to do the same. You need to survive. Once you've worked out a way to do that, you can think of what to do next.' She shot me a fierce look, her high cheekbones gaunt in the deep shadows of the candlelight, her lips pursed.

Katie talked of the riding times, the centuries when families banded together for mutual protection and lived their lives at the point of a spear, becoming what history came to know as the Border Reivers. When war crackled along the southern horizons and distant smoke was seen from the roofwalk outside where we sat, families drove their animals into the hills and hid from foraging, rapacious soldiers. 'You are all outlaws now,' she said, 'and you will need to find a way of living, surviving, beyond the reach of those who are hunting you.'

As the whisky bottle was passed round and we risked a second candle, the stone chamber seemed less chill. We talked of fighting spirit, of how the Borderers had distinguished themselves in battle again and again. In the regiment there was a distinctive, thrawn, can-do sense of independence. Suddenly, an unlikely example swam into my head.

'Do you remember Private Sinclair, Willie Sinclair?' I asked Wilson and Campbell.

'Aye, sir, not the sharpest knife in the box'.

'True, but he did have a bit of spirit. He used all his leave to go back home to Coldstream to look after his old mother. Do her garden, chop logs, all that sort of thing.'

I could see from Campbell and Wilson's widening smiles that they remembered the story I was about to tell, but Katie had not heard it. 'One afternoon in Berwick, I saw him in civvies with his suitcase waiting for the bus to Coldstream in Golden Square. When I pointed out to him that he was half an hour early, he puffed out his chest: "Aye, sir. But it won't take me long to wait half an hour." Now that's the kind of spirit we need.'

After a little more whisky, I could see that Wilson and Campbell were at the end of any energy they had left. They knew it, too, and as a strange version of decorum circulated in their heads, they levered themselves upright, saying they would find a corner in the chamber below.

When they were gone, I said to Katie, 'It's probably . . .Well, it really *is* too late and too dangerous for you to cycle home through the dark tonight. Isn't it?'

She was enjoying my discomfiture, smiling, cocking her head to one side, waiting for me to blunder on with this hesitant invitation to sleep with me. Even though there was no bed and we could see our breath plume into the air around the candle flame.

'And don't worry. I'll keep my distance.'

Still she said nothing.

'Anyway, you said I had a certain aroma.'

After a few seconds that seemed to stretch into an eternity, she raised an eyebrow and then took my hands. 'Listen, you idiot, I'm not going anywhere. Not without you. Anyway, it's bloody cold and we both need a hot water bottle, even a smelly one.'

Keeping our coats on and covered by Katie's mother's cashmere, we lay like spoons on the straw, my face inches from her hair. With my arm pulling her close, I hoped the moment would last forever, but we fell asleep almost immediately.

'Charming' was the word that woke me. Katie was looking out of the window at Wilson and Campbell urinating off the edge of the crag the tower perched on.

'And bloody stupid!' I said, running down the spiral staircase to get them out of sight.

Moments later, Katie wheeled her bicycle down to the wrought-iron gate to the eastern track. We had agreed that she would ask her father for his help. We could not risk another night in the tower. Someone was bound to notice activity and toing and froing around a place that was supposedly uninhabited. Would it be possible for the three of us to spend the night at her father's farm, in the hay barn, before moving on? And could I please use the telephone?

*

Having been beaten very badly, the four prisoners were scarcely able to walk.

With their hands tied behind their backs, they stumbled up the steep steps of the Guild Hall in the Marygate, not far from Berwick Barracks. The guards pushed and kicked at them until they reached the top. If any could still see through the bleeding mess of their faces, they would have made out the shape of a gallows set up just below the top step. On a cross beam, four nooses had been tied. The Germans dragged the soldiers into a line to face the crowd that had been forcibly marshalled in the street below. There was a hushed, horrified silence as the little commandant stood forward and shouted.

'These men were prisoners of war and they escaped from the barracks. They were, of course, quickly recaptured. Resistance of this sort is useless and you would all do much better to cooperate. Do not forget what you are about to see. Tell everyone you know what you see today. Everyone! *Heil Hitler*!'

The guards hung a sign on each of the men: *Our wives and children are all dead because of us.*

And then as the commandant walked behind the row of prisoners, a noose was tightened around their necks. So that this grisly spectacle lasted as long as possible, he booted each man in turn off the step to swing and suffer an agonising death. The crowd gasped at the long minutes of choking, wriggling on the end of the rope, scrabbling to get a foothold back on the top step, each soldier finally pissing himself while the others waited and watched. After about half an hour, this obscene spectacle ended. The gallows and the bodies hanging from the crossbeam were left standing for seven days as the gulls circled above them.

*

'No, David. I am going nowhere, and that's an end of it. We've been here for centuries and if these appalling people think . . .'

'Dad,' I cut in, 'please. Listen to me. They are coming. They'll come for you soon. Because they want to find me, because they'll think you know where I am. They'll beat you and probably worse. Please, please, Dad, you have to leave.'

Katie's father had kindly let me use his telephone but, understandably anxious about nosey operators listening in, he warned me not to be too long.

'No. I will not leave, and if they do come, they won't get in without a fight.'

I was despairing. 'Okay. Then please do one thing for me. Put some water and some food in the priest hole, and if they bang on the door in the middle of the night, hide there.'

Both Jacobites and Catholics, my family had survived persecution in the long and dangerous centuries before emancipation, and next to a grand fireplace was a very cleverly concealed hiding place for a priest. Reluctantly, my father agreed to do as I asked, muttering something about being a rat in a trap, before hanging up.

Although we rarely agreed on very much, my father and I were closer than we had ever been. But that was not saying much. When I was eleven, I can remember sitting at the top of the main staircase in Abbey House, looking through the bannister as my parents held their Christmas drinks party for tenants and neighbours. I think my father must have drunk too much whisky, for I heard him talking a little louder than usual to two friends. Loud enough for me to hear every word. He was complaining about someone, saying they were faint-hearted, weak, perhaps a little effeminate and, even worse, uninterested in the important things in life, like family, the land and the church. After a few moments it dawned on me that the person who had disappointed him so much was me. He was talking about me. Shocked and winded at my own father running me down, his only son, in front of two friends, not even members of our family, I never forgot those words of betrayal, and I never told my mother, or my father, that I had heard them coming out of his mouth.

Away at school, I enjoyed languages – German, French, Latin and Greek – something my father could not begin to understand. 'Useless, simply useless. Complete waste of time.' Looking back, I think part of the reason I enjoyed learning about other cultures, and how they viewed the world, was an unconscious reaction to my father's disapproval. The person he talked to his friends about was clearly not good enough, but in German or French, I could adopt an alternative identity, be someone else. And the truth is that I also took those subjects precisely *because* of my father's disapproval of them. When our modern languages master said I had the best German accent and pronunciation he had ever heard from a non-native speaker, the transformation was complete. Although I did not realise it at the time, I had found another person I could be, someone who was *not* faint-hearted, weak, effeminate and disappointing.

Where I think I did meet with his approval was on the rugby field. Probably the only innate, natural gift I was given was the ability to play this game very well. At fourteen, I was six foot one, the same height I am now, with a big frame, the ability to sprint, kick goals, and I had what our house master called 'adhesive hands' because I never dropped the ball. When I was older and came home during the Christmas and Easter holidays, I was immediately drafted into the Melrose 1st XV. But even though I knew he enjoyed rugby and came to watch me, my father never uttered an encouraging word.

At St Andrews University, I rather gave up the game, preferring to spend as much time with Katie as possible. One Easter, Melrose had selected me to play in a home game against Kelso and my father was told that a Scotland selector was coming to watch me. But he chose not to tell me – why, I don't understand. I had a slightly stiff shoulder, decided not to play and went up to St Andrews to be with Katie. Since I gave up playing, several people have said to me that I was international class, but my father never did.

Why he was so closed off, I do not know. His upbringing was severe, I believe, but that is a poor excuse. The cycle should be broken. But one thing did cheer me. My mother's love was completely unconditional, and she encouraged and supported me until the awful day when she crashed her car avoiding a child who ran into the road. The little girl survived but my mother did not. I know that my father loved her very much and he never found a way to accept his loss. A friend once told me that when he was waiting for me in the drawing room at Abbey House, he overheard a very flirtatious conversation between my parents. Unaware of his presence, they embraced and kissed passionately in the hallway. I was glad that, after some pressure, my friend had told me what he had inadvertently witnessed. At least that was a fulfilment for my father: real happiness. He was a hard man to love and would, in any case, have recoiled if I had expressed any emotions like that. But he was my father, and no doubt I played a part in the sterility of our exchanges. Although what that part was, I cannot be sure.

'Bleaklaw Moss,' said Katie's father, apropos of nothing anyone else had said, probably a link to a conversation conducted in his head until that moment. 'No one will ever find you, even if they know you're there.'

After the first hot meal any of us could remember, Wilson, Campbell and I sat by a crackling fire with Katie while her father poured generous tumblers of whisky, something we were going to miss.

'So far as I understand things, it seems to me that you have no option but to disappear, at least until something else catches the attention of those thugs at Berwick.' He went on to explain that Bleaklaw Moss was a wide plateau of dangerous bog-land, much of it covered by willow scrub and colonised by self-seeded sitka spruce blown from a vast plantation on its eastern flank. 'I know an old shepherd, Sandy Ormiston, who can show you the safe paths. I think there's a bothy there. I'm pretty sure there is, but I've no idea what state it's in.'

'Where is it?' I asked, never having heard the placename, wondering just how bleak it might be in winter.

'About twenty miles south of here, in the foothills of the Cheviots.'

Christmas Eve, 1944

As a farrier in a former life, Angus Wilson knew a great deal about horses but, to my total amazement, he had never sat on one.

'Sit up!' barked Katie. 'You look like a sack of potatoes.' She walked around the placid Highland pony Angus had managed to mount after more than a few grumbles, tightened the girth, placed the big man's feet in the correct place in the stirrup irons and showed him how to thread the reins through his fingers, between his pinkie and ring finger and then index finger and thumb. 'Their mouths are sensitive and you won't need to haul this old chap around. He knows his job and plenty worse than you have sat on him.' And last of all, she buckled on a neck strap, explaining to Wilson that 'the technical term for this is the holy crap strap. When those words come into your head, grab it.'

Quite how Katie had persuaded her neighbour to lend us four of her shaggy Highland ponies, I was not sure. Perhaps her riding school was not busy, perhaps she needed a break from feeding them through the hungry months of the winter. But with twenty miles to cover in a day, we needed transport, and to move fast in daylight. Walking through the night was much slower, more dangerous and it would be very easy to get lost on our way to a place none of us knew.

When Alan Grant suggested we take refuge in Bleaklaw Moss, he had better reasons than inaccessibility for choosing it. He knew how to get from his farm to the foothills of the Cheviots without much risk of us being seen. Very well read, and a farmer who saw the land itself as a text, as more than simply a place where crops grew and stock grazed, Katie's father had spread a map on his kitchen table. 'The Germans will use the roads. There aren't yet enough of them to do anything else and they'll see only what they see from their vehicles. But there is one long road that's invisible to them, a ghost road, one that will make you disappear.'

Smiling, knowing that he had our full attention, Alan traced his finger across the old Ordnance Survey map. 'Do you see this straight line? It's not just a lot of field ends. It's a Roman road, built by the legions almost two thousand years ago, and it'll take you very nearly all the way to where you need to go.' Because the Romans had hammered down the hard standing of gravel and fringed it with kerbstones, no farmer could ever get a plough through it. Almost impassable in summer, choked by hawthorn and blackthorn, it opens up in winter. 'You can see where it runs,' said Alan, 'but the die-back is high, nothing flattens it and in lots of places there are big trees on either side. All of that will give you cover.'

An overnight blanket of cloud had caused much of the snow to melt, only white fringes remaining in the lee of dykes and in ditches. As the grey dawn edged from the east, our band of four riders clopped down the Grants' farm track in the shadow of a shelter-belt of Scots pines.

Katie rode in front, leading us west to join the ghost road where the legions had once marched. Teasing us as we were tacking up the ponies, she had said that real Border Reivers would not have been so weedy. They would not have hesitated to ride their surefooted little ponies by night. 'Ill met by moonlight' was the phrase she used.

Breasting a rise, we could see below us a long line of hardwood trees, their naked, leafless limbs gaunt against the morning sky. There was no wind, nothing moved, and no sound except the crunch of the ponies' hooves on the frosted ground.

'That's it over there' – Katie pointed – 'and about half a mile beyond is the main road.'

The night before, we had agreed that in the unlikely event that we saw any traffic on Christmas Eve, we should stop, dismount and stay as still as possible. The placid Highlands would immediately drop their heads to look for a bite of something. But we could make out no engine noise carrying in the clear air as we joined the line of the old Roman road.

Spear-straight, it made for the shoulder of a distant hill that was topped with a monument that can be seen all over the Border country. More resembling a land-locked lighthouse, it had been built at the end of another war by French prisoners to honour the Duke of Wellington's victory at Waterloo. As our ponies plodded quietly between the avenue of trees, the path winding uphill around bushes and fallen branches, it occurred to me how history shifts. In 1815, the Germans were our allies against the French and Napoleon's vaulting ambition to dominate Europe. In fact, the arrival of Field Marshal Blücher's Prussians at Waterloo had turned defeat into victory. Perhaps the lighthouse should have been dedicated to him.

Alan Grant was right about the road. Between the lines of trees and bushes, most of them thorns, nothing but shallow rooted weeds and tall grass grew. Almost two thousand winters had done little damage to the road-bed laid down by the Romans.

Katie turned in the saddle. 'We'll have to dismount when

85

we reach that wood up ahead. There's no gate and we'll need to move quickly down a tarmacked back road to get out of sight again.' She smiled. 'You manage a trot, Angus?'

I could not see his face, only imagine the horror on it.

Just as we turned down the road, I fancied I could hear engine noise. Bouncing around in the saddle, slewing from side to side, Wilson was hanging on grimly as his pony trotted, grabbing for the holy crap strap. And was only saved from a heavy fall on tarmac by Katie doubling back to grab his reins. 'Stand up in the stirrups and keep your backside out of the saddle!' In a sudden dip in the road by a little bridge, there was a gap in the fence and a dense wood behind it. Moments after we were all through it, a very stately car glided past. Was it a Rolls Royce or a Bentley? There were several grand houses in the vicinity and perhaps a chauffeur had been sent out on an errand.

Below the wood flowed our first real obstacle. Thankfully, there was no winter spate speeding the River Teviot towards its junction with the Tweed at Kelso, but it still would not be easy to cross. We could have diverted by a road bridge about a mile to the west, but that would have been a very last resort. There were clearly people about. Katie reckoned that the easiest way across was below an old cauld. Where the low dam diverted part of the flow of the river into a mill lade, there were some islets and she felt the ponies would be happiest crossing where they could see some slivers of land rising up out of the water.

'Kick! Kick!' Katie shouted at Wilson. 'If he thinks you won't, he won't go.' After more refusals, she splashed back, took the reins and led the reluctant Highland and its sorry rider to the far bank. For some doubtless suspect reason, perhaps memories of boarding school, I liked severe, bossy Katie.

But it was at that moment I first felt we were being watched.

There were no buildings nearby, not even any field shelters

or barns, only a strip of dense and dark woodland on the ridge above the southern bank of the river, in the direction we were going. Was there a flicker of movement in the woods? Or was it just birds fluttering amongst the debris?

When we crossed another stream, the land began to climb noticeably. This stretch of the road was open, not clogged by the winter die-back of weeds and thorns, clearly maintained and used as a farm track to reach out-bye fields. Its unnatural, geometric straightness impressed me. Without machines or the internal combustion engine, with only picks, shovels and baskets, the Romans had been able to write their story indelibly and enduringly on this landscape.

Looking sideways at Angus Wilson, Katie suggested we trot where the going was good. It was mid-morning and only three days after the winter solstice, the shortest day, so we needed to make better time. There were perhaps only four or five hours left for us to reach Bleaklaw Moss before the light faded. With Katie riding alongside, Wilson managed to stay on as we moved into the upcountry.

Passing through woodland on either side, much of it evergreen, we were well hidden. But when we came to a crossroads, where a tarmacked C-road cut across, it was much more open. And it would be like that for about a mile. Too risky. We dismounted, led the ponies across a stripy ploughed field with snow-filled furrows and found cover behind a long shelter-belt of pines and spruces. With no time to stop and rest, we ate what the Grants had put in our saddlebags as we walked south towards the Cheviot Hills. We had agreed to meet Sandy Ormiston at Five Stane Rig. An old shepherd whom Alan Grant knew well, and trusted completely, he would show us the lie of the land, open the bothy and then take Katie home in his car.

Where the Roman road spurred away south off the tarmac surface, the views behind us to the north and east opened dramatically. A watery sun blinked between the clouds. Remembered sights like that had been a salve for my soul on the hardest days of the hunger march and after bullets had flown around us on Queen Beach. I gazed for a few moments at the three Eildon Hills that rise above the Tweed at Melrose, over the fertile fields of Berwickshire and east to the flat horizon of the North Sea coast. This was my home place, and I was damned if it was going to be taken from me and all the people who made it. I was damned if I was to be nothing more than a fugitive, a casualty of a lost war.

Katie pulled up her pony beside me. It was as though, without knowing it, both of us shared the same prayer at that moment and, for both of us, it was answered at the same time.

She turned to look at me, fixing me steadily, not smiling, and I said, 'We will fight. I don't yet know how, but we will fight.'

Sunk down between two parallel dykes, the old road seemed pristine, unchanged, the course of its metalling clearly visible, dropping slightly on either side so that the frequent rains could run off. Only the curlews could see us passing through the landscape as they wheeled in the updraughts and we trotted on in the hoofprints of history. On the hills on either side of this raised valley, sheep were moving slowly across their flanks, searching for a bite of bitter winter grass amongst the gorse.

With perhaps two hours of light left, Katie encouraged us to kick on for Five Stanes Rig, only a mile or two further. But when we came to the shoulder of a hill and could see the course of the Roman road run a long way to the south, well past the place where Sandy Ormiston's car should have been visible, we could see no sign of it or him. Perhaps he was late, or had been stopped, or had hidden his vehicle somehow. The five stones of the little circle are not monumental, more like something you might sit on than be in awe of, but their location is clear. It was also clear that the old shepherd was nowhere to be seen.

Katie pointed to a plantation some distance off the road, over to the west. With my binoculars, I thought I could make out the shape of a small, low building half hidden in the fringes of the trees.

'Perhaps that's the bothy my dad meant?' she said. 'Even if it's not, you should use it. I need to start back very soon.'

We headed over the tussocky grass, looking for a sheepwalk that might make for easier going through the dips and sudden hollows. And when we reached what looked to me to have been a shieling, little more than a rudimentary shelter used by shepherds summering out on the high pasture with their flocks, we were sure this must be the place that Alan meant. In the wide and open landscape around the road, there was nothing else to be seen.

'Don't worry,' Katie said, kissing me, 'this old pony has plenty of gas left in the tank and we can canter on the good stretches. I'll be home before the night closes in. It's Christmas Eve! I had better be.'

As we dismounted, and Wilson and Campbell unlatched the door of the bothy, I watched Katie ride away, turning in the saddle and waving.

And then, in a moment, she disappeared. The pony reared. They both fell. And were gone.

VI

Having leapt into the saddle and dug my heels in as hard as I could, the Highland almost threw me as it took off over the tussocky grass, into the gallop after only a few strides. In the gathering gloaming, I found it difficult to judge distance and could see nothing of Katie and her pony. A rising panic was fought down by the certain knowledge that they could not possibly have disappeared. The ground could not have simply swallowed them. But it seemed that it had.

Then I almost rode right over them. In a deep and sudden dip, both horse and rider lay side by side. Neither was moving but I could see that the pony's flanks were heaving as it breathed. Racing across to Katie, I felt for a pulse. Thank God. And she too began panting. Perhaps it was shock. For both of them. Then she let out a faint groan and her forehead furrowed. Coming round after being knocked out, she turned on her side.

'Don't move, darling,' I whispered. 'You might have broken something.'

Ignoring me, she grunted, opened her eyes, and sat up. And then pointed her finger past my shoulder. 'Look, David. Look!'

Turning slowly around, I saw what I first took to be a child, a young lad. Clothed from head to foot in various shades of brown and green and with a hat stuck with feathers, he was aiming an arrow straight at me. Standing at point-blank range, with his bowstring fully drawn back to his shoulder, he was utterly still and made no sound. Having no weapon with me, not even a knife, I raised my arms slowly.

'No, no,' Katie said to the boy, 'it was an accident. I know that. We didn't see you.'

Still silent, and still pulling back the full draw-weight of his bow, the lad slowly edged around us so that he had both of us and the pony in view.

Watching him closely, wondering if he would shoot, I could see that he was no boy, but a small, very spare man with a heavily lined and weathered face.

The pony snorted and began to rock back and forth where it had fallen. Katie got to her feet, still unsteady and woozy.

'Please,' I said, 'I'm not armed. I have nothing. I won't harm you.'

At that moment, Wilson and Campbell appeared on the edge of the hollow. This disconcerted the strange little man very much. I realised that he realised he could not fire arrows fast enough to cover all of us, and more than that, the two soldiers carried shotguns. When the pony whinnied once more, the little man slowly lowered his bow, darted over to the pony, took hold of both its forelegs, made a low clicking sound and with tremendous, unsuspected strength, pulled it round onto more level ground.

Open-mouthed at this, we watched the old Highland roll onto its belly, tuck in its hind legs, get up and shake itself. As we watched the miraculous resurrection of the horse, none of us noticed the little man disappear.

*

'Now look, Sandy, there's nothing I can do about this.'

In the only cell in St Boswells police station, Sergeant Bell explained that he was bound to file a report. Even though it was Christmas Eve. After a phone call from a neighbour, some-one the policeman refused to name, his only patrol car had stopped Sandy on the road to Jedburgh. After searching the car, the constable asked him to come back to the station to answer a few questions.

'You see, Sandy,' said Sergeant Bell, 'it doesn't make any sense. You said you were going off to feed some out-bye ewes for a friend. But you won't say who, or where. And you can't explain why your collies weren't in the vehicle and why the constable found no bags of feed in the back. Your neighbour saw you get in the car without them. And that's what we found. Nothing to back up your story.'

Sitting on the bench along one wall, Sandy Ormiston just shook his head and said to the sergeant, 'What are things coming to, Bill? What are you doing, helping these people?'

Sighing, the policeman went on to explain that he had been forced to put in a call to Berwick. 'If I hadn't, your neighbour would have made a formal complaint and I'd have been for the high jump. They'll be here shortly.'

The old shepherd blew out his cheeks, shook his head and leaned back against the wall of the cell. At seventy, he was too old for these sorts of capers. And what would Mrs Ormiston say? It was well past suppertime.

An hour later, the shepherd heard loud voices followed by the clatter of boots down the stairs. The door of the cell opened and two black-uniformed Germans came in. 'Stand up!' one of them shouted at the old man.

And when he did, the other punched him hard in the stomach.

*

What troubled Katie more than her concussion was that she would not be at home for Christmas. And that instead of celebrating, enjoying some much-needed cheer in this, the darkest winter any of them had known, her parents would be worried, not knowing where she was.

'We'll get a message to them somehow,' I said, having no idea how.

Before darkness fell, we had foraged outside for some firewood, and then cleared the debris off the floor of the single-room shieling, stuffing some straw into the gaps around the rotting window frames.

Katie had turned away the four ponies, saying, 'They'll not stray far, and Highlands can find food in a desert.'

Their saddles would make decent seats or even pillows, and far from any habitation, in the deep midwinter dark, we risked a fire in the blackened grate. John Campbell had snapped small branches over his knee and stacked them to one side. A fallen limb from one of the Scots pines, its rich, red bark still on it, had been too thick to break and so he fed one end into the flames, sliding it a few inches further in as it was consumed, making bright orange flames. The sharp scent of the resin in the sparking bark filled the room and made it seem fresher, less musty and much warmer.

We shared some food and the last of Campbell's stolen whisky. Sitting in a semi-circle around the fire, leaning on the pony saddles, we were quiet after a long day, staring, enjoying the hypnotic flicker of the flames, perhaps unconsciously absorbing the extraordinary events of the last few days. At the time, we heard nothing, not a whisper, but outside there was movement. One of the ponies looked up but made no sound as the little man stole silently out of the cover of the trees behind the shieling. Making a low, nickering sound and crouching to make himself even smaller, no threat, the man scratched the withers of the old Highland and opened his fist to feed it a handful of beech-mast. Soundless, his tread gossamer-soft and fleeting, the man approached the lit window of the shieling and, with his back pressed against the wall to one side, he listened.

'If we try to resist, or begin to organise some resistance,

93

our people will be made to suffer in reprisal.' I was thinking aloud, as much as inviting discussion. 'The Germans know they are too few to control the countryside with anything much of a military presence. There will be no patrols or roadblocks. Instead, they'll do it with terror.'

'We heard stories,' said Angus Wilson. 'Whole villages in France destroyed; women and children machine-gunned; men herded into churches, shot in the legs so that they could not try to escape, and then burned alive. And it was the SS, the same lot as these bastards in Berwick . . . Sorry, miss. They won't hang back.' Campbell and I nodded. 'And they have the atom bomb.'

Quiet until then, still staring at the fire, Katie said, 'They'll only use that in very exceptional circumstances. Like mass resistance. Insurrection. Something really big. They've already turned London and much of the south-east of England into a worthless desert. What's the point of conquest, of dominating Europe, if you destroy it? I think they'll react to any local resistance with violence, like in the French villages.' She shook her head. 'And what's the point of resisting? We'll just get our people, and probably ourselves, killed. I don't know what we should try to do – except survive, at least for now.'

Christmas Day, 1944

The morning dawned clear after a sharp overnight frost. The slanting sun lit the high valley and the sheltering pines cast graphic shadows around the shieling. When she went out to look for the shaggy Highlands, Katie shivered, her footprints leaving a green trail in the frosted grass. The ponies would have found somewhere out of the icy east wind, what Katie imagined had blown all the way from Siberia. In the wide moorland between the shieling and the Roman road, there were swales and hollows; Katie found the ponies at the bottom of one, scuffing at the cold ground, snuffling after a bite or two of bitter winter forage.

Before she could catch up her old pony in a halter, all four flicked up their heads at a thin, piercing whistle. Like no bird call she had ever heard, the sound seemed more like a signal, and Katie turned in the direction of the pine wood, where it seemed to come from. When it changed pitch, the whistle prompted the ponies to trot towards it, like four huge dogs summoned by a handler. It was then that Katie saw him, the little man, squatting on his hunkers, not far from the shieling.

'Where did you learn that?' she asked him.

The man smiled and brought a fistful of wild oats and mast out of his pouch, feeding each of the ponies in turn. And then, looking directly at Katie, fixing her with extraordinary deep brown, almost black eyes, he patted his chest with the palm of his hand and motioned for her to follow him into the wood.

After only a few moments, they had left behind the copse of tall pines and the shieling, and were enveloped by the tangle of the moss. Immediately, it felt different. There seemed to be no wind and it was warmer. Were she not following the little man, Katie would have become quickly lost, as a canopy of thick wands of willow scrub closed over her head. Pools of brown, brackish water, some with leafless bushes growing directly out of them, lay on each side of a path that was little more than a series of raised tussocks, like green and wobbly stepping stones.

When they heard the plaintive *piou-piou* of a buzzard, the man stopped, stretched out his arm no higher than his shoulder, and then, to Katie's astonishment, a huge bird glided towards them. Canting its wings to slow its flight, it alighted on the little man's forearm. Startled by the buzzard's stern gaze, Katie stepped back, lost her footing and almost toppled into a pool before the little man clasped her wrist. He steadied her, smiled, clicked his tongue and the great bird lifted effortlessly into the air.

Like an island made entirely from woven willow withies, bracken, a lattice of branches and bark, and reached by a narrow causeway, the shelter was invisible until the little man had led Katie very close. Inside, it was snug, almost circular, and on a central hearth laid with interlocking stones the embers of a fire glowed. The shelter smelled smoky and fishy, and the deer pelts and what looked like fox fur suggested that this man was a skilled hunter. Feeling no sense of threat, Katie understood that she had entered a different, singular place, an oasis, a relic of an ancient world, that of the hunter-gatherers who had rustled the leaves of this landscape more than four thousand years before.

The little man beckoned for Katie to sit on a low bench covered with pelts while from under another, he pulled out a leather pouch the size of a saddlebag.

'My name's Katie.'

He put the pouch on his lap and smiled. 'Know your name,' he nodded. 'Watched you ride here. You looked after the big man. You are kind.' His voice was little more than a whisper, but nevertheless an effort that seemed to require great concentration. 'Ponies like you.'

'What's your name?' Katie asked.

The little man shook his head. 'Don't know.' He looked away and sighed.

Katie waited, saying nothing more.

'Animals know me.'

There was no awkwardness, no sense of an interrogation or indeed any reticence. They sat under the willow bower and the silence of the wood settled around them. Katie noticed that the little man's clothes were made from animal pelts sewn with thongs of rawhide. He wore a buckskin tunic and leggings, and a short jerkin, more pale green than brown and trimmed with fox fur.

After a time, Katie smiled again and asked the little man how long he had lived in the wood.

'Not sure. Here for many winters.'

It struck her that he spoke deliberately, weighing his words, perhaps because it was a long time since he had spoken – to anyone.

Having undone the rawhide ties of his pouch, he tipped its contents on the floor. There were scores of gold and silver coins, some of them bearing the heads of emperors, a gold ring, silver clasps of some sort and, most spectacular, a small golden torc.

'All mine. Found them here. My wood, my home.' He picked up the torc. 'For you. Know what day it is today.' He smiled. 'No one comes here. Except you. And you are beautiful and kind. Heard what you said last night. Know you are in trouble. I help you.'

*

'You make our Christmas Day difficult. Yours too.' The German grabbed Sandy Ormiston by the hair and pulled up his bloody head. 'Give us the name. Tell us who sent you out yesterday.'

The old shepherd was barely conscious and his breathing was halting, rasping. After a severe beating the night before, and refusing to say anything, not even giving his own name, Ormiston was almost beyond pain. They had punched out his front teeth, leaving little more than bleeding shards, blinded him in one eye and pounded and squeezed his testicles until he passed out. But still, he would say nothing.

At that point, the evening was late and abandoning the ruin they had made of the old man, the Germans locked the cell door, left the police station to find some supper and perhaps something to drink. After all, it was Christmas.

*

Her extraordinary gift in a saddlebag, Kate was making good time, perhaps good enough to get home in time for Christmas dinner. The old pony seemed not to be injured after the previous day's fall, when the little man, the woodsman, had appeared from nowhere and caused it to rear. It was only by the time that they splashed across the Teviot that Katie felt the pony sag a little. When she saw the cupola of the Waterloo Monument glint in the winter sunshine, they were almost there.

'My God. Where have you been? And how did you get that shiner?' Katie's father hugged her as she shut the stable door, having stuffed a rack full of hay and hung up the old pony's tack.

In the farmhouse kitchen, Eileen Grant was busy at the Aga with Christmas dinner, enjoying a glass of sherry, trying to create some seasonal cheer. 'Darling, you worried us,' she said. 'Even though we knew you were with David. But you're here now. Maybe something stronger than sherry? Looks like someone took a disliking to you.'

Playing on the gramophone in the drawing room, at full volume, was a surprising festive favourite of her mother's, a recording of a Welsh male voice choir, forty blazered men belting out *Bread of Heaven*, *Rock of Ages* and *Land of my Fathers*. Katie smiled when she heard it, enjoying her mum's eccentric tastes, casting her mind back to Christmases past, times when the world was kinder.

'I don't know what happened to Sandy,' said Alan Grant. 'He's normally so reliable. Perhaps he had a flat tyre, or took ill. Maybe too many drams! But you found the shieling anyway.'

98

When Katie brought out the golden torc, it surprised her as much as her parents. It felt like an unlikely, tangible relic of a dream. When she talked of the little man, they both shook their heads.

'I suppose Bleaklaw is a wild place, and a wilderness has its secrets,' said Alan. 'I knew of a couple, years ago, who lived in the woods around Kelso. They used to gather kindling, stooking it like corn so that it dried. And the local children left the stooks alone, dared not touch them. They were terrified of these two. Dressed in rags, their faces unwashed, black as crows, they would appear suddenly, out of nowhere. One moment the path was clear, and the next, they were walking silently behind you. Their dogs were savage but instantly obedient, no collar, no lead needed. And when they sold their kindling round the doors for pennies, off the back of a rickety handcart, the dogs barked to let the street know they were there. They seemed better able to communicate with animals than people. They could tame wild birds with whistles and lures. They lived out all year round, and John Agnew up at Galloway Law used to let them sleep in his hay barn through the worst of the winter; in return, the dogs cleared his steading of rats. For the rest of the year, they bivouacked under the trees, their sleeping places invisible under sloping layers of branches. The rumour was that they were not man and wife but brother and sister, the children of another brother and sister. And no one ever knew their names.' He shook his head at the memory. 'They were wild, feral people and knew the land and its creatures better than anyone.'

After Eileen and Katie cleared away the plates and cutlery, they all sat by the drawing room fire and the male voices from the 'valleys of song' were given a break.

'It's difficult to cut through the propaganda we hear on the Scottish Home Service,' Alan said. 'It isn't news anymore, just a series of announcements and, before and after, a hell of a lot of Beethoven, Brahms and Wagner. Wasn't Beethoven Dutch?'

Katie smiled as the words tumbled out. Her dad had always spoken quickly, often breathlessly, moving his hands, giving emphasis, underlining his points.

'Anyway, the Germans have been talking about something they're calling "resettlement". Reading between the lines, I think that means many people from the cities, and perhaps from the south, coming to live here. I expect someone who knows nothing about Scotland has looked at population statistics and concluded there's plenty of room.' Alan Grant grunted as he leaned forward to poker up some flame in the log fire. 'The other thing they have started banging on about is Scottish independence and the right of self-determination. They apparently include us in what they call the "Nordic races". My guess is that Mosley's government, such as it is, will try to create support for the new regime by appealing to nationalists on the one hand, and to returning soldiers by chopping up all the big estates and farms. Parcels of land will be dished out as smallholdings. Those who get them won't have a clue what to do, thinking that managing ten acres is like gardening. Apparently, the "king", as we must learn to call him, is going to say something about this later on in his Christmas message on the wireless.'

Alan Grant's face was flushed with rage. '"Our German friends and allies", by God! What does that little upstart think he's saying? Hundreds of thousands have died at the hands of our "friends" and "bloody allies". They incinerated London, killed his brother and his family. King Edward VIII, indeed! Send him back to the bloody Bahamas with that frozen-faced wife of his. Little German puppet.'

Katie had rarely seen her father so angry, and after his outburst, he sat back, sighed loudly and stared at the fire.

Boxing Day, 1944

In the early morning, four workmen bumped their lorry across the grass of St Boswells Green. In the back were several stout lengths of timber. Having dug two holes through the frosted ground and erected two uprights, making sure they were plumb and properly aligned, they chocked each one with stakes and hammered in supporting struts to keep them steady. From ladders, they pulled up and fitted a crossbeam, hammering long nails through it and into the uprights to give the whole structure rigidity.

Last of all, they slung two nooses over the beam, leaving them to dangle in the cold wind.

'Out! Now! All of you!' In the middle of the village, by the post office and the butcher's shop, a German soldier was barking through a loudhailer. 'Everyone. Out now!'

An armoured car had been driving around the lanes, honking its horn as people emerged from their houses, buttoning their coats, wondering what all the fuss was about.

'Go to the Green immediately. Go now! All of you!'

Couples with children, small groups and then dozens walked down the long, straight road towards the hotel. When they saw the gallows set up at the corner, close to the busy main road, many gasped and exchanged fearful glances. By late morning, around three hundred people had gathered, their breath pluming into the air, not many of them talking.

After a time, the armoured car appeared and behind it was the local police patrol car. Sergeant Bell pulled up by the side of the armoured car and opened one of the rear doors. With her hands handcuffed behind her back and her face disfigured by ugly red bruises, Agnes Ormiston was pulled out.

'Oh, my God, no!' Agnes blurted when she saw the gallows looming over the Green and a hushed crowd gathered.

Around her, eight German soldiers formed up, all of them

carrying submachine guns. And then out of the back doors of the armoured car, his Gestapo interrogators dragged the lifeless body of her husband.

The crowd grew agitated, but in a moment were quietened when the little commandant of the SS garrison at Berwick began to shout, reading from a paper that fluttered in his hand.

'I am Kommandant Schneider from the headquarters of the allied security forces at Berwick. We are here to defend you good people from our common enemies. You may think of these two people as your friends, but they are guilty of treason, of collaborating with the enemies of Scotland.' He motioned to the interrogators, who then dragged the old shepherd's body across the grass, his heels leaving a trail through the frost.

His wife began to sob, turning her face away, unable to watch as Ormiston was strung up, both men hauling up the corpse until it swung clear of the ground before tying off the rope on one of the struts. Shock rippled through the crowd, mothers hid their children's faces, pulling them towards them. There was a sign pinned to the old man's chest: *My wife will die because of me.*

'No! No!' Agnes Ormiston screamed as she was dragged to the gallows, stumbling, held up under her arms by two soldiers. 'Please, no,' she panted, 'it's not right. We've done nothing wrong.'

She saw neighbours, old friends: 'Jamie, Archie, help me! Help me! Please!'

Many turned away but the crowd seemed to surge forward as the old lady was made to stand beside her husband's body. One of the soldiers rattled a volley of machine gun fire over their heads.

'No, no!' Agnes screamed before another smashed her in the face with the butt of his gun.

Moving quickly now, following Schneider's orders, knowing

that if they rushed them, the crowd could overwhelm the execution detail, the soldiers pulled the noose over the woman's head and savagely pulled it tight around her neck, silencing her screams. When they began to haul her upwards, she wriggled when her feet left the ground, her legs kicking, one shoe falling off. Warm urine ran down her legs, dripping.

As Agnes Ormiston began to choke to death and her face turned purple, it seemed to some that what they saw was so unbelievable that it could not be happening. It was a waking nightmare. An old lady, well known and liked in the village, had been beaten and then executed on St Boswells Green, where the fairground stalls set up each summer and the gypsies came to tell your fortune.

It was an impossible sight, and act of appalling cruelty, but in the new Scotland, it was far from unbelievable.

*

'My God,' I said when Katie related what had happened on St Boswells Green. 'I feel responsible. It's my fault. It's medieval, utterly ruthless, sadistic. But effective. Someone has already been talking to the Germans. Otherwise, how did they know to stop Sandy Ormiston?'

The news of the atrocity at St Boswells had crackled like wildfire around the Borders. When Katie and her parents heard about it, they knew they had to act straight away – the Germans could be at the door of the farmhouse at any moment.

Katie had run to the stables and threw a saddle on the old pony. The bitter east wind bleared her eyes as she kicked on the sturdy little Highland up the Roman road to Whitton Edge, the place where magnificent views opened. Ignoring them, intent on getting to the shieling at Bleaklaw Moss as quickly as possible, Katie paid attention to nothing except the ground in front of her.

Relieved to see that there was no telltale smoke blowing from the chimney of the shieling but anxious that none of the ponies could be seen grazing anywhere nearby, Katie pushed open the wooden door. The room was completely empty: there was no sign of any kit and the saddles and bridles had gone.

'Gone this morning.'

She whirled round to see the little man crouched in the doorway.

'I show you.'

With that, he turned and began running across the wide moorland, beckoning Katie to follow. His agility in skipping across the ridges, swales and dips of what was awkward ground was astonishing and even on her surefooted Highland, bred for this kind of country, she struggled to keep up.

They joined the old road about a mile below the shieling and made even better time. Beyond a dyke, Katie made out the rectilinear banks and ditches of what she thought must be a series of Roman camps. At the foot of a gentle slope, she exhaled with relief when she saw Wilson, Campbell and myself by the banks of a wide stream. Delighted we had come to no harm, she turned to thank the man, but he had vanished.

Whistling as loud as she could – and that was loud – Katie stood up in her stirrups and waved at us.

'It's barbaric, what they did to Sandy and Agnes Ormiston, utterly barbaric. It brings it home, the savagery we saw in Europe,' I said.

Wilson and Campbell were still open-mouthed at what Katie had described.

I was angry, but also fearful, very anxious about all of our families, and I could see that both men were thinking of their own people.

We mounted our ponies and trotted briskly back up the old road.

'Others will talk,' I said. 'Someone will give up the names of your mum and dad, and my dad. Even if they are three amongst many, the Germans will be thorough.'

*

Never having imagined that they would be forced to leave their farmhouse with an hour's notice, Alan and Eileen Grant had to think quickly. Grant's father had moved out of his draughty old house and gone to live with a widower neighbour. They would stop at a telephone box en route and call him to tell him they had left the farm but not where they had gone. And his son would insist that he went nowhere and would not give away his whereabouts.

Food, drink, changes of clothing and weapons was the rubric as they packed as much as they could into their car. What about valuables, apart from money? Forget that. Maybe some jewellery. But waterproofs, definitely. They would need those when they reached the coast.

Moored for the winter in the tiny inner harbour at St Abbs, next to the launch ramp of the lifeboat station, there bobbed Alan Grant's passion: what he called a masterpiece and his wife called a floating gin palace. As often as farming allowed, Alan sailed his little wooden yacht through the spectacular coastal waters of Berwickshire, its cliffs unrivalled, its skerries dangerous.

One of about four hundred made at the yard of an American designer, Nat Herreshoff, the yacht was only sixteen and a half feet long – too small for a gin palace but big enough for two berths. Single-masted, it moved sleek and steady through the water, and could turn on a sixpence to catch the wind. If Alan and Eileen could get to St Abbs, they could conceal themselves in the cabin for the night and then, if the weather was good, move on up the coast the following day to find an anchorage where they would not be seen.

'Surely these thugs can't take reprisals just because someone disappears?' said Alan as he fired up his bronchitic old Vauxhall.

'Don't be so sure,' said Eileen. 'And if they come here and find a locked and empty house, they'll know that they have probably found the link with Sandy Ormiston. Then they'll come after us.'

Instead of driving down to the main road, the Grants followed a loaning, a bumpy farm track that wound its way close to the Waterloo Monument, and from there they would cross the Teviot below Nisbet. Avoiding the towns and larger villages, the plan was to thread their way around the foothills of the eastern ranges of the Cheviots and then dash for the coast.

*

Travelling in the opposite direction, we were making good time. But it was late afternoon when we stopped about half a mile from the Grants' farm. While Wilson and Campbell kept the ponies quiet, Katie and I moved close enough to see lights burning in the farmhouse.

'Good. That's good,' said Katie. 'We can feed the horses and find comfort and food for one night.'

But as she made to stand up and run towards the house, I pulled her back. Angrily, she tried to free her arm.

'Listen,' I said, 'just listen.'

And faint in the quiet of the gloaming, we heard the harsh snap of commands given in German.

'Oh, my God. My God. Mum. Dad,' whispered Katie.

Begging her to stay put, I made my way even closer, edging along the shelter-belt and managing to get across the track by the steading. After a few long minutes, I heard car doors slamming and engines revving. Risking revealing myself, hoping no driver was looking in a rear-view mirror, I saw an armoured car and what might have been a black Mercedes bumping down the farm track to the main road. And there were no longer any lights on in the farmhouse.

When Katie and I pushed at the half-open front door, the beam of my torch lit a scene of devastation. A hall cupboard had been pulled over, chairs lay upended on the floor and, in the drawing room, it seemed that everything breakable had been smashed. Papers from Alan Grant's desk had been strewn all over the floor. Katie was stunned. Upstairs it was the same, chaotic and, it seemed to me, willfully destructive mess.

'Oh God,' gasped Katie, 'they've taken them. They'll kill them. Help me, David. We must go after them.'

But I was not so sure. Perhaps the Grants got away before the Germans kicked in their front door. The mess looked to me more like frustration than an organised search. And when I showed Katie that the Vauxhall was not in its usual place, under an arch in the cartshed, she almost wept with relief.

*

It was nearly dark when Alan Grant turned down the steep hill to St Abbs. The sight of it perched on the cliffs, and the quiet, dark sea beyond, lifted their hearts. No one seemed to be about.

Little more than three parallel lanes with most of the houses facing out to sea, the little fishing village was ancient. Its rocky haven had been used since the seventh century, when an Anglian nunnery had been founded by a princess, St Aebbe.

Although everything about his appearance – his square shoulders, calloused hands and weathered face – said farmer, Alan Grant was also deeply interested in history, in the land and its stories. He had read everything he could find about the village and loved the story of St Cuthbert, who, as a visitor to the community, decided one night to go down to the shore so that, like many of these ascetic old saints, he could mortify his flesh in the ice-cold waters of the North Sea, sing psalms and offer up prayers. A curious novice monk followed him and watched a miracle. When the saint emerged from the water, two sea otters dried his feet.

A gentle tale that ran through Alan's mind as he and his wife fled from savagery.

*

Before we left the farmhouse, I took one of Katie's father's overcoats and a black trilby hat.

'What do you want those for?' Katie asked.

'It might be helpful at some point not to look like a British soldier in dirty old fatigues.'

By the time we rejoined Wilson and Campbell, I had decided that we needed to get to Abbey House and my own father as soon as possible. If the Germans had made a link between Sandy Ormiston and the Grants, they might make another one. The little commandant at Berwick knew my name and he would still be smarting at the breakout. His soldiers and the Gestapo men who had beaten Sandy to death would be asking questions. And the terrified people they spoke to would be giving them answers – anything to make them move on, leave them alone.

Our difficulty was the Tweed: Abbey House was on the far side and not only would the bridges be watched, the winter snows made the fords impassable.

'What about the railway viaduct?' suggested Angus Wilson. 'I reckon that if we can get onto the railway track, we wouldn't be seen, at least not easily.' With his huge hands, used to holding up a horse's hoof and banging clench nails through a shoe, the big man was animated, pointing the way. 'If we lead the ponies, don't ride them' – the relief was etched on Wilson's face as he said this – 'we'll not be seen, not in the dark.' Seeing the sense of this as he spoke, the words came tumbling out of the normally taciturn farrier's mouth, and I was glad to have someone else take the initiative. 'I'm pretty sure the line goes through cuttings mostly,' he went on. 'When we get to the big viaduct over the Tweed, we should keep to the far side, the western side. That way, we'll not be seen by sentries down on Leaderfoot Bridge. It's a lot lower and on the east side. If we keep low, they'll not see us.'

It was risky but I could think of no other way to get across the river. And the railway line was only half a mile north of the Grants' farmhouse.

A gusting east wind blew in flurries of snow as we climbed down the shallow slopes of the embankment onto the track. We had nothing to cover the ponies' saddles and when, or if, we remounted, they would have to be dried somehow, otherwise Wilson and probably everyone except Katie would slither off. Walking between the rails and on the gravel between the sleepers was awkward, and even though we were concealed I felt that we were making a lot of noise. The mass of Eildon Hill North loomed up out of the mirk on our left-hand side. When the railway line at last emerged from a cutting, we found ourselves approaching the river and the high bridge across it.

We could see no lights on the parapets and no barriers. But below us to our right was the road bridge and, sure enough, we saw two sentries light cigarettes. They were close, less than a hundred yards away, and we needed to move slowly and silently.

The wind and the snow made progress dangerous. Because only trains on a single track crossed the viaduct, it was narrow, and the parapet was low with only an iron railing between us and the black waters of the Tweed below. What made it more perilous was that the space between the track bed and the parapet was a raised concrete walkway wide enough for human beings but challenging for chunky, four-legged ponies. They turned out to be very uncertain, and kept stopping, planting their feet. Katie, the most confident and experienced rider, led us but had often to double back to coax a hesitant pony. She scratched their withers, quietly clicked and cooed at them until they finally put one foreleg in front of another. Wilson was behind her, and since the big man was not confident, that transmitted itself and made his pony refuse to go on. Katie had to pull one foreleg forward and then another. And all the time, two German soldiers patrolled the bridge below us.

And then Wilson's pony snorted loudly. We froze. But no challenge came from the sentries. After an agonising twenty minutes or so, we finally reached the northern bank of the river and left the vertiginous heights of the viaduct behind.

After fording the Leader Water, we turned east. I felt as though I had at last entered home territory, my own beloved countryside, farms that had been in our family for generations. Even in the darkness of midwinter, I sensed it, knew exactly where we were. I had thought about this moment hundreds of times in the previous year, but never imagined that after the war I would return home like a thief in the night.

We made our way up Bemersyde Hill to a place where people often stopped to gaze west to the three Eildon Hills. One of these people was reputed to be Walter Scott, and the charabanc trade eventually dubbed this vantage point Scott's View. Before the war, many often assumed that such places were the great beauty spots of the Borders, along with the ruined abbeys and the grand houses and castles. But none of these lifted my heart as much as the fields around Dryburgh. Best seen in an evening sun, they are beautiful to me. Settled, peaceful – except at harvest time – productive and made by the day-in, day-out labour of generations, the fields seem gentle, unassuming, not statements like castles or a great church. Such buildings are thought of as grand, and it is precisely because the fields are not that I love them so much. And even though his name was given to a view and his house at Abbotsford is considered picturesque, I think that what Scott liked about the view from Bemersyde Hill was not just the rising majesty of the Eildon Hills but the cultivated, cared-for detail of the patchwork of fields around them.

When we reached the steep slope of the road that passes the home farm, I pulled up my pony and motioned for us all to dismount and keep quiet. I handed my reins to Katie and climbed up the bank by the road. As a child, I had roamed across every inch of this ground and I knew that we were still high enough to look down on the ruined gable of the south transept of Dryburgh Abbey and, beyond it, my father's house. Not absolutely certain, I thought I could see a pinprick of light, perhaps the lit window of the drawing room.

Skirting the abbey, and the hotel between it and the river, I wanted to approach Abbey House from the east. There were trees and welcome dark shadows on either side of the drive. By the time we were close enough to be sure that the lights were indeed on in the drawing room, I could not make out the shapes of any vehicles in front of the house. And there was no sign of my father's old Bentley. While Wilson and Campbell held the reins of our ponies, Katie and I crunched over the gravel to the front door.

What greeted us inside was more wreckage, more wanton destruction. Just as at the Grants' farmhouse, the Germans had left a trail of gratuitous violence, smashing mirrors, vases and pulling out and emptying every drawer on to the floor.

But in the dining room, next to the grand fireplace, the concealed entrance to the priest hole was closed, had not been discovered. Thank God.

In case my father was armed, and almost certainly badly frightened, listening to all the commotion that had raged around his house, I knocked gently on the panelling.

'Dad. It's me, David. Are you okay?'

There was silence. No movement I could hear. I knocked again. No response. When I pressed on the place in a corner of the linen-fold panel by the mantelpiece and the narrow door swung open, the priest hole was empty. On a shelf there was a bottle of water and a biscuit tin, unopened.

They had taken him.

*

'Your lordship' – Sergeant Bell was wide-eyed with surprise to see my father walk into St Boswells police station out of the snow – 'it's long after curfew, sir.'

The shoulders of my father's long raincoat had epaulettes of snow and the brim of his hat was rimmed with white. 'I am here to see the commandant who was in charge of the business on the Green today.'

Just as the sentence ended, Schneider appeared beside Sergeant Bell behind the counter. 'Ah, Lord Erskine, I take it. We've been looking for you. Your son has caused great difficulty and, I am afraid, is guilty of treason. Have you come to give yourself up?'

My father stared for a silent moment at the little commandant, pulled his shotgun out of the folds of his raincoat, fired both barrels at point-blank range and blew the German's head off.

VII

A gentle breeze drifted in off the sea, clinking the halyard against the top of the mast, a sound that made Alan Grant smile, no matter the circumstances. And echoing in the distance, he could hear the eerie calls of the seals. Hauled up on the sandbank in Coldingham Bay, a little way down the coast, scores of them howled in the wind, like sea-wolves. It was low tide at St Abbs and the inner harbour had emptied completely, leaving Alan's beloved yacht yawed to one side. It was late when they parked their car by the pier, and there seemed to be no one about. As in most towns and villages, the curfew was respected. But who knew who was watching?

The tang of salt seaweed filled the night air as Eileen Grant quietly unloaded all that they had thrown into the back of the vehicle only two hours before. Having made his way carefully down the sea-steps to the soft sand in the little harbour, her husband began to untie the canvas cover that had kept the worst of the winter weather off the open deck and out of the cabin.

By the time everything had been stowed and the Vauxhall parked out of the way up at the Creel Road, they sat down at last in the cabin, sliding the window shutters closed. With his hand torch, Alan rummaged under one of the berths for the primus stove. It was very cold indeed. Carefully pouring paraffin into the small reservoir and making sure the mantle was square and secure, he pushed the pump in and out a few times to create some air pressure. The stove lit with a flash and a puff of flame but soon Alan had adjusted it to a stable and warming glow.

Sitting opposite each other on the berths, Eileen looked at Alan, her eyes filling with tears. 'What is happening to our world? Madmen are everywhere. Terrible, terrible, cruel things are being done. Where can we run to? There's nowhere.'

Alan leaned over and took her hands in his. Small and delicate, her hair beginning to turn grey, Eileen seemed suddenly fearful and uncharacteristic tears brimmed. 'Try not to worry, darling. David will do his best to look after Katie.'

In no mood to heat any food, relieved to feel the edge come off the chill in the cabin, they ate some cheese and pieces of Eileen's Christmas pudding, washed down with the remains of the brandy she had flamed it with. Consoled and sustained by such solid fare, the Grants climbed, exhausted, into their sleeping bags to wait for the morning tide to lift the boat, and perhaps lift their spirits.

*

Acrid smoke filled the room and Sergeant Bell staggered sideways, his face spattered with blood, the grey debris of Schneider's brain and fragments of his teeth.

Roused by the sudden thunder of the shotgun blast, two soldiers rushed in, looked in astonishment at the decapitated body of their commanding officer and then at my father, holding his shotgun in one hand by his side. They quickly disarmed him, handcuffed him and marched the old man to the cell downstairs. The same cell where Sandy Ormiston had been beaten to death.

*

Throwing all caution to the wind, I raced back from Abbey House to where Wilson and Campbell held our ponies. Riding hard for the footbridge that crossed the Tweed near the home farm, Katie chased and caught up with me.

'David! David!' she shouted, clattering across the bridge behind me. 'Wait. Stop.'

When we reached the far bank, only about a mile from St Boswells and my father, she grabbed my reins and pulled the pony's head around. 'You must think! If you ride through the village straight to the police station, you'll be outnumbered and probably outgunned. Think! Think!'

*

'I am Oberführer Manfred von Klige from the Waffen SS detail at headquarters,' I said in faultless German. 'I am here to meet Kommandant Schneider and interrogate his prisoner.'

What the Gestapo officer saw in front of him was a man in a long, heavy overcoat with a black trilby hat pulled down over his eyes, and he heard a perfect, faintly aristocratic German accent. What Sergeant Bell saw, however, was David Erskine standing in front of him. For an uncomfortably long moment we stared hard at each other.

I barked at the Gestapo officer, 'I served as a colonel with the SS Panzer Division Leibstandarte Adolf Hitler and you will stand to attention when I address you, and you will not keep me waiting! What is your name and rank?'

'Kurz. Lieutenant Reinhard Kurz.'

We had left the ponies to graze on the golf course above the river while I pulled on Katie's dad's suit, overcoat and hat. After only a few minutes looking around the village, we found my father's Bentley parked by the church hall and the keys were still in it. While Katie, Wilson and Campbell ran back to the golf course to saddle up the ponies and get ahead of us, I took the car keys and walked into the police station.

'The prisoner will accompany me to Berwick immediately

and one of you will come as an escort,' I said, making a statement and not a request.

The Gestapo officer explained what had happened an hour before and I pretended to be outraged instead of absolutely astonished. Sergeant Bell said nothing, even when the German left the reception room to go down to the cells, and he busied himself with cleaning up the considerable mess on the counter and the wall behind it. Only when we heard footsteps approaching did Bell look up at me. 'If I don't do what they want, they'll kill my wife.'

My father had not been beaten but he did look stunned, almost catatonic, his gaze downcast. A stocky man in his prime, he had shrunk with age and grown round-shouldered. The loss of my mother had weighed heavy.

Suddenly, Sergeant Bell came around the counter and, standing between my father and me, clearly realising that the old man might recognise his son, asked, 'Will you give me the car keys, sir? I'll see that the prisoner is in the back seat with Herr Kurz when you come out.'

I waited for a few unnecessary moments, looking at the blood-stained wall behind the counter, trying to imagine how rage at the execution of Sandy and Agnes Ormiston had built volcanically in my father and erupted almost exactly where I stood.

When I opened the driver door and slid onto the smooth leather of the seat, a memory of childhood flashed through my head. My father loved cars and his Bentley Vanden Plas was more than a joy, it was an engineering miracle – a British engineering miracle, made in Crewe.

The rear-view mirror sat on a slim pedestal on top of the cherrywood dashboard and I had difficulty in adjusting it so that I could see both of my passengers. Kurz sat directly behind me and was clearly visible, but my father seemed to have slumped down. Perhaps he was unable to lever himself higher. I could not risk suspicion by asking the Gestapo officer to remove his handcuffs. I pulled the starter and pushed down on the throttle too firmly with my right foot, gunning the engine in neutral. Driving lessons around Abbey House were not a happy memory and for a mad moment, I waited for a comment from the back seat as I pushed the gear selector into drive and we glided off to find the coast road to Berwick.

It was dark but clear, and a crescent moon was rising behind us. I had agreed with Katie and the others that I would follow the road to Kelso that took us past the track leading up to the tower where we had spent the night, just a handful of days ago. It seemed a long, long time since then. The Bentley's huge, dish-like headlamps cast a wide, extended beam, bright enough for them to see us coming from a distance, flag down the car and stage an 'ambush', for the benefit of Kurz.

Once out of St Boswells, we cruised along the night road at thirty miles an hour. 'Perfectly adequate,' my father would say, in different circumstances, 'and with all of those damned potholes, slow enough to avoid them.' It would take little more than an hour to reach Berwick Barracks, in theory. I glanced at Kurz sitting in the back seat, but with only the glow of the instruments on the dashboard, I could not make out his features or expression. My father seemed to be asleep or, at any rate, very quiet and motionless. If he was conscious, he must have been thinking that nothing good awaited him in Berwick.

'Where did you serve with the Leibstandarte, sir?'

It had not occurred to me that I would need some biography to back up my impersonation of von Klige, everything had happened so quickly. And so I opted for brevity. 'I was taken prisoner at Caen in Normandy.'

Kurz shifted a little on the leather seats. 'Ah, yes,' he said, 'I too was captured in France. Where in Britain were you interned?'

I could not hesitate, equivocate or shut down what was a perfectly natural exchange between a German soldier and a member of the Gestapo. 'At what the British called the Black Camp, in the mountains.' The only POW camp I had ever heard of was near Comrie in Perthshire, and it was so called because it held many Waffen SS men. Fanatics who refused to believe that the war was lost, they were categorised as dangerous and were therefore closely confined. Vindicated in their blind faith in Adolf Hitler, many of them now led units in what had become an army of occupation.

Kurz grunted, made no reply. A moment later, I felt the press of cold metal on the back of my neck, the business end of the barrel of a pistol.

*

Even though the night sky was open and there was a sliver of a crescent moon, Katie found it difficult to make out more than dark shapes. There was no detail anywhere in the landscape and the only horizon she could be sure of was the watershed ridge of the Cheviots in the south.

With Wilson and Campbell, she had found some cover at the end of a long straight on the St Boswells to Berwick road so that they could see the headlights of the Bentley soon enough to mount their ponies and drag an old field gate out of a ditch.

Clicking on her torch for only a moment, Katie looked at her watch. The lights of the Bentley should have been visible by now. There was no traffic at all, nothing else moving in the darkness and no leaves on the roadside trees or hedges to obscure a car on the road.

*

'I myself was held prisoner at the Black Camp, at Comrie,' said Kurz, 'and I never saw you there. All of the Waffen SS were held in one compound, guarded by Polish soldiers who wanted to shoot them. But you were not there. Why are you lying? Who are you?'

He pushed hard at my neck with the barrel of his gun. I reckoned we were two miles from the track that led to the tower, only five minutes. Soon Katie would see the lights. If I could stall, think of something, spin out what had become an interrogation, we might make it.

'Slow the car down now!' barked Kurz.

With as much venom and authority as I could muster, I said, 'You are interfering with business you know nothing about, and your behaviour will be severely punished. But if you put away your gun now, admit that your memory is faulty, then I may be lenient.'

With the barrel of the pistol, Kurz hit me very sharply on the side of the head. And just at that moment an apparition suddenly loomed huge in the headlights. A white barn owl, its wing-spread more than three feet, flew directly towards the oncoming Bentley before lifting over it at the last moment. I swerved instantly. Kurz was thrown to one side and, looking for a second into the rear-view mirror, I saw my father grab for his gun. There were two shots. The big car fishtailed but I managed to keep it out of the roadside ditch and came to a halt.

I turned to see Kurz's blood-covered face rear up behind me like a hellish phantom, and he hit me again with his Luger before scrambling out of the car.

I quickly looked at my father. The German had shot him in the head.

Pointing his gun at me, Kurz opened the driver door. And when he tried to pull me out, I punched him and we rolled to the ground. Ablaze with rage, I fought like a demon. But Kurz managed to pull free, aimed low and shot me through the thigh.

A few minutes later, I found myself slewing around in the

back seat, handcuffed, with my father's blood-soaked head leaning against one of the rear doors next to me. My thigh wound was bad, bleeding profusely, but I had no hands to exert any pressure on it. It forced Kurz to drive as fast as possible to Berwick to avoid arriving at headquarters with two corpses and no answers. Passing in and out of consciousness, I heard him on a walkie-talkie or a radio of some kind, telling his superiors that he had two prisoners and that he had seen riders on the road. He was sure there was some connection with Lord Erskine. I felt myself slipping away, not thinking rationally. Perhaps this would be how it would end, a rollercoaster journey into the bowels of hell.

My father had tried to save me and I could not save him. I felt the fight ebbing out of me and closed my eyes.

*

Through the still night air, Katie, Wilson and Campbell had heard the gunshots. Abandoning any thought of ambush, they kicked on their ponies and made their way back along the road towards St Boswells as fast as they safely could.

Swinging uphill and around a corner, Kurz was driving the Bentley at breakneck speed. Somehow, the three riders had managed to get out of the way of the wildly careering car, but Wilson's pony reared and threw him.

In the paddock at the foot of the tower we had slept in a few nights before, Katie and John Campbell caught up two of the ponies. Wilson had fallen hard, and Campbell and Katie suspected he had broken several ribs on his right side. 'You'll need to stay here,' said Katie, giving him all of the food and water they had left. 'I had a bad fall once and if you can bear it, try to continue breathing deeply. That will hurt, a lot, but it will get your ribs in alignment so that they begin to set properly. Wait a day before you try to move. We'll come back for you.'

A dense and welcome mist made the land seem ghostly, only the treetops showing above it in places, but it hid them from sight and discouraged other traffic. It meant that Katie and John Campbell could move quickly, perhaps reaching Berwick in three hours if the ponies were not too blown. And frankly, without Wilson to delay them, they would make much better time.

*

'More bloody Beethoven.'

Both of them unable to sleep, Alan Grant had reconnected the battery to the yacht's radio and was fiddling with the dial, looking for something they could listen to. The Scottish Home Service and the Light Programme were unrelievedly dull, with only approved music playing, most of it classical and German, certainly nothing from the American and British big bands and singers so popular during the war. And then with another flick of the dial, a familiar and now sickening phrase filled the little cabin. 'German calling. Germany calling. Germany calling.'

Popularly, infamously, known as Lord Haw Haw, a former British fascist, William Joyce, had made weekly broadcasts on Radio Luxembourg for most of the war. It was not against the law to listen and millions in Britain did, not because they agreed with what he said but rather to discover something of how the Nazis saw the world.

In his thin, nasal whine, Joyce was crowing about how Jewish-dominated capitalism in Britain would change, how Germany would reorder the world with its Italian and Japanese allies and how the Axis powers had cowed the USA and the Soviet Union into defeat. Without explicitly mentioning the atom bomb that had destroyed London, Joyce reminded listeners about Germany's total military dominance: 'Be in no doubt, the Führer will not hesitate to act if irreconcilable elements

121

threaten our undertakings with our new friends and allies in Britain.'

'I've had enough of this,' muttered Alan, and he poured two generous tots of brandy. 'Let's see if we can find something worth listening to.'

With the volume turned low, he tried to find new frequencies. Through several bands of static and gurgling noises that sounded as though they came up from a deep well and not down from the airwaves, he began to pick up a strong signal. But it was not from a radio station. It sounded more like a conversation. Two men were speaking quickly in German, but he could make out some words, including several mentions of the name of Berwick. Was this a military frequency?

Then he heard one of the voices mention St Boswells, and after that – he was absolutely certain about this – the other said 'Lord Erskine'.

Alan Grant turned to his wife. 'I'm sure I heard someone say "Lord Erskine". Absolutely sure.'

They felt the hull of the yacht shift as the incoming tide began to fill the inner harbour.

Alan and Eileen Grant looked at each other and she said, 'We can't move until first light, can we? How far south is Berwick? About six or seven miles?'

Alan Grant smiled. 'About that. But we can't just blithely drop anchor in the harbour, in full view of the walls and the garrison.'

He unfolded a chart of the coastal waters. His yacht had a minimum draught of about four feet and could sail further inshore than most without running aground. 'I've never dropped anchor there, but Fisherman's Haven must have got its name because you can.' He pointed to a small, sheltered bay that lay no more than three hundred yards from the Elizabethan walls and the barracks. 'As soon as there's enough light in the east, we'll make our way south,' he said. 'But let's get some sleep first.'

27 December 1944

They must have assumed that I did not understand English.

A local doctor and nurse were replacing the dressing on the wound in my thigh. 'He's been lucky that the bullet passed straight through, missed his femur and a major artery, but he has lost a lot of blood,' the doctor said.

Instinctively maintaining my fictional identity, I kept muttering, '*Danke, danke schön*'. Woozy with what I imagined was morphine, I asked, '*Wo ist die alte Mann?* Where is the old man?'

They shook their heads. 'Soldiers come soon,' said the doctor and, with practised hands, they rolled me off the examination couch onto a stretcher on a trolley.

When I turned my head, I could see through a window that a misty day was dawning. Perhaps a haar was floating in off the North Sea, I thought, as I closed my eyes.

*

'Attention!' Every soldier in the courtroom of Berwick's grand Guild Hall stood up immediately, except for Oberführer von Klige. '*Heil Hitler!*,' barked the sergeant by the double doors. With Katie's father's overcoat around my shoulders and my heavily bandaged leg extended, I had been permitted to sit.

When Kurz came for me earlier, I had made a tremendous fuss. Having had time to think and work out a strategy, I insisted that if he had suspicions, then they ought to be tested in a courtroom and not by some Gestapo torturer. 'I am your superior officer!' I shouted. 'I served in the SS Panzer Division Leibstandarte Adolf Hitler. Some of my comrades were once the Führer's personal bodyguards. And you will respect my rank!'

I could see doubt flicker across Kurz's face. What, after all, would be the harm of a court martial? Perhaps more information might be extracted by questioning rather than other methods. It would also mean that responsibility for the fate of this man, and what he might or might not have done, would be shared. Schneider's deputy, Captain Müller, could preside. And he would suggest they could involve this new militia raised from British soldiers who had seen which way the wind was blowing – the Department of Public Safety, or whatever it was called. Directives to include them as much as possible had been sent to every garrison in the occupied territory.

The courtroom of the Berwick Guild Hall had seen centuries of grand ceremony in the long history of the town, and civic portraits of men in ermine, wearing chains of office, lined the walls. As we waited for the presiding officers to arrive, I looked around at this gallery of well-fed dignitaries from a long bygone age, from another country, a lost world. Suddenly the double doors behind me were thrown open and I heard the approaching clatter of jackboots on the wooden floor. Two soldiers walked purposefully past me and up to the dais where a long table had been set up. '*Heil Hitler*,' said a German officer I did not recognise. But when I saw the other man, I was stunned.

It was Colonel Murray, my commanding officer in Normandy. He took off his hat, laid it on the table, looked up at me for the first time and gasped, 'My God. David!'

*

'There will be road blocks and sentries on all the approaches into Berwick,' said John Campbell. 'There were when it was still our regimental depot. The Germans will have probably strengthened them.'

The two riders had kept to the north bank of the Tweed, skirting around Kelso and Coldstream, and they had at last pulled up their ponies at the entrance to the grand driveway leading to Paxton House, just a few miles from Berwick.

'I have an idea,' said Katie, thinking of the summer festivals – known as common ridings – held in Border towns. While there was much invented, mainly Victorian, tradition, the core of the unique events was ancient and involved a ride around the boundaries of the common land that belonged to each burgh, to check that surrounding lairds had not encroached. 'Before the war, I rode the Berwick Bounds, the line of the border between England and Scotland. If memory serves, the Bound Road is not used at any other time. It's well hidden by high walls and hedges on both sides and it takes riders very close to the town walls. It'll take longer but be much safer.'

Their ponies had sagged a little but because they had stopped to let them drink from streams, they were not yet blown. Katie and Campbell skirted Paxton village, splashed across the Whiteadder Water and quickly found the Bound Road. It climbed steeply up a slope above the flood plain with high banks on either side before it began its wide circuit around the common land known as the liberties of Berwick. Katie reckoned it would take only half an hour to reach the town.

*

'There is some mistake!' I insisted, playing up the aristocratic gloss on my German accent. 'My name is Oberführer Manfred von Klige and I have never seen this man before.'

Kurz was smiling, shaking his head.

In halting English, Captain Müller turned to Colonel Murray: 'You know this man. You must tell us who he is.'

For a long moment, Murray looked at me, and instead of answering the question, he asked one: 'What has he done?'

Müller explained that I had obstructed an officer of the Gestapo in making an arrest, falsely claimed that I had been

125

sent to interrogate a prisoner, Lord Erskine, who had shot and killed Kommandant Schneider. And I fought with an officer of the Gestapo and attempted to disarm him.

Murray and I looked at each for a moment, and I made a decision. 'I am Captain David Erskine of the 1st Battalion of the King's Own Scottish Borderers,' I said as calmly as I could, 'and I was privileged to serve in Normandy with Colonel Murray.'

They would find me guilty whatever anyone said. What would be the point of Murray denying he knew me after blurting out my name? If he had, they would surely punish him too. And they could easily replace him in whatever role the Germans had invented.

'There is nothing to be gained by continuing,' said Müller, closing his wallet file. 'You have admitted your guilt.' He looked around the courtroom as if to invite comment and then banged down his gavel as a full stop to the proceedings. Except it was not quite the end. 'Captain Erskine, you are guilty of spying and of treason against the state. The punishment for that is death by hanging.'

Colonel Murray shook his head and, speaking very deliberately so that the German could understand, said, 'Captain Erskine is not a common criminal. He should not be sent to the gallows. He is an officer in the British army and he is entitled to a soldier's death.'

I could see that Murray was playing for time, trying somehow to delay my inevitable fate. But at the time, it all seemed so distant. I had the sense that this was happening to someone else. I was a spectator, not the victim. From far away, I heard Müller say, 'The war is over, Colonel. The sentence is clear.'

At that, Murray exploded, banging his fist on the table. 'I insist that a military punishment is carried out, a firing squad.'

Somehow taken aback, and perhaps anxious to exhibit at least the show of cooperation with the new Department of

Public Safety, Müller shrugged his shoulders. 'It makes no difference to me. One o'clock today. At the parade ground.'

*

The haar had slowed the Grants' progress down the Berwickshire coast. Between St Abbs and Eyemouth, there are many skerries, jagged reefs hidden just below the surface of the water. Alan did not want to avoid them by navigating further out to sea than he had to, both because it would make the short voyage longer and also there was a risk of being run down by one of the big merchant ships that plied the east coast sea roads. But to get his bearings, he needed to see the shoreline and only occasionally did the dark shapes of the high cliffs loom up out of the mist. After they had rounded the entrance to Eyemouth harbour, tacking with what wind there was further out to sea to avoid the vicious reefs at the harbour entrance, Alan set a course due south.

*

Levering himself up to the window embrasure, screwing up his eyes in extreme pain, Angus Wilson managed to sit down on the ledge. Breathing hard, his shirt soaked with sweat, he slowly stretched out his legs, looking for relief from his broken ribs. How he had managed to climb the spiral staircase of the tower, in total darkness, he could not say. Driven by the need to lie down flat, he had dropped down to his knees and failed to avoid crying out when he rolled to one side. Wilson had been completely unaware, dead to the world, when Campbell and Katie left the tower in the early hours.

After drinking deep from a water canteen they had left him, Wilson looked out to the south over the crag and the fields below it. Mist still lingered in the river valley, clinging to the trees like smoke, forming and lifting as the breeze swirled. At

127

the foot of the tower and around the crag as far as the eastern track, there was a fenced paddock, a handy place to turn out the ponies overnight.

But it was empty. Wilson could see no sign of his pony, and when he turned to look around the upper chamber, his saddle and bridle had gone.

*

'Is there anything I can do, anyone you would like me to inform?'

Colonel Murray had not been permitted to talk to me alone in the guard room next to the parade ground. We both glanced at Kurz and then the two soldiers standing on either side of the door. If I mentioned any names, they would be noted.

'Would you please at least attempt to ensure that my father has a decent and respectful burial? His ancestors are waiting for him at Dryburgh, but I imagine that will be out of the question.'

Murray nodded and told me he would do all he could.

So much had been destroyed. London obliterated. A puppet king and a fascist government installed. It seemed trivial that I should grieve not only for my father but for the breaking of a line, a link with a long past. And soon it would end entirely, with my execution, the extinguishing of the last of the name.

*

'That's my dad's boat! The gin palace.'

Katie and Campbell were leading their ponies past the Nissen huts of a deserted army camp close to Berwick's walls, perched on the cliffs above Fisherman's Haven.

'I'm sure it is!' She pointed to the yacht bobbing at anchor in the little bay. Excited, relieved and anxious all at the same time, but unable to see for more than two hundred yards, Katie

128

looked around but could make out no one and nothing in the eerie silence. Pulling her riding mac tighter and making sure her shotgun was completely concealed, she turned to John Campbell. 'I just don't know what we'll find. Nothing good, I expect.'

He nodded and, for some shred of reassurance, gripped the stock of his own shotgun tighter through the slit-pocket of his mac. 'Just make sure the safety is on, miss, until you need it to be off.'

Having been a soldier at Berwick Barracks, Campbell knew the ground well, even when the winter haar had set in. 'We can't risk trying to get into the town through the Cow Port, the gateway under the walls. It will be guarded. But I know another way.'

When they climbed up onto the Elizabethan walls, Campbell led Katie past the graveyard of a squat little church. The haar seemed patchy, lifting in places as the sun climbed. Through a wrought-iron gate, they made their way between rows of headstones. And then it seemed that, like a stage curtain rising to reveal a set and a cast of actors, the haar disappeared.

The silence was abruptly broken when a soldier shouted an order in German and a detail of six soldiers marched smartly out of the gates of the barracks. Very quickly, the Parade area began to fill with people. Katie grabbed a posy of flowers out of a jar by one of the gravestones. She noticed that there were soldiers mixed in with the gathering crowd, and that they were armed.

'Look!' Campbell pointed.

Out of the gates came a further four soldiers, each carrying a corner of a stretcher. An officer walked beside them. They turned immediately left and stopped at a stretch of blank wall. Opposite them four more soldiers formed up in a line, at a distance of about ten yards.

129

And then Katie and Campbell saw who was on the stretcher. Katie gasped.

With one leg heavily bandaged, I was lifted out of the stretcher and made to stand unsteadily against the wall. The crowd of more than a hundred people were slowly marshalled into a semi-circle and, with her emotions churning, Katie joined them, with Campbell just behind her. They gently pushed their way to the front, the reluctant crowd parting willingly.

'Miss,' Campbell whispered, 'there are an awful lot of them and only two of us.'

At that moment, time suddenly seemed to shift and events took place in a dizzyingly rapid sequence. Captain Müller took up a position next to the four-man firing squad. He barked an order. They raised their rifles.

Campbell and Katie thumbed off their safety catches.

Müller raised his hand.

And was shot through the throat by an arrow.

VIII

His throat gurgling, blood spouting like a fountain from his carotid artery, Müller pulled at his shirt collar, his mouth agape. As he fell, more arrows found their marks in seconds, one flying after another in rapid succession. Two of the firing squad fell to their knees, a third tried frantically to pluck an arrow from deep in his chest while a fourth soldier shot wildly in the air before his neck was also pierced. After a moment of stunned astonishment, chaos broke out. The soldiers in the crowd sprayed bullets from their submachine guns at the surrounding rooftops without any clear idea where the deadly archer was. Silent, almost invisible in flight, the arrows seemed to come out of nowhere.

Behind the crowd, high on the roof of a tall church at the corner of the Parade, the archer suddenly revealed himself.

Ululating, hollering and whooping, the little man fired more arrows, nocking each one with lightning speed, bringing down more soldiers. As others turned to fire on him, he scampered along the ridge of the church's roof and the Germans raced across the Parade to give chase.

Winded, open-mouthed at what had happened in less than a minute, Katie and Campbell ran over to the wall where I stood and carried me bodily towards the Cow Port.

'Here. Let me help!' Alan Grant ran out of the crowd, most of whom were following the German soldiers.

Between the three of them, they carried me across the old golf course, scrambling down the cliff path to Fisherman's

Haven. Having splashed through the shallows and bundled me over the gunwale into the yacht with Eileen's help, Alan hauled up the little anchor. With Campbell, he rigged a spinnaker sail to catch the wind once they had sculled out of the little bay.

Meanwhile, a merry dance around Berwick's huddled rooftops was leading most of the German garrison up and down the town's narrow streets.

With an extraordinary, animal-like agility, the little man scampered over the orange pan tiles, jumped across alleyways, leading the Germans in a wide circle, away from the cliffs and the coast. Then he raced at great speed along the top of the Elizabethan walls to the most northerly bastion. Skipping down the stone revetments to the open grassland and the abandoned army camp, he leapt on Wilson's pony, gathered up the other two and galloped with them up to the beginning of the Bound Road, pausing to make sure the Germans continued their pursuit. He knew exactly where he was going and those behind him would find out, to their great cost.

*

Having sipped a fiery tot of Eileen Grant's brandy, lying on one of the berths with my injured leg slightly raised, I found myself unable to hold back the tears. It was the shock, I think, rather than the pain, although that was bad enough. I wept for my father, for his stubborn courage and biblical sense of justice, for all the things we had left unsaid, for the destruction of our world and the triumph of evil, and for the violent death he had suffered trying to come to the aid of his only son. Facing the firing squad, less than an hour before, I found myself unafraid to die. And that was because I felt that all my courage had left me, all the fight had gone. Katie kissed my forehead and I began to freefall into a deep sleep.

'We can't dress that wound.' said Alan Grant,'and it'll need to be kept clean. All we have is a first aid kit.'

Having caught a westerly wind, the yacht was scudding over a calm sea, making good progress northwards, past the high cliffs, the ramparts of the spectacular Berwickshire coast.

'There are only two hours of light left. If we can get around St Abbs Head soon, with the wind directly behind us, we might make it to Pease Bay. There's a good, secluded, sandy beach where I can run her aground.'

*

By the time the little man reached the edges of Bleaklaw Moss, he had left his pursuers behind, but not too far behind. Once he had untacked the ponies and stowed their saddles and bridles in the shieling, he quickly set to work. In a wide semi-circle around the old cottage, its sheltering copse of Scots pines and the hidden entrance to the moss, he had spent time in the summer digging into the peat banks on the moorland. Having cut out a series of long, rectangular clefts, he had stuffed them with dry moss and lichen, brittle leaves and twigs.

The light in the west was failing fast, the sun falling behind the Cheviot watershed and so he lit a pine resin torch. At each cleft, he fired the tinder so that by the time he had finished, there was a long arc of dark and billowing smoke stretching across the moorland.

In the long night to come, the fire would reach far into the peat beds between the Roman road and the shieling, making them smoulder, making the very earth burn. When morning came, the Germans in their armoured cars would be able to see the smoke from far away. And then they would come for him.

He would be waiting.

*

When the tide began to ebb from the broad sands of Pease Bay, Alan Grant was dismayed to find that his beloved yacht was becoming increasingly uninhabitable. It was not designed to carry five people and it must have been the extra weight that made it slew to one side on the wet sand.

Darkness was gathering fast and Eileen and Katie took as much food and drink and as many blankets as they could carry. 'We used to picnic at the foot of the Old Red Sandstone cliff when you were small,' said Eileen. 'There's a deep recess that will keep us out of the worst of the wind.'

After they had helped me out of the boat and deposited me with my back against the sandpaper-like rock, Campbell and Alan went off to forage for driftwood. My job was to sprinkle some paraffin over the few sticks and twigs they had picked up near the mouth of the recess. I smiled at their thoughtfulness in involving me, making me feel useful in whatever piddling way. The recess where I sat was an impressive, elemental place, worn out of the high cliff by aeons of high tides.

As I rested, the throbbing in my leg eased. We agreed that the dressing should come off in the morning and Campbell volunteered to help me wade into the icy seawater as the tide came back. It was not a moment I was looking forward to but the water would help clean the wound and we would redress it with any clean bandaging that could be salvaged and the cotton wool and antiseptic from the yacht's first aid kit.

After half an hour of dragging driftwood across the deserted beach, a decent blaze was crackling, sending sparks spiralling up into the darkness. Campbell had been on a commando training course at Spean Bridge, near Fort William, and had been taught how to build what he called a 'lateral fire'. Instead of the traditional cone shape, he set out a longer and narrower fire so that the big branches that he and Alan could not cut would be burned. With our backs to the cliff and out of the winter wind, we sat more or less in a line, our faces lit by a generous glow. The yellow sandstone at our backs danced with shadows. Instead of gin in the gin palace, Alan Grant kept a supply of Glenlivet, and Eileen found some decent glasses. Soon, more than the fire was glowing as we passed around drams and what had come from the Grants' Christmas larder.

For a while, little was said. Staring through the sparks from Campbell's ingenious fire, I could see that it was an open sky, the Plough clearly visible in the north. Perhaps the shock of all that had happened was still distorting perspectives but I imagined I could see our bright fire by the shushing waves and the recess below the ancient cliffs from a great distance, high in the dark, winter sky. While I dozed for a few moments, dreaming of endlessly falling, the others sorted out blankets and the spare foresail we might need to rig if it began to rain.

Katie sat next to me and, thank goodness, very close. 'Come on, sleepy head, wake up. We all need to talk. We can't stay here like five Robinson Crusoes. We have to work out what to do.'

What followed was a sobering, realistic appraisal. 'Our old life is gone,' said Alan Grant. 'None of us can ever return home.' We had all survived, at least, and Campbell assured me that Angus Wilson would be all right – he had a huge extended family and somehow he would find his way to the help he needed, either from them or from close friends. But the world we now inhabited had no place for us. Campbell made a bad joke about Robin Hood and Maid Marion in the greenwood. But he had a point. We were outlaws. And it was not only the Germans we needed to avoid. Good and decent people like Colonel Murray had persuaded themselves that there was no option but to collaborate.

'I saw the atom bomb explode. And I was two hundred miles away,' I said. 'What can we do with that sword of Damocles hanging over us?'

Katie sat up suddenly, an expression of extreme annoyance creasing her brow. 'I'll tell what we can do, you great lump. We can have children. You and I. Somewhere. We will find somewhere. And we can bring them up as good and decent people. That's what we can do, you idiot.'

My mouth opened and closed again. Alan Grant roared with laughter and Eileen smiled.

'Well,' I stuttered, 'that certainly is a plan.'

Katie punched me hard in the shoulder. 'But we'd have to be married first.' She punched me again, even harder.

'I've only got one good knee, so if it's all right with you, I'll sit still and not kneel.' There was a moment of hushed silence, it seemed. 'Katherine Elizabeth Grant, will you marry me?'

28 December 1944

When the dawn light crept across the moorland on a windless morning, the smoke spiralled high into the sky, visible for miles around. In the air floated the tang of peat, and the dense, earthy scent greeted the little man as he emerged from the tangle of Bleaklaw Moss. He did not have long to wait. Having climbed like a cat up one of the tallest of the Scots pines, he looked east to the line of the Roman road. He could see movement, about a mile and half away. They were coming. Two German army vehicles had pulled up at Whitton Edge, where the C-road carried on and the old road made by the legions branched off towards the hills. The smoke would bring them, the little man was certain, and he was ready for them.

Bent on vengeance, determined to make an example after their humiliation in Berwick in front of a crowd, the Germans had also prepared. One of their vehicles was an armoured car, known as a *Panzerwagen*. It was equipped with a turreted cannon that that could fire a withering blast of two hundred rounds a minute and over a much longer range than a submachine gun. Its crew of four had seen too many of their comrades skewered by arrows on Berwick Parade and were furious that this man-boy had led them up the Tweed Valley, laying false trails, sometimes evading capture at the last moment. Maybe they had at last run him to ground.

Behind the *Panzerwagen* trundled a small truck carrying twelve grenadiers and their sergeant. Feldwebel Horst Bultmann had endured the dishonour of captivity at the Black Camp at Comrie after his regiment surrendered in France. The taunts of the Polish guards stung him often, especially after the failure of the Ardennes offensive. But in the end the Führer had not failed them.

Through his binoculars, Bultmann could make out a low cottage sheltered by pine trees on three sides. When the *Panzerwagen* and the truck came as close as they could, having ripped through the Roman road-bed that had endured for two thousand winters, he called a halt. The smoke over the moorland had cleared as a breeze blew down from the western hills. Between the road and the cottage lay about four hundred or five hundred yards of more or less level ground, tussocky, perhaps boggy in places, but no real barrier. Bultmann climbed up on the turret of the *Panzerwagen* and, focusing his binoculars more sharply, he was astonished by what he saw. Sitting cross-legged on the ridge of the cottage roof was the little man who had killed so many of his comrades in Berwick.

And he was waving.

*

Raking through the embers of the fire at the foot of the sandstone cliff, Alan Grant added more kindling and set a billycan to one side, to warm some water.

Waking slowly, with Katie folded close under a quilted

137

blanket beside me, I smiled and asked if he and Eileen had got much sleep.

'Glenlivet helps. I see your fiancée is still sound asleep.'

Carefully cradling her sleepy head to one side, I managed to lever myself upright. With Campbell's help, I unwound the dressing on my thigh and braced myself for the icy waters of the North Sea. The wound had closed, mercifully, but there was a worrying yellow tinge around it. 'That's from the bullet,' said Campbell. 'Close range.'

The tide had refloated the Grants' yacht and we decided to wade out to it, hang onto the gunwale for a moment and wade back. When we made it back to the beach, I was gasping with the shock of the cold.

After Katie accepted my proposal – with a kiss, not a punch – and we raised a glass to celebrate something good, there was a discussion and a decision. Eileen Grant made the excellent and obvious point that we would soon run out of food, to say nothing of Glenlivet. We needed resources, and also somewhere safe to lie low. I added that my name would have been circulated around the German garrisons in Scotland and the north of England, and anyone with me would be assumed to have been complicit in the remarkable events in Berwick.

'What about Aunt Jenny and Uncle Robert in St Andrews?' said Katie, stirring immediate undergraduate memories of summer drinks in their garden. 'They have a big house and we can reach the town by boat.'

Alan Grant remembered that his sister had said something about St Andrews being fortified, trenches dug on the banks of the Swilken Burn, across the fairways of the Old Course. 'I shouldn't think we can just sail into the harbour,' he said.

*

Bultmann was enraged at the cockiness of the little man, but he tried to think like a soldier. The cottage was beyond the range of the *Panzerwagen*. They would need to get within at least two hundred yards, closer if possible, for its devastating rate of fire to be anything like accurate. But would the moorland be sodden, boggy and treacherous? Was that why the little imp on the roof was taunting him and his men? Arrows would not fly further than his weapons would shoot, and so this would be a game of caution and patience. All the Germans had to do was get close.

Bultmann did not notice that the smoke had clung to some of the tussocky patches and that it lingered in the hollows.

As a line of soldiers, their submachine guns at the ready, began to move, a high-pitched whistle pierced the clear air. Over the trees flew four buzzards, calling *piou-piou* to each other. Bultmann shouted to his men to ignore these distractions and look to their fronts, and he signalled to the driver of the *Panzerwagen* that he should advance. The engine noise seemed to break into the quiet and the line of soldiers moved slowly. The little man sat motionless on the roof. Very soon, he would be in range. But still he did not move. Surely they had him now. Bultmann looked along the advancing line, waved his arm for them to speed up, charge towards the cottage and begin firing.

That was when the first soldier fell into the inferno.

For many hours, the little man's invisible peat fire had been burning underground across the moorland. Where the surface crust was thin, a man's weight would break it and he would fall into a red-hot fire.

The first soldier screamed as the ground seemed to crack under his feet and he was taken down into hell. He had fallen up to his waist, smoke puffed out around him, his face blistered in the updraught and the fierce heat roasted his legs and lower torso. When a comrade ran to help him, he too broke though, this time sinking up to his chest, his arms waving frantically.

Where the blazing layer of peat was thin, some men burned only their legs and could scramble out, very badly injured. The cries of others lasted only a moment as they were completely submerged in a smouldering pit of unspeakable agony.

Bultmann stopped dead in his tracks, not moving, staring at the ground around him. But he had the presence of mind to turn round and signal to the driver of the *Panzerwagen* to stop immediately. Terrified, retreating from a landscape of dead and dying men, roaring with pain as their bodies burned alive, he tested the ground with every step, petrified that the fires would claim him. He reached the safety of the vehicle and climbed onto it as the awful sound of living death echoed across the moorland.

*

'We'll have to cross the Firth of Forth at night,' said Alan Grant. 'There's too much traffic during the day.'

Earlier, he had walked up to the village of Cockburnspath to make a reverse charge call to Jenny, his sister, in St Andrews. She had warned him that the town was crawling with soldiers – 'unpleasant thugs' – and that the harbour was closed. In fact, the university was also closed down. These thugs had arrived one morning at Robert's office in the physics department and instructed him to move and to hand over the keys to all the laboratories. All of his colleagues were also summarily ejected and instructed not to return, for any reason.

Alan asked Jenny to make a call for him. He knew Alistair Charters from the Royal Forth Yacht Society, and could he please arrange a berth for him at Crail harbour, assuming these things were still possible? With fair winds, helpful currents and a great deal of good luck, they might arrive in the small hours of tomorrow morning. And from Crail, they would somehow find their way to St Andrews.

Few of the soldiers trapped in the blazing peat died quickly. With a submachine gun, from the turret of the *Panzerwagen*, Bultmann put those going through a living hell out of their misery, close comrades all of them. In the Black Camp at Comrie, the loyalty of all the SS men to the Führer, and to each other, had become even more intense. With one exception. Sergeant Wolfgang Rosterg had visited great dishonour on all of them when he said he believed the war was lost. After a court martial, he was hanged. The British and the Poles made some arrests but no one betrayed their oaths. These men had understood the meaning of honour.

'We need to get closer,' Bultmann shouted to the driver. 'Go slowly and be prepared to reverse. Do it!' Surely with three axles and six big wheels, the armoured car would not sink. The question was: fast or slow? 'Maximum speed, now!'

When he saw the vehicle begin to move, the little man stood up on the ridge of the roof, walked to the chimney and climbed onto the mantle so that he could see better what was happening. And, suddenly, the turret cannon of the *Panzerwagen* opened up. It was devastating, shattering the windows, flattening the door and ripping away stonework. And making the man lose his balance and fall backwards off the roof.

Bultmann had realised that the ring of fire was not broad and the armoured car came to a stop by the walls of the shieling. Behind it, the German found the body of the man, curled in a tight crouch, as though he was asleep. For some reason, Bultmann was reluctant to touch this strange creature, even though he wanted to feel for a pulse. It would be much better to take a captive rather than a corpse back to Berwick. When the German prodded the body with his boot, two buzzards exploded out of the sky, dive-bombing him, making him stagger backwards until he caught his heel on a root and fell.

When he got back up, the little man had gone.

*

'We'll do it by the lights.'

Gloaming had fallen and Alan Grant was tacking against the wind, guiding his yacht out of Pease Bay and into the busy sea roads of the Firth of Forth. In the half-light, Alan could not have too many lookouts. Fearful that we might be seen by the coastguard, he had not rigged bow or stern lights. The light he really needed came from the string of lighthouses on the shores, rocks and islands of the great firth.

'It's exciting, David.' Katie was perched on the edge of the berth where she'd made me comfortable. 'Back to St Andrews. Trips down memory lane. Even if everything else has changed, the three streets won't have.'

That thought, and the gentle swell of the sea and the sway of the boat, lulled me. Our time at university was like a Christmas scene in a glass bubble: captured forever, unchanging and idyllic.

On deck, Alan blessed the good weather. Winter storms could blow up suddenly in the firth, whipping blinding spindrift off the tops of big waves driven by the strong east winds across the North Sea. But that night they had little more than a stiff breeze coming out of the south-west, enough to billow out the sail but not soak the open deck. It was cold, though, and in her yellow oilskins, Eileen was shivering. 'Go below, darling,' Alan said. 'John and I will manage.'

We made good headway up the East Lothian coast, passing the Barns Ness light on the left-hand side, prompting Alan to peer through the darkness for his next seamark. Soon, the pale white cliffs of the Bass Rock loomed up, the ancient guano of thousands of generations of gannets visible even on a winter night with only a crescent moon. Taking a bearing on the light that flashed on the flank of the rock, Alan began to change course, moving almost due north. This was the trickiest part of the short voyage. He guided his yacht into the sea lanes over the Rath Grounds, where many tons of herring were caught during the August draves. But this was December and a very different sea might be waiting out of the lee of the land.

Very carefully, Eileen lit the primus stove and, in its glow, she looked for a moment at Katie dozing. How beautiful her girl was, how content amidst all this turmoil: together now with her true love. Even though the war meant they saw little of each other after graduation, she never thought theirs was just a university romance, something that would not survive the winds of the real world. In fact, it had been the brutality of an all too real world that had brought them together. There was at least that consolation. Having brewed some hot cocoa and put away the primus, Eileen took two mugs on deck for John and her husband.

Alan pointed to his right. Through the darkness, there was a scintilla, a tiny pinprick of light. 'I think that's May Island. We should see the harbour lights of Elie, Pittenweem, Anstruther and Crail soon.'

But no sooner were the words out of his mouth than a huge black shape seemed to rear in front of the yacht out of nowhere. Travelling east, picking up speed before it reached the open sea, a merchant ship was bearing down fast on the much smaller vessel.

Shouting at Eileen and Campbell to duck, Alan pulled the boom around sharply. To have any chance of avoiding a collision, he had to shift his course north-west. Thinking they were about to be overwhelmed, they looked up at the lights on the big ship's prow. And then we were hit hard by its huge bow-wave. But mercifully, it did not knock us down. If the wave had hit us abeam, on the side of the yacht, it would have probably capsized. But instead Alan kept his own bow straight enough to the north-west to meet it and cut through. However, when we careened down the other side of the wave, as the merchantman passed us, the sea almost washed all three of them off the open deck.

Holding onto lines Alan had rigged along the gunwales, Eileen and John Campbell began bailing as fast as they could. Katie insisted I stay put in my bunk. On one leg, I'd be more than useless – a liability. Katie emerged from the cabin with a billycan and they frantically scooped up as much water as possible from the slippery deck. At the same time, Alan saw that, somehow, the near accident had pushed us much closer to the cliffs of May Island and, pulling the boom back over, yelling at the others to duck once again, he reset his course northwards.

John Campbell's Morse code was rusty but when he saw the dot-dash of a torch being clicked on and off, he thought he could read C-R-A-I-L.

'That will be Alistair Charters on the harbour wall,' Alan said. Even though it was black-dark with no street lights on in the fishing village, he risked his powerful lamp and it played off the ancient yellow sandstone blocks that had kept the sea at bay for centuries.

After threading his way through the narrow entrance, Campbell pushing at the sandstone wall with a paddle to keep the hull away from it, we tied up close to the sea-steps. At the top, Alan shook hands with Charters, the torchlight making introductions a little theatrical. 'Thanks for turning out so late. We much appreciate it.'

I managed the steps with difficulty, Campbell behind me in case of mishap. Katie stayed in the cabin with Eileen, gathering together what we might need and stowing what we would not.

'Well, now,' said a voice from the darkness behind Charters, 'what a jolly little party.'

In an instant at least half a dozen powerful torches snapped on. My heart sank. After all we had been through.

'You are all breaking curfew. And by some distance. You are all under arrest,' drawled an aristocratic, very English voice. 'Good evening. We are officers from the Department of Public Safety. Bit of a mouthful, I know,' continued the polite, invisible man. 'Some people call us the Vigilantes. Rather prefer that.'

A tall man in a black uniform emerged into the light. A beret with what looked to me like a British regimental badge was crammed over his floppy hair. The deliberate, even languid manner matched his voice. 'You will all accompany us to the Tolbooth. Immediately, if you please.'

I turned to look at the top of the sea-steps, but Katie and Eileen must have heard the exchange and they stayed hidden in the yacht.

IX

29 December 1944

When we reached the old Tolbooth in the centre of Crail, we found that Alistair Charters had somehow become detached from our group. He was nowhere to be seen. Had he simply slipped away? As we were ushered into what seemed like a rather grand council chamber, no one made any comment on his absence. Had it been him who betrayed us?

The rest of the Vigilantes simply disappeared, no doubt pleased to get to their beds. This strange set of circumstances prompted me to challenge our captor, who seemed quite at ease to be alone with three people he had just arrested. I noticed that he was armed with a British Army issue Webley revolver. I also noticed the cap badge of the Royal Scots on his black beret and asked him why a soldier from a cavalry regiment that fought at Waterloo was now collaborating with the German army of occupation.

'Just following orders, old boy. No change, really. Same old thing.' His manner was languid, almost effeminate. 'By the way,' – he held out his hand – 'I'm Jamie Griffith-Smith. I know who you are. Sorry I had to take you in in the middle of the night. Orders from up the road.'

After we had shaken hands, I decided to press a little harder, test his new allegiance. 'These people didn't hesitate to obliterate London, kill hundreds of thousands of people, including the king, the man to whom you swore loyalty as a Royal Scot.'

He raised an eyebrow. 'Well, the RAF didn't hesitate either, Captain Erskine. The firestorm raids on Hamburg and Dresden were pretty severe.'

For a few minutes, we exchanged arguments until Griffith-Smith appeared to tire of the conversation. 'Look here. There's no real debate worth the name. They have the bomb, and that is, sadly, that. Nothing else to be said.'

'There's a great deal more to be said.' For some reason my time at the Château de la Muette swam into my head. 'They'll do much worse and have probably already done much worse.' Even though I had only ever discussed it before with Squadron Leader Godwin, I told Griffith-Smith about the memoranda I had seen from Lieutenant Colonel Adolf Eichmann, with their vague talk of mass deportations of Jews from Hungary, earlier that year. There was also a list, compiled by him, of the number of Jews in each European country. For England (meaning Britain), there were 335,000. Estonia was *Judenfrei*, Jew-free.

These revelations immediately caught Griffith-Smith's interest, the charm peeling away like a mask, but he made no comment.

'I think the Nazis are killing many Jews or working them to death in their labour camps. And they could do the same here. What is to stop them?' I made this last point as emphatically as I could.

There was a pause and Griffith-Smith looked hard at me for a moment. 'Well, can't stand here chatting all night. I'll see you all bright and early.' And with that, he turned on his heel, closed the chamber door and locked it.

*

Careful to keep hidden in the shadows of the medieval lanes leading up from the harbour, Katie and Eileen had followed us.

Noticing that when Griffith-Smith left the Tolbooth, he

147

did not seem to lock the main door, they decided to take a chance. They waited until he had walked some way down the Marketgate, got into a little sports car and driven off up the St Andrews road, and then the women walked quickly across to the old building. Were any of the posse of Vigilantes guarding their prisoners? Probably, but Katie and Eileen had concealed shotguns under their overcoats. If they surprised any guards, they might be sleepy and would not make trouble if they were staring down two double barrels. But there might be bloodshed, or possibly worse, loud bangs in the middle of the night that would bring people running. Katie turned to her mother and smiled grimly, 'Just do what I do.' She turned the huge wrought-iron door handle.

At the same time, just a few hundred yards away, Griffith-Smith braked, did a rapid three-point turn and drove back close to the Marketgate, hoping that the two women who had followed them up from the harbour had taken the bait. He concealed himself in the pillared portico of one of the grand townhouses opposite the Tolbooth and waited.

Katie and Eileen found no guards at the Tolbooth, the main door unlocked and the key still in the lock of the council chamber, where Griffith-Smith had left it. It seemed that the Vigilantes in Crail were very relaxed about their duties.

*

'I think we should split up,' I said. 'A group of five wandering around the countryside will be noticed.' I suggested that the three Grants should go together, and Campbell and I would follow. I wasn't looking forward to the hike: my leg was painful, but at least the wound had closed and the bandaging on it seemed to be holding everything together; when it didn't, I would have Campbell to support me. 'We should try to get a couple of hours' sleep before these people come back. And before first light, we'll all become pilgrims on the path of right-eousness that leads to the holy city.'

When we were students, Katie and I had walked part of the pilgrim road to St Andrews. In the university library, it had been my first real research project and I read everything I could find. Endowed by the earls of Fife in the twelfth century, a ferry brought the faithful from North Berwick across the Forth to Earlsferry. From there, bands of psalm-singing penitents made their way north, to be close to the relics of St Andrew. He was a man who knew Christ, and to pray in close proximity to his bones made those prayers powerful.

Katie and her parents joined the path near a farm about three miles south of the town, and Campbell and I stayed back, about half a mile behind them. Since the Reformation and the ban on pilgrimage, the path had withered, sometimes become entirely lost, its route broken where it had been ploughed over. That was what recommended it to me. Few knew of it and even fewer would be walking or watching it.

Until bands of pilgrims reached the summit of Wester Balrymonth Hill, the spires of St Andrews Cathedral, St Regulus' Tower and the many other churches remained hidden from sight. From the hill, a wide panorama of sanctity was at last revealed to those who had made their weary way from the ferry. The vast cathedral, ruined by the Reformers must have seemed as though it perched on the edge of eternity, for beyond stretched the vast horizons of the North Sea. I had asked the Grants to stop on the hill, and if they were unobserved and the path ahead seemed clear, Campbell and I would catch up.

'It looks as though the Germans have indeed fortified the place, just as Jenny said.' Alan Grant pointed to what seemed to be a timber palisade on the far bank of the Kinnessburn. Flowing into the sea at St Andrews harbour, the stream marked a southern boundary. The good thing was that Aunt Jenny's house was to the west of the town centre, beyond the medieval walls, and we should be able to find our way there if we were careful.

But we were not careful enough. We had no way of knowing it at the time, but Jamie Griffith-Smith watched us as we stood on that hill. He hoped that we would lead him to our destination. And there, perhaps, all of the rats would be caught in one trap.

*

Colonel Kritzinger did not deal well with anxiety or pressure from his superiors. When he summoned Griffith-Smith to his headquarters at College Gate, the former administrative centre of the university, he banged on his desk several times and marched around the room, glancing out of the windows that looked up North Street to the ruins of the cathedral. Commandant of the German garrison in St Andrews, he was a small, fidgety, excitable, irritable, highly intelligent man with flawless English.

'Erskine will try to become the focus of a resistance movement. I am certain of this. Stories about him and his friends will spread. But before we arrest him and – unlike those bunglers in Berwick – execute him, we need to understand something of his network. Before it grows, we can, as you say, nip it in the bud. Find out who his contacts are. And why he has come here.'

*

'I haven't the slightest idea what a yardarm is, but I am certain that somewhere in the world the sun is over it.'

Katie's Aunt Jenny and Uncle Robert were dispensing drinks from a sideboard that seemed unaffected by wartime shortages. Even in the chill of a deep December, Jenny radiated sunshine, warmth and excellent manners. John Campbell was the only bedraggled arrival she did not know, and she took great trouble to make him feel welcome and at ease. Asking him about himself, she topped up his glass of whisky and sat next to him during an improvised but excellent supper. Her smile seemed to bring him to life. When younger, she had been a great beauty, and she still was. But unlike most beautiful women, Jenny did not keep her distance. Naturally and instinctively, she touched people, a reassuring hand on an arm, or a hand held. After a hot bath and having my wound redressed, and an hour or two of conviviality, good wine and Jenny's good food, it was possible to believe that all of our troubles were out there, far beyond the walls of the MacDonalds' hospitable house.

'I have an announcement.' I tinkled a glass with a knife. 'I would like to introduce you to my fiancée, your niece, the most beautiful, kind, clever . . .'

But before I could complete my string of adjectives, Jenny whooped and said, 'About bloody time!' and kissed us both. For some misplaced reason, Robert shook Alan's hand, kissed Eileen and Katie and then remembered to shake mine.

When we took our drinks through the double doors to the sitting room with its vast, pillowy sofas, and Robert had pokered the log fire into life, he and Jenny began to tell us what had taken place in St Andrews and what had happened at its ancient university. Robert MacDonald had held the chair of physics – or natural philosophy, as he preferred to call it – for ten years and had spent the war working on various research projects for the government. He had become used to soldiers, to the necessarily abrupt nature of military methods and the demands of deadlines, but when the Germans began to arrive in November, their behaviour shocked him: 'Complete thugs. Always on the edge of violence, shouting, frenetic, and explaining nothing. They love uniforms as well, don't they? Perhaps they think they're intimidating, too, especially when dressed in black.'

Robert took a sip of his whisky and carried on. 'Completely out of the blue, unannounced, this SS colonel – Kritzinger is his name – came to the Bute and demanded a tour of the labs and the facilities. He spoke excellent English, even understood scientific terms. Claimed to have been a scientist before the war. Then, without any reason, any explanation at all, he threw us all out, the whole department, everyone. I was forced to leave behind all of my work, notes and correspondence in my office. All we were allowed to take were personal effects. And we were on no account to leave the town, any of us. What annoyed almost as much as anything was this man telling me not to worry. We'd all still be paid.'

Jimmy MacRae, the university Bedellus – in effect, the head of security – told Robert that the Germans had also ejected the Principal and taken over his vast, rambling house and cordoned off North Castle Street. All of the residents of those beautiful old houses were summarily evicted, forced to leave their furniture and allowed to take only their clothes and other belongings. A few days later, a dozen or so Americans had arrived with, it seemed to the Bedellus, their families in tow. All of them were installed in North Castle Street or the Principal's House. With no explanation and no idea who these people were, MacRae had to hand over all sets of keys for these university properties.

'You can only get into town through the West Port,' said Jenny, 'or at the bridge over the Kinnessburn, below the cathedral precinct.' She added that there were hundreds, perhaps a thousand, soldiers on patrol and that the Bute Building, St Mary's Divinity College and the university library had been completely sealed off. The only access was through the old arch into the library quadrangle. 'You know, the one with the quote above it, *In Principio Erat Verbum*.' Parliament Hall and the university courtroom above it had been converted into offices, a huge radio mast had been erected in the corner of the quad and scores of telephone cables had been fed through the upper

152

windows. 'The town has become a fortress,' said Jenny, 'and the Bute Building seems to be its citadel. What on earth is going on? We have absolutely no idea.'

*

When Jamie Griffith-Smith returned to his car, parked not far from the short but secluded driveway that led to Jenny and Robert's house, he felt very uneasy. His parents knew the MacDonalds, had done for many years. When his father sat on the university court, they had been dinner guests at their house near Kingsbarns and, as a boy, he had been dazzled by Jenny MacDonald. And kind as she was, she had made a fuss of him, making the boy blush.

Suddenly, life had become a little more complicated than simply following orders.

30 December 1944

'I understand very well what your requirements are, Professor Feldman,' Colonel Kritzinger snapped. 'But I am a scientist, not a magician!'

Small, balding, peering through spectacles with thick lenses and wearing a scarf wound twice around his neck, Feldman sat by the fire in the German's office, warming his hands. 'It is very simple, Colonel. If we do not have the materials, then we cannot do what you wish in the time that you wish it.' The little professor seemed not to be at all flustered by Kritzinger's anger and bluster. He stared at the yellow flames; there was no more to be said to this irritable man. Well, perhaps one thing. 'It's New Year's Eve, tomorrow, Colonel. When I was a child in Vienna, and as an adult in New York, we celebrated St Silvester with a party. May we be permitted to do so here?'

Kritzinger made no reply as he stood looking out of the

window. It had begun to snow. There was no breeze off the sea that morning and big flakes floated gently down on the town, tilting and swaying as they came to rest on the roofs and the streets.

'Colonel Kritzinger,' said Feldman, jolting the German out of his reverie, 'I'm sure that your family used to have sauer-kraut, raclette, cakes and marzipan sweets on St Silvester. And perhaps a few bottles of Sekt or some fiery punch? May we hold our party in the Principal's House? You are, of course, invited. We hope to foregather at the evening service at St Salvator's Chapel.'

Kritzinger looked for a moment at the little scientist's round face and sighed. 'Yes. Yes. I suppose we are all far from home. The families will of course have to be escorted. And your people will be at work in the Bute laboratories in the morning as usual.'

'Thank you, Colonel. Forgive me, but I had another matter to raise with you. I hope you have a moment. We have yet to hear from our colleagues in Germany. We are anxious to consult with them. As I have explained, our facilities at Los Alamos were purpose-built for our work, but here we're having to improvise. And that can be dangerous. As you know.'

*

The snow was lying now, piling precariously on the tops of gateposts and fence rails, falling in lazy flurries on the windless morning. Clutching a steaming cup of strong coffee in both hands, Katie watched her aunt's garden transform. From the French windows in the kitchen, she saw the lawn blanketed white, and the high hedges and ring of sheltering trees seem to close in. So long as you were snug, warm and indoors, snow could be comforting, making the world shrink as everything outside fell silent and still. All of the people she loved were in this house and, closing her eyes, she offered up a prayer that the evil that lay beyond it would recede and that decency would somehow return.

'I know, Father. I know this is a highly irregular request.' Upstairs, in Robert MacDonald's study, I was talking to Father MacKenzie of St James' Church. 'But we live in extraordinary times. I'm sure that God's love will smile down upon us.' I laughed when the priest qualified my certainty, perhaps with the German garrison in mind. And then he very kindly, somewhat reluctantly, agreed to my request.

'Thank you, Father, thank you. We'll see you there at 6 p.m. tomorrow.'

31 December 1944

Griffith-Smith was cold. Despite a cashmere pullover under his Vigilante uniform and his old army greatcoat over everything, his feet were like blocks of ice. Perhaps it would be better to get out of his car and stamp some warmth back into them. He had parked close to the university playing fields, on the opposite side of the road from the driveway to the MacDonalds' house. In the early darkness, he had been almost invisible inside the little sports car, but if he had stood out on the pavement, against the white background of the snow, he might have been more easily seen. However, he also needed to pee, urgently. No wonder, with such freezing feet. Once out of the car, he half-hid himself in some bushy rhododendra by the gates into the playing fields. Gasping with relief, Griffith-Smith turned to look at the MacDonalds' driveway.

'Bugger,' he whispered, 'bugger, bugger.'

A car was moving down it, the headlights embarrassing him profoundly. He quickly turned his head away in case he was recognised.

Once the car turned down Hepburn Gardens on its way

into the town, Griffith-Smith rushed over to his vehicle, kicked the snow off his boots, fired up the engine and followed it. They were breaking curfew. What were they doing? No civilian cars were permitted to pass through the West Port, and so if this was the Grants, the MacDonalds and Erskine, they would have to find somewhere to park, discreetly. From there, he would follow them on foot.

When he had rustled his way out of the rhododendron bushes, looking at the tail-lights of the car disappearing down the road, Griffith-Smith did not notice a figure in a dark overcoat slip out of the driveway and follow it. John Campbell had agreed with me that he would use all of his commando concealment skills while following us into town and keeping an eye out for anyone who might be on our tail.

*

When we walked under the arch of St Salvator's Tower, Katie slipped her arm through mine and it seemed that the years fell away. Memory is often unreliable, it being almost impossible to recapture the atmosphere and myriad details that make a moment unique. Instead, it seems to me that places can be the deposit of experience and to go back to them triggers memory, often drawing up feelings – and even incidents long forgotten – from the deep.

Katie and I had often walked under the old arch and into the quadrangle for lectures. On two sides were the schools, the lecture theatres of tiered benches and scuffed desks where both modern languages and English literature were taught. We first met, or rather sat near each other, in one of the most tedious, tired and hilariously badly delivered lectures on early English drama. A grey, careworn, dusty professor in an ancient black gown talked to us about a sixteenth-century comedy called *Ralph Roister Doister* and its cast of characters, such as Dobinet

Doughty and Madge Mumblecrust. Rambling, disconnected references to writers none of us had ever heard of, and the fact that most of the time the professor spoke so quietly – mumbling about Mumblecrust, addressing his remarks, it seemed, to his tie – made for an hour that itself became a comedy. Students who had long since ceased to take notes looked wide-eyed at each other, shaking their heads. But it was Katie who cracked first. After a shapeless succession of remarks about the play's links with Roman comedy, the professor revealed that the play had probably never been performed. What started as a giggle from Katie quickly became infectious and built into an outburst of uninhibited laughter. 'Yes, yes,' said the professor, looking up and apparently startled to see a hundred students sitting in front of him, 'very amusing.'

When we pushed open the heavy oak door into St Salvator's Chapel and turned to walk up the nave, Father MacKenzie was waiting for us at the altar steps. He had lit two tall candles on the altar and one on a small table at his side.

'Thank you,' I said, shaking hands. 'I much appreciate your taking the trouble to do this,' and I introduced Katie.

'Now, you do realise that a ceremony of betrothal has no status, especially since you belong to different churches?' he said, 'And it's a number of centuries since a mass was said in this one.'

We all smiled and Father MacKenzie began.

'Beloved of Christ. It is the dispensation of Divine Providence that you are called to the holy vocation of marriage. For this reason, you present yourselves on this day before Christ and His Church and before His sacred minister.'

He then recited the rubric, which I repeated: 'In the name of our Lord, I, David Erskine, promise that I will one day take thee, Katherine Grant, as my wife, according to the ordinances of God and Holy Mother Church.'

Katie repeated her version of the vow and when I slipped a ring borrowed from Aunt Jenny on her finger, Father MacKenzie placed the ends of his stole over our clasped hands and we kissed. And from the dark shadows of one of the back pews, someone began clapping their hands.

'This is not my church either,' said an American voice.

A small, bespectacled man with a scarf wound twice around his neck walked into the candlelight. 'Please forgive me intruding. But may I be the first to congratulate you both?' As Father MacKenzie folded his stole and put on his overcoat, for the chapel was chilly and he was anxious to be away, the man went on, 'And now that this beautiful ceremony has told me your names, may I introduce myself? I am Isaac Feldman. And your guess that I am not a Catholic – or a Protestant – would be correct!'

He went on to explain that his own faith did not prevent him from coming into the chapel for a few moments of peace, and that he had not wished to disturb us by getting up to leave. 'Are you coming to the evening service?' he asked. 'It begins, I think, in an hour. Afterwards, my colleagues and I will be having a New Year's Eve party to celebrate St Silvester. Would you like to join us? It seems that you have something to celebrate, too.'

When I replied in German, prompted by the reference to St Silvester, to thank him, he smiled broadly, 'How good it is to hear my native tongue so softly and gently spoken, for once, Mr Erskine.'

*

While we were at St Salvator's, the MacDonalds and Katie's parents had paid a flying visit to friends who lived just outside the military perimeter, and we promised to rejoin them quickly at home and not take unnecessary risks. Father MacKenzie invited us to come back to St James and the chapel house on the Scores. It would be much better and safer to telephone from there than be seen walking around after curfew, even though the evening service had been permitted.

Up in the choir stalls, Jamie Griffith-Smith had heard every word spoken in the echoic old church.

He decided to stay put. When Erskine and his fiancée returned for the evening service, there would be soldiers in the quadrangle and in the streets – the escorts that Kritzinger had organised for the Americans and their families. It would be a straightforward business to make arrests then and with more than three hundred worshippers, many of them women and children, it was his judgement that Erskine would not risk resistance and the shooting that might involve.

*

Stille Nacht, heilige Nacht,
Alles schläft, einsam wacht.

The service started with a young boy, his voice not yet broken, being introduced – and encouraged – by Professor Feldman: 'This is a carol from Austria, where some of us grew up as children. It is really about Christmas Eve, but I hope you will forgive us. I hope it will be good to hear it on the eve of a new and perhaps better year.'

I felt the tears prickle as the crystal purity of the melody floated high in the nave of the old church and beyond it, over the rooftops of the snowy town. It was the sound of another, better, Germany and Austria. St Salvator's Chapel was full, with many standing at the back and the choir stalls were crammed. And between each precious line of the carol, the congregation seemed barely to breathe.

Christ, der Retter, ist da,
Christ, der Retter, ist da.

In a gesture that caught the moment perfectly, the university chaplain, a gruff old Highlander who used to referee rugby matches and penalise swearing, shook hands with the young boy. And in as emphatic a voice as the Reverend Ruaridh Macleod deemed appropriate, he said, '*Danke, danke schön*'. And then the chaplain raised his hand for the benediction, to bless us all in English, and in his own Gaelic, and to encourage us to hope that 1945 would bring joy.

As the congregation began to shuffle towards the narrow doorway and out into the snow-covered quadrangle, I put my arm round Katie's shoulders.

'No kissing in church, now,' she whispered. 'The rest of us are all Presbyterians here, even if you have plighted your troth.'

The chapel took a long time to clear and an exasperated murmur seemed to be building as the congregation filed out into the cloister. It was very cold and the evening was growing late, but no one was moving very far. When Katie and I eventually made it out and into the quad, we saw that the great doors under the arch of St Salvator's Tower had been closed, and frustrated people were rattling at the two wrought-iron gates in the west and north walls. In the gap between the schools and the east end of the chapel, there was a large detachment of soldiers.

Katie and I looked at each other. 'Quick, back into the chapel.' There was a little-used door on the street side, beyond the tower. We might be able to force that open.

But before we could move, a series of arc lights clanged on, very brightly illuminating the quadrangle and the milling, confused congregation. Then a voice crackled through a loud-speaker. 'We have information that the traitor, David Erskine, is hiding among you. If he does not immediately give himself up, then we will open the doors under the archway.'

There was another loud murmur, more confusion amongst

the crowd, trying to make sense of what they had just heard. I realised that the Germans did not know what I looked like.

'And as you all pass under the archway, we will begin counting. We will begin the process of decimation. Unless Erskine comes forward now, every tenth person, be they man, woman or child, will be removed and immediately shot.'

Amidst the gasps, I turned to Katie. 'This is the end. There is no choice. I have to give myself up.'

X

Before I could reach the archway and the waiting soldiers, the sky was suddenly lit by a flash of bright yellow light. A moment later, the night air was rent by an explosion like a clap of thunder. The roiling tumult of the crowd in the quad froze, and then there was another flash, a second explosion and, in the stunned silence that followed, I could hear Professor Feldman shouting, 'Herr Colonel! Herr Colonel!'

Out of the archway marched an officer, a long, black leather coat over his SS uniform. He met Feldman only yards from where Katie and I stood.

'It's the laboratory,' Feldman said to the officer. 'I'm certain. We must go immediately. God knows what's happened. I need my people. They're all being held here.'

As both men turned to leave, Feldman saw me and stared for a moment before rushing off with Kritzinger. Over his shoulder, the colonel shouted, 'No one else leaves.'

And just as they reached the cobbled pavement beyond the arch, John Campbell appeared, as if from nowhere, stood directly in front of the German officer and said, 'I am David Erskine.' In the shock and rush of the moment, Campbell turned, sprinted across the street and disappeared down an alleyway.

'Find him!' roared Kritzinger. 'And bring him to me alive.'

When the soldiers set off in pursuit, the crowd surged under the archway and dispersed very quickly in all directions like frightened animals running for their lives at the sound of gunfire. For many minutes, chaos streamed around the streets of St Andrews as people frantically sought the sanctuary of their homes. The colonel and the professor got into a car that sped up College Street towards the Bute laboratory.

'Who is David Erskine?' asked Feldman.

'A former British officer who is responsible for the deaths of too many of our soldiers.'

*

Weaving in and out of the many narrow alleyways that link the three arterial streets of the old town, pausing, hiding in the shadows, waiting for groups of soldiers to pass him before moving on again, Campbell came to the cathedral precinct. In the darkness, crouched over, using the hundreds of headstones for cover, he thought it a good place to evade capture at least for an hour or two, or until the hue and cry calmed down. The soldiers looking for him had torches but in the undulating ground of the graveyard, he was not confident he would see them before they saw him. Behind him ran the high precinct wall, ancient, but now part of the fortress St Andrews had become, and beyond that lay cliffs and the sea. Realising that he had fled into a cul-de-sac, Campbell needed to find a hiding place, and quickly.

*

Sirens wailed and fire engines raced up to the West Port – only to discover that the medieval gateway was too low and narrow to pass through. At the western end of Market Street, soldiers were frantically dismantling and dragging aside the wooden barricades, erected only a few weeks ago, to allow the firemen to get to the blaze at the Bute laboratory. Moving in the opposite direction, Katie and I sought the camouflage of the crowd that had rushed out of the quadrangle and we stayed in their midst. Soldiers made no attempt to stop us and, not long after, we were running up Hepburn Gardens.

'Thank God,' said Jenny MacDonald as she opened her front door. 'The town is in uproar. What on earth has been going on?'

From what he could see from the upstairs windows, Robert was sure that the fire and the explosions that may have caused it was consuming the Bute Building.

When I related the meeting with Isaac Feldman and the astonishing events after the service at St Salvator's Chapel, Robert reckoned that he must be one of the Americans that the Bedellus, Jimmy MacRae, had told him about. From the brief conversation I had overheard between him and Kritzinger, I judged that the professor led a team of American scientists.

'Whatever they're doing, the Germans seem to think it's extremely important. Vital. But they have won the war. They're holding the world to ransom. What could be so important? What makes them behave with such brutality?' said Robert as he reached the bottom of the stairs. 'And what happened to cause the explosions and the fire? And where's John Campbell? He must still be somewhere in the town. I hope he's all right.'

I tried to reassure Robert. 'He can look after himself. He trained as a commando. I expect he'll find his way back.'

After a bewildering, exhausting day, we sank into the sofas in the sitting room, grateful not to be out there and involved. Katie and Jenny fortified themselves with stiff drinks and went through to the kitchen to marshal a very late supper.

'Erskine!' Griffith-Smith walked into the sitting room and pointed his pistol at me. 'Get up. Now! You will come with me immediately.'

Robert MacDonald also stood up, his mouth agape at this sudden intrusion, unable to speak.

As I got to my feet, Jenny came into the room. 'Jamie, isn't it?' she said quietly. 'Jamie Griffith-Smith.'

He turned to look at her and, as she smiled at him, that distracted moment gave me a second to lunge across the room. Grabbing his wrist, I punched him as hard as I could in the stomach and when he doubled over, the gun rattled across the parquet floor. Katie picked it up and pointed it at Griffith-Smith.

'No, no,' said Jenny. 'Please, put that thing away.' She turned to the winded intruder and said, 'What are you doing here, Jamie? Why are you wearing that uniform?' She took his arm very gently. 'What's happened to you? I don't know what has persuaded you to work with these terrible people, but I want you to tell me.'

*

By the time Kritzinger and Feldman reached the Bute Building, the firemen had begun to play their hoses on the blaze. 'It's gas,' one of them shouted above the din of the pumps, 'I can smell it.' Having drenched the façade of the building and soaked some of the interior as water poured through the smashed glass windows, the firemen were attempting to quell a blaze that had consumed a wooden annexe close to the laboratories.

Feldman turned to Kritzinger. 'I think the firemen are correct: the explosions were from gas containers. The electrical wiring here is very old and in need of constant maintenance. Some of the light switches spark when they're used. It could have been something as simple as that.'

Kritzinger was clearly agitated, shifting from foot to foot, not really listening, perhaps mentally composing a report for his superiors in Berlin that assigned blame to anyone but him. He knew that would not matter. What mattered to them were results, and this fire, accident, whatever it was, would inevitably cause delay. He would be blamed for that.

'Sabotage,' the German said to Feldman. 'Was it sabotage? That's what I want to know.'

The flames were beginning to die down as the hoses soaked the fire.

'All of my people were at the chapel, Herr Colonel. How could it be sabotage?'

Kritzinger turned to face the little professor. 'All I am interested in is progress. And if there is no progress, then I will have no choice but to take action. That is why your families are all here. We did not bring your wife from America to cook your supper, Feldman. She is here as a guarantee that you will make this work as soon as possible. And if you do not, she will suffer. Am I making myself clear?'

*

John Campbell could see two groups of soldiers, or at least two groups of torch beams, on the far side of the railings that ran on the town side of the cathedral precinct. In a few minutes, they could be amongst the ruins and the headstones, searching for him. If they did the sensible thing and formed a line to sweep the ground, it would be very difficult for him to outflank them and make his way back into town. The snow had stopped falling but any movement would be more easily seen against the pristine white background. And he was leaving tracks. Sitting with his back against a particularly grand memorial, he looked around the graveyard. To the right of the high east gable of the cathedral stood a tall, square-sided slim tower.

When he reached what looked like the walls of a small church at its foot, Campbell saw that there was an entrance. Pushing open the heavy door, he plunged into the black darkness of the windowless tower. With one hand on the outer wall, feeling for the steps with his feet, he realised that he was turning up a spiral staircase. The exit at the top came up so quickly that Campbell stumbled and almost fell over the low parapet. Below him, he could see the soldiers' torches shining in the graveyard, swinging from side to side, their beams sweeping across the headstones, punctuated by the occasional shout in German. It was illogical, but Campbell imagined height to be an advantage, even though there was only one way out of the tower and many more of them than him.

From his high vantage point, Campbell could see the lights of the town spreading out in the distance. South Street and North Street radiated from the cathedral and he could make out activity in both: vehicle headlights and the occasional patrol of soldiers lit by a streetlight. But the glow of the dying fire at the Bute Building seemed to be a focus of activity with many comings and goings. The line of searchers below him washed past the foot of the tower, more interested in looking into the nave of the roofless church on its eastern side. Campbell brushed away the snow that had collected on the platform at the top of the tower and sat down with his back to the parapet. Despite himself, and despite the cold, he fell asleep.

*

Surrounded by the Grants, the MacDonalds and me, Griffith-Smith suddenly seemed a forlorn figure and at first he made no response to Jenny MacDonald's question about his loyalties and working for the Germans. Staring silently at his feet, he let out a long sigh and looked at the beautiful woman who had made him blush as a boy and was now holding his hand. Perhaps memories of a lost, sunlit past flitted through his head. Perhaps he remembered a lunch under the apple blossom in the orchard at Kingsbarns. A sea breeze blew some of the tiny white petals into the air. Long ago, in another time, Jenny had smiled at him across the table. Now, she made him cry. Tears began to run down his cheeks.

Jenny squeezed his hand. 'Sit down here by me. Robert, can you please find Jamie a glass of brandy?'

Griffith-Smith sniffed, wiped his cheeks with his fingers and looked at me. 'When you told me about those memoranda you read about Jewish deportation from Hungary, and about labour camps, I was listening carefully.' All of his languor, polish and ease had evaporated, and when he turned to Jenny, his voice was trembling. 'My wife, Miriam, is Jewish. Last night, her mother telephoned from Glasgow to say that they had received a letter from the Department of Internal Affairs. I had no idea such an organisation existed. It told the Levinsons – my wife's family – that they had been selected for resettlement in Perthshire and that arrangements for transport would be made as soon as a departure date was set. They should be ready to travel at any time and bring only one suitcase. Everything else would follow. Several of their friends and neighbours received identical letters.' Griffith-Smith shook his head and went on, 'Because their mother is Jewish, all of my three children will be considered to be Jewish.' And the tears came back.

Jenny put her arm around his shoulders and asked me to explain, to relate as much as I could remember more about the memoranda I had read in Paris.

'Because they have the atom bomb, these people and their perverted, obscene ideas will now dominate Europe and perhaps further afield,' I said. 'They truly believe they are the master race, and that events have proved that. From the jaws of defeat, they snatched victory over us, the Russians and the Americans, and they dictate to the Italians and the Japanese. Now I think they won't hesitate to do terrible things in pursuit of what they call racial purity.'

Without saying a word or asking a question, Robert MacDonald had been listening intently to these exchanges. He put forward a simple proposition: 'Jamie, your position as an officer in the Vigilantes is not going to save your wife's family, or indeed yours, from whatever the Germans are planning. But it might help us to understand what is going on here in St Andrews.'

*

After more than two hours of continuous hosing, pumping water up from the Kinnessburn, the fire at the Bute had been extinguished. At that point, the firemen forced their way into the main building to ensure that there was no structural damage, so far as they could judge by torchlight. But when they attempted to move through to the laboratories, Colonel Kritzinger sent soldiers in to prevent them going any further. With Feldman, he himself would make a full inspection in the morning. They agreed to meet at first light.

'One more thing, if you would excuse me, Colonel,' said the professor as Kritzinger made to leave. 'May I wish you a happy new year.' The colonel whirled round but before his scowl could become an insult, the little professor went on, 'No, I mean it. Nineteen fourty-four was terrible for all of us. All of us. I hope that somehow we can make this year a better one.'

Kritzinger grunted, refused Feldman's proffered hand, and climbed into the staff car without offering to take the professor back to North Castle Street. He would not be able to sleep. A report for Berlin needed to be written. Perhaps the use of the phrase 'minor setback' would mitigate their wrath? No, it would not.

Although he was not surprised at the German's routine rudeness, Feldman walked up Westburn Wynd sensing that something had changed, something in his own head had shifted. Even in the midst of the madness of the world, the old town he now found himself in was somehow consoling. Its stones spoke of generations, of the ebb and flow of events, the passing on and the getting of knowledge, the acrid smoke of religious martyrdom, the wash of history on the cliffs below the cathedral ruins and, above all, of continuity. A New Yorker for most of his life, the professor had been surprised to find moments of peace and reflection in St Andrews, in the chapel and amongst the ruins. But it was the streets and alleyways he especially liked and felt comfortable in. Unlike the hard angles of the grid, the numbered avenues and the skyscrapers of New York's cityscape, this town had not been organised or planned. Instead, it had grown like an organism, edging westwards from the cathedral and the university and petering out on the edge of the farmland beyond. Feldman had no faith, his Judaism departed long ago, but as he walked down the pleasingly awkward cobbled pavement of North Castle Street, he realised that he believed in something, that somehow the upside-down world would right itself. But he had no idea how.

*

Robert MacDonald was thinking aloud. 'Your rank and uniform means that you have access to the town through the West Port, but does it allow you to penetrate the cordon around the Bute and the old library quadrangle?'

Griffith-Smith shook his head.

'All right. Jimmy MacRae told me that the Americans were billeted in the university houses in North Castle Street and in the Principal's House. Can you find out where Professor Feldman and his family are living?'

When Griffith-Smith agreed that he could, he went on to make the excellent point that the American might immediately contact the Germans and betray him. After all, their families were here, probably as hostages of some sort. Feldman would always choose them.

I had been watching Griffith-Smith closely, his face and his gestures. He seemed accepting and receptive. If the Germans discovered, as they probably would, that his wife and children were Jewish, they could in turn blackmail him into revealing our whereabouts. 'There's a risk everywhere,' I said. 'It's a risk to contact Feldman, but if we don't know what it is the Americans and the Germans are doing at the Bute – what they're going to great pains to hide – then what do we do? Run and hide? Frankly, we've been doing rather too much of that recently.'

Alan Grant laughed, somehow releasing the tension of the moment.

1 January 1945

Both the Vigilantes and pairs of German soldiers had toured the streets of St Andrews, both inside and outside the perimeter wall. Through loudhailers at each corner, they had demanded attendance at St Salvator's Tower in North Street at midday when Colonel Kritzinger would address them.

A few minutes before the appointed time, Professor Feldman, his wife and several colleagues, two of them with a child, left their houses in North Castle Street, curious to know what announcement they would hear. By the time they reached the cobbled area below the tower, hundreds had gathered, spilling into the street, including Katie Grant and her parents. At the back of the main body of people, their breath pluming into the January air, stood Jamie Griffith-Smith.

When Kritzinger appeared from under the arch, Katie noticed that he did something generations of students had avoided. Set into the cobbles are the letters 'PH', marking the spot where Patrick Hamilton was martyred in 1528, burned at the stake. To stand on the stone letters was reckoned to bring the worst of bad luck and, as the German set foot on them, Katie prayed that superstition would turn into fact.

'Some of you were in the quadrangle yesterday evening

when we demanded that the traitor David Erskine should give himself up. This morning he was arrested and condemned to death.'

Katie shivered. She knew that this was not true but nevertheless the words gripped her heart.

Kritzinger continued, 'Your presence here is important. You should understand that we are protecting your community vigorously. You should witness justice being done, see for yourselves the fate of those who, like Erskine, threaten the peace that Germany has brought to your country. Look up. Now!'

Katie put her hand over her mouth to stifle a scream. Her mother gasped. With his hands tied behind his back and a noose around his neck, John Campbell was standing on the parapet at the very top of St Salvator's Tower.

'Now!' shouted Kritzinger, and a soldier pushed Campbell in the back. The fall at the end of the long rope must have broken his neck. Alan Grant prayed it had broken his neck.

John Campbell's body swung obscenely, like a pendulum, across the red face of the clock on the tower. At the back of the crowd, Jamie Griffith-Smith grimaced. All around him there were cries of distress, some from children whose parents had not reacted quickly enough. Since the days of the martyrs, nothing like this had happened in St Andrews. Professor Feldman put his arm around his wife as they walked away. And Griffith-Smith followed them.

*

'Mind your head, Professor MacDonald, Mr Erskine. The roof is very low.'

Feldman sat on a stone block at the sloping entrance of a mine. Almost four centuries before the appalling events at St Salvator's Tower, violence had flared only yards from the professor's front door, where the ruins of St Andrews Castle clung to

172

a headland of steep cliffs above the waves of the North Sea. In 1546, the castle had been under siege. Protestant lairds manned its walls while Catholic forces, many of the soldiers French, bombarded them with artillery, but to little avail. Frustration had led to a spectacular attempt to tumble the walls by other means. Through the living rock, a mine was dug to undermine the gatehouse, but the defenders foiled this subterranean attack by digging a countermine above it that would allow them to rain down all manner of things on their enemies. This relic of the tumult of the Reformation fascinated Professor Feldman.

When Griffith-Smith asked him to meet me and Robert MacDonald in secret, he did not hesitate to agree and immediately suggested the mine – to our amazement: Feldman was not permitted to go beyond the walls around the town without an escort, and in any case he was often followed. But the entrance to the mine was very close to his house, and he was certain the Germans had no idea it was there and he could easily get to it before us and wait.

'I was sorry to see your fiancée witnessing your supposed execution, Mr Erskine. I'm assuming you knew the poor man who died,' said Feldman as we shook hands again and I introduced him to Robert MacDonald.

'A dreadful, terrible exhibition of cruelty,' I said. 'Something I fear will become a feature of our daily lives.' Griffith-Smith had told me that, in exchange for any information Feldman might be prepared to divulge, I would have to tell him all I knew about the Eichmann memoranda. Knowing Feldman was Jewish, I had unashamedly used what I had read in Paris as a lure, certain that he would want to know what was going on in occupied Europe.

'Yes. Thank you, Mr Erskine. For some reason, none of that comes as a complete surprise. We knew that the Nazis had enacted legislation to remove all sorts of freedoms from

Jews and that widespread destruction and beatings in the street had taken place. That sort of thing has, sadly, been part of our history for centuries. But we began to hear stories in America, what seemed like wild tales of mass murder and state-sanctioned brutality. The scale of what these memoranda hint at is vast. Why would the Nazis need a list of the number of Jews in each country if they weren't to be a target of some kind?'

*

More than fifty miles west of St Andrews, in the foothills of the Highland massif, the villagers of Comrie had watched lorry after lorry arrive at Cultybraggan Camp. For more than a month, they had been coming to what was better known as the Black Camp. It was a sprawling network of paths, roads and rows of Nissen huts where the most fanatical of the SS prisoners of war had been held. But after the destruction of London and the capitulation of British forces, all prisoners were released to form the core of the army of occupation in Scotland. Now it seemed that they had returned.

Long trains began to arrive at the railway station carrying soldiers who marched through the village to reoccupy the camp. Soon afterwards, the first prisoners came. Clothed in black-and-white-striped uniforms that more resembled pyjamas, they were set to work even in the worst of the winter weather. Some of the villagers thought they recognised several of the men; they were sure they had been the Polish soldiers who guarded the camp before the surrender.

When rainstorms and snow blew over the Perthshire mountains and down into Strathearn, gangs began digging a cutting, a spur from the railway line that came west from Crieff. Using only picks, shovels and barrows, they shifted many tons of muddy soil before reaching the banks of the River Earn. Winter spates meant that the construction of a new bridge would have to wait. It seemed clear that the Germans intended there to be a railway that reached right into the camp.

South of the Earn, more digging went on at Cultybraggan. In a new compound between the old camp and the river, long rectangular pits were excavated. Thousands of bricks were unloaded from lorries at the sides of the pits to wait for better weather in the spring when building could begin. The camp was extended far beyond its original perimeter, perhaps tripling in size. Trees were cut down and farm fields appropriated. Local people were not permitted to come near the new camp, but they could see developments closer at hand. Around Comrie station, on the eastern edge of the village, a high barbed wire fence was erected that left a gap only for the track that led westwards towards Lochearnhead and the West Highland railway lines. The prisoners also made a sign above the main gate out of the station. It read, *Welcome to Comrie Resettlement Camp.*

No one in the village dared to ask what that meant.

*

'The Germans brought us here to St Andrews not only because you have a university with laboratories and some facilities, but also because the town lies on the North Sea coast,' said Feldman. 'And I assume that, unlike the city of Aberdeen and its university, they thought that this place was easier to defend and could be made very secure. They also chose to bring us here, I imagine, because the south-east of England is said to be little more than a desert. Thousands are dying of a sickness caused by the atomic explosion and the cities of northern England have been flooded by refugees.'

I had brought a torch since I remembered that the smooth rock of the floor of the mine could be slippery. Robert and I had come at gloaming, and now a dense darkness had fallen.

The beam of the torch lit us all very theatrically, but there was already sufficient drama in these exchanges, and plenty of jeopardy if we were discovered. I offered Feldman a cigarette and for some reason the tobacco smoke seemed to introduce a note of normality to this strange tableau.

'I believe that I now work in your office, Professor MacDonald, but I can assure you that all of your papers and your notes have remained undisturbed.' With that, Feldman sighed and his train of thought seemed to peter out.

Robert MacDonald leaned forward and touched the little professor on his knee. 'Thank you. I appreciate your consideration in leaving my things untouched. It must be difficult for you, too. But I sense that you yourself are a little disturbed.'

Feldman looked up at us both and nodded. 'Yes. Perhaps I should tell you a little more.'

The professor went on to explain that he and his colleagues had been instructed to leave their laboratories and travel with their families to Scotland. To refuse to do so would have left the Germans with no option but to carry out their threat to destroy New York City. They would have detonated the bomb carried in the U-boat that had surfaced in the Hudson River and they promised that the devastation would have been even greater than in London. 'I have family and friends in New York. What else could we do but agree to leave?' He talked about how he and his colleagues and their wives had tried to make the best of things, and indeed some, like himself, had become genuinely interested in the old town of St Andrews. It was unlike anywhere else they had ever been.

'Why does it matter,' I asked, 'that we're on the North Sea coast?'

Feldman replied that it was because ships from Norway could reach us directly and quickly, as though that was somehow obvious.

176

Robert MacDonald was nodding but I persisted in my puzzlement. 'What comes from Norway that you need?'

'It's heavy water, isn't it?' interjected Robert, and Feldman nodded.

'Forgive me, but what is heavy water?'

Between them, the two scientists explained that it contains more deuterium, a kind of hydrogen, and that heavy water is manufactured in Telemark in southern Norway. 'One of the main reasons why the Germans invaded in 1940 was to gain control of production,' said Feldman. He told us that since its discovery in 1934, it had become clear that it was easier to split an atom of deuterium and control the chain reaction. 'That is the important thing. Splitting an atom serves no purpose, indeed it's very dangerous, unless you can control it,' said the professor.

'So what you're doing at the Bute,' said Robert, 'is building a nuclear reactor?'

There was a moment of hesitation and Feldman said nothing, looking at both of us, perhaps weighing an answer, or no answer. Suddenly remembering his cigarette, he dropped it on the stone floor and ground it out. 'If the Germans knew I was here, talking to you about our work, they would not kill me or even beat me. But they might do to my wife what they did to your friend today. As we have seen, they're capable of anything.' He stood up to leave.

But before he could move past us to the entrance to the mine, Robert MacDonald asked if he would wait another minute or two. 'What do you think will happen to you and your wife when your work here is complete?'

The little professor made no comment.

'You won't be allowed to return to the United States. By the time your work is over, you'll both be expendable, perhaps even a liability. And by then the Germans will have whatever it is that they want from you. I know this is an appallingly difficult business. It is for all of us. I think I know what you're doing at the Bute. But we need you to tell us. Please, please do not leave.'

*

'May I use your telephone, please?' Instead of barging in brandishing a pistol, Jamie Griffith-Smith had rung the doorbell at the MacDonalds' house. 'I am sorry to bother you, Mrs MacDonald, but I need to make an urgent telephone call. I tried on our phone but there was no ringing tone at the other end. To be honest, I also wondered if someone was listening.'

Jenny brought Griffith-Smith into the hallway, but before leaving him to his call, she said, 'You seem very anxious. Come and talk to us when you've finished.' But he had already picked up the receiver and had begun dialling. Jenny left him to it, saying, 'Join us in the sitting room when you can.'

*

As the wind freshened and began to whistle around the ruins of St Andrews Castle, I shivered in the damp of the mine and, as he sat down again, I offered Professor Feldman another cigarette. Cupping a match in my hand, I leaned over to light it.

'We are indeed building a nuclear reactor,' he said. 'That's why we need so much heavy water, and I've told the Germans that we don't have enough. And I've told them that I fear that last night's fire will cause delays. Perhaps six months to a year. That's why, I am certain, the Germans are behaving in the way they are.'

Robert MacDonald nodded and asked, 'Once the reactor is working, it will begin to use the deuterium as fissile material, splitting its atoms? This isn't my field, and that's about as much as I understand from what I've read in the literature.'

I understood very much less and, with the directness of the ignorant, unhampered by knowledge, asked, 'What is the nuclear reactor for?'

Feldman lifted his head and looked directly at me. 'And so, now we come to the point of the exercise, the point of all this brutality and bloodshed. We'll use the reactor to make plutonium. It's much lighter than uranium, and we'll need to make ten kilos of it, at least. That will take some time – and can only happen after the reactor is working smoothly.'

Feldman paused but must have known that the conversation had reached a point of no return. 'That amount of plutonium can become a warhead mounted on a missile. What we are making at the Bute Building, Mr Erskine, is an atomic bomb.'

XI

Griffith-Smith put down the telephone and for a minute or two tried to gather himself. His tears the previous evening had embarrassed him, especially in front of Jenny MacDonald. He still retained shreds of the schoolboy that needed to be a grown-up, to impress her, and he feared that tears would not do that.

With Katie, Jenny sat by the fire and when Griffith-Smith came into the room, she gave him a glass of whisky. There may have been no tears but his face was creased with anxiety. 'What's wrong?' Katie asked as he sat down beside them.

'Miriam has been telephoning her parents in Glasgow all day. Every hour. She wanted to wish them a happy new year. But there has been no answer at all. They go nowhere – they're retired, too old for restaurants or nights out. When Miriam telephoned the Greens, their neighbours across the road, thinking they might have been with them, there was also no reply. And no reply from two other numbers she called. Something strange is going on. Miriam is worried, very worried.'

*

'Why do the Germans need you, a group of Americans, to make atomic bombs?' Despite the fact that, in the cold, dank air of the mine, we were all becoming chilled, I kept on with my daft laddie questions. 'They seem to have at least two more bombs: those in the U-boats that sailed to New York and to Leningrad. And, presumably, they are making more?'

Feldman smiled and shook his head. 'I've been wondering the same things. Perhaps they want as many atom bombs as possible? You said the Germans "seem" to have at least two more. No one who has seen the awful, apocalyptic photographs of London can doubt that they successfully built and delivered one bomb. Every week, I've been asking Colonel Kritzinger to put us in touch with the German scientists who made the London bomb, but he keeps telling me they're too busy.'

Robert MacDonald interjected, 'But that makes no sense. Their experience and expertise would be of enormous help to you, and save a great deal of time.'

'Yes,' said Feldman, 'undoubtedly. And there's something else I don't understand. From ships lying off the harbour here, we're receiving large shipments of heavy water from Norway. I know their volume of production is very limited. What are the German laboratories using to make plutonium?'

It was at that moment I blurted out what the professor seemed to be driving at, what was hanging in the air above this exchange. 'There is no second bomb! No third bomb. Sending those U-boats was a huge, monstrous bluff. But after London, one that nobody wanted to call. There are no more bombs!'

Feldman agreed. 'Yes. That is what I've come to suspect. My guess is that the German laboratories were bombed in the last day or two before the London attack and perhaps many of their scientists were killed. That is why Kritzinger is so desperate. It may be that my team and I are the only people who can make a new atomic bomb for the Germans.'

I finished the train of thought: 'And, until you do, the bluff has to be maintained. The rest of the world has to believe that Hitler has more bombs and that if threatened, he would not hesitate to detonate them.'

In the silence that followed, Feldman looked at both of us as though he was weighing up what he might, or might not, say next. 'The truth is,' he began, 'that I believe we're much closer to being able to produce a prototype bomb than I have said to the Germans. My estimate of six months is not a fiction – things may go wrong – but it's a gross overestimate, I think.'

What hit me like an express train in that damp tunnel was that there was hope. At last. If – and it was a gigantic if – there were no more bombs and Feldman's team could make enough plutonium sooner rather than later, then that made resistance not only possible but essential. At that moment, everything changed.

*

'Dr and Mrs Levinson. Come forward. Quickly!'

After a long, cold and bewildering journey huddled in the back of a lorry with their neighbours, Miriam's parents stood at the head of a queue. Behind them a line of families, couples, widows and widowers stretched the length of the hangar-like building. At a desk with a ledger opened in front of them sat an SS officer and a clerk. Flanking them were two soldiers, each with a rifle.

'Where are we, please?' pleaded Dr Levinson. 'We do not . . .'

But before he could finish the sentence, a soldier cuffed the old man hard around the head, sending his black Homburg hat flying across the concrete floor. 'You will speak only in response to a question!' shouted the officer. 'Do you have your instruments with you?'

Dr Levinson hesitated. 'No. I am retired. And you said that we could bring only one suitcase.'

The soldier hit the doctor again, this time with the butt of his rifle, drawing blood from his lip. 'Then you are of no use to us. Or to your people. Stand over there, behind the yellow line.' He pointed to the corner of the hangar. 'Next!'

Many of Glasgow's Jewish community had been forced into

the convoy of lorries that left the city early on New Year's Day. The soldiers had pulled down the rear tarpaulin and secured it tightly to the tailboard in each vehicle, making the interior dim. Facing each other on benches, some friends and neighbours were too stunned to speak. Others did nothing but speak: babbling, protesting uselessly to each other, asking questions that none could answer. Torn out of the warmth of their houses, leaving behind all that was familiar, all that they owned, saying goodbye to their lives in the city they grew up in, all were filled with great foreboding.

Sitting at the end of one bench, close to the tailboard, Rafael Levinson could see through a narrow gap in the tarpaulin and was able to get a sense of where they were going: 'Great Western Road,' then, later, 'I'm sure that's Loch Lomond,' followed much later by, 'Crianlarich, I think.' But after that, the snow had rendered the Highland landscape anonymous. By the time the trucks came to a halt and the soldiers herded the prisoners into the makeshift reception hall at Cultybraggan Camp, it was late in the day.

*

For the first time in months, since the moment before I saw the mushroom cloud from the crane at Antwerp, I felt a surge of optimism, even the return of some confidence. Instead of constantly reacting, running, of allowing the Germans to mould and define the future, perhaps the initiative was swinging towards us.

I was convinced that there were no new bombs, but the odds against being successful in using this information – or, more correctly, this hypothesis – to defeat the Germans were mountainous. And the consequences of being wrong could be absolutely calamitous. In their BBC broadcasts, they had threatened more of our cities with atom bombs if we did not comply and accept the unconditional surrender that had been forced on us.

But we did have some time, perhaps six months if Professor Feldman's fictional estimate could be maintained, to work out a plan of action. It seemed to me that the American government was central to anything we might do with what we knew. If they could be persuaded to act, to challenge the Germans, then the bluff could be called. *If* it was a bluff.

*

By the time the SS officer and his clerk had recorded all of the new prisoners from Glasgow, most stood at one end of the hangar and others, including the Levinsons, were gathered behind a yellow line painted on the concrete floor. A double door at one end opened and in came four men, all wearing black-and-white-striped uniforms and caps. They pulled two barrows filled with identical clothes.

'Pay attention!' shouted the SS officer. 'You will remove all of your clothes, pile them neatly in front of you and await further instruction.'

There were gasps, and cries of no, no, no. The officer ignored these as more prisoners came into the hangar. Each of them carried a chair and a set of hair clippers. Within a couple of hours, more than two hundred men, women and children had been dramatically transformed. From well- and warmly dressed people, they had become shaved, shivering, frightened captives who stood shocked and cowed, in striped uniforms, waiting to be told what to do.

Tables had been set up near the exit from the hangar and soldiers pushed and shoved the prisoners into a shuffling queue. Almost unrecognisable to each other, shamed by their forced nakedness and quietly obedient, each was given a piece of bread, some cheese and a cup.

'Those who stand behind the yellow line will be escorted to Hut 21. Everyone else will go to the work camp. Move quickly. Now!' shouted the officer as the soldiers herded the two groups out of the reception centre.

Lit by a single, naked bulb suspended from the centre of the roof, Hut 21 was spare and so cold that the Levinsons' breath clouded in the air. Along each side were rows of low wooden beds and against one wall stood a woodburning stove and its flue. It was not lit. The semi-circular curve of the corrugated iron formed both walls and ceiling, and two windows, both heavily frosted, were let into each side. With the Levinsons were eight other couples and two widows, all of them retired, all of them friends or acquaintances. But no one dared speak as the German soldiers allocated beds. None wanted to earn the beating the doctor had suffered. Even after the soldiers switched off the light, locked the doors and left, there were only whispers in the darkness. After a few minutes, Jane Levinson got out of her bed, took her threadbare blanket and climbed in next to her husband. They might keep each other a little warmer.

'Rafael,' she said quietly, 'will we die here?'

*

A world away from the cold and misery of Hut 21, in the warmth of the MacDonalds' home in St Andrews, I sat at the kitchen table with Robert, Katie and her father while Jenny and Eileen made some supper.

'We have some time,' I said, 'but not enough time to build any sort of organised resistance. We cannot do what the Maquis did in France. In any case, what would we achieve? We might hamper them a little, but that would just irritate the Germans into bloody and brutal reprisals. We've seen what they're capable of. And so, I think, if we can, we should be bold: gamble everything on one throw of the dice.'

Thinking aloud, doing most of the talking, enthused by the hope we had found, I suggested that the nine American scientists led by Professor Feldman were the key to any effective resistance. If there really were no more bombs then it was clear that the Germans needed the scientists and their work desperately. If we could find a way of removing them, and their families, so that hostages could not be taken – a way of kidnapping them, in effect – then that would deal a tremendous blow to the Germans.

'Supposing you succeed, and at the moment I can't see how you could, what would you do then?' asked Alan Grant.

I smiled at him and shrugged. 'I don't know, but if we could somehow get them out of St Andrews, it would buy time.'

We agreed that Feldman might be sympathetic, though probably fearful, and we had no idea of the mood or circumstances of his team. Or, indeed, how the removal of twenty or so Americans, as well as six of us, might even be possible.

*

Jamie and Miriam Griffith-Smith sat close, side by side, in front of their fire. The children were all upstairs in bed, stories read and heads on their pillows. They took turns to go into the hallway and stand at the foot of the stairs to listen for chatter or restlessness, but the little ones seemed to have settled.

Staring into the flames, a handkerchief knotted in her hands, Miriam went over once more what she had discovered. From an afternoon phone call to a non-Jewish neighbour, it seemed that a truck had drawn up in her parents' street and soldiers had gone knocking on doors. A few minutes later, Dr and Mrs Levinson appeared in their overcoats and hats with a suitcase and were bundled into the back of the lorry. As were the Greens, the Henrys, the Levys and all of the other Jewish families in the street.

'They are doing it,' said Miriam. 'They're rounding up the Jews. It's beginning.'

Until now, having accepted the fait accompli of the surrender and the crushing threat behind it, and believing that service with the Department of Public Safety might help to make the best of a bad job, Jamie Griffith-Smith had gone some considerable way into the process of reordering his world. But if the Germans had any idea that he had become involved with David Erskine, then he would immediately be shot. And now his family was threatened by something he had taken no account of. Everything was now at stake. Inaction was not an option.

*

'I have an idea,' said Jenny as she poured some coffee, 'and it's a long shot, in every sense. But it just might work. In fact, something like it will have to work if Professor Feldman and his people are to be persuaded. They'll not only need to agree to the very dangerous business of leaving St Andrews, however that can be managed, they will also want to know where they're going. And if their families will be safe there.' Jenny smiled at Robert, Alan and Eileen. 'I think you know what I'm going to suggest.'

Out of a drawer in his study, Robert MacDonald produced a worn, much-consulted Ordnance Survey map, marked 'Mallaig and Glenfinnan'. Having carefully unfolded it, he pointed to a scatter of islands and skerries off the Atlantic shore of the Morar peninsula. 'You see the little bay marked Camas Geal? It means "white bay", because the sand is not yellow but a brilliant ivory colour.'

I could see that it lay on the southern shore of a small sea loch whose narrow entrances were protected by a series of rocky reefs. To the north and east was the village of Arisaig and its railway station.

'You remember it, Katie?' Robert asked his niece. 'You first visited when you were very small.'

He pointed to a building marked on the shore of the White Bay. 'Darroch House is no palace but it has eight bedrooms, a comfortable sitting room with views down to the loch and a kitchen that could cater for a regiment.' He explained that the house and some land around it had come down to him through a complicated path of Highland inheritance, and in case we began to see him as an absentee laird, he explained that at such a distance, it was difficult and expensive to maintain. But there was one road in and one road out. That made it difficult for anyone to arrive without being seen. And Arisaig was little more than a mile and a half away from it. 'But the problems start here, in St Andrews,' said Robert. 'We go to Darroch House in the summer vacation. And I know that it's exactly one hundred and seventy one miles by car, door to door. How will you get twenty or so people there in one piece, and quickly?'

I argued that these difficulties would be academic for the moment if Feldman could not be persuaded or he could not persuade his colleagues. But now we had a destination, a remote place, a wild harbour we could run to. If we could get there, it would at least delay the building of the bomb, buy time and allow breathing space to find a way forward. We could not dither or do nothing. And Robert and I had to get a message to Feldman.

2 January 1945

'Up, Jews! Get up!' roared the soldier as he ran his stick up and down the ridges of the corrugated iron of the Nissen hut. 'Roll call in thirty minutes. Do not be late!'

Rafael Levinson looked at his wife and shrugged. The Germans had taken everyone's watches. 'Best get to the toilet quickly, my dear,' said the doctor. He used his thumbnail to scrape at the ice that had formed on the inside of the window-panes. Although it was barely light, he could see that it had snowed overnight.

'Rafael, Rafael, please,' a voice rasped from a bed not far from the window. It was Morris Gerber, a neighbour. 'I can't breathe. Please help me.'

Dr Levinson helped the old man to sit more upright, so that his airway was clearer, and took his pulse. It was very irreg-ular, missing beats and then racing for short periods. 'Morris, you're experiencing tachycardia – irregular or fast heartbeat. It's uncomfortable but it won't kill you. I promise.' But the cold and the shock of what has happened might, thought Levinson. 'Try to take deep breaths. You'll probably feel better once you get moving.' Anything to calm the old man.

Outside Hut 21, the prisoners were ordered to stand in two rows and an arm's length apart. When their names were called out, they were told that the correct response was, 'Present, sir.' The soldier who had hit Levinson with the butt of his rifle walked up and down behind the two lines, waiting to pounce on and punish mistakes. But there were none. All were present and correct. It was bitterly cold and an icy wind blew over the mountains and down Strathearn.

'And now,' said the soldier taking the roll call, 'we will do all of this again. We want no mistakes.'

By the time they finished, the twenty prisoners had been standing outside for an hour, with only their striped uniforms to keep them warm. Behind him, Levinson heard what sound-ed like a long sigh and then a groan as Morris Gerber crumpled to the ground. The soldier who had prowled behind the lines kicked the old man viciously, again and again. Paralysed by fear, all of the others did not move or turn to look at what was happening, even when Gerber's helpless, heart-rending moans ceased after the terrible beating.

'You two,' said the soldier in charge, pointing at Levinson and Peter Green, another old neighbour from Glasgow, 'take the body away. We will show you where to dispose of it.'

*

'Will we see people wearing kilts, perhaps? Hear bagpipes?'

The little professor's jaunty response amazed me.

Robert MacDonald had described to me what he thought might be a blind spot in the southern perimeter around St Andrews. The Germans had built a timber palisade across a bridge over the Kinnessburn, but had not noticed that there was a narrow shelf at the foot of the piers. With care, it was possible to pass under the bridge and the perimeter without being seen. Griffith-Smith had passed a message to Feldman and we met at the mouth of Crail's Lane in the warren of alleyways that link the streets of the older, eastern end of the town. We agreed to walk up and down these and avoid being seen on the wide main streets.

'What option do we have?' said the professor, before going on to point out the obvious difficulties of getting more than twenty people out of St Andrews unseen and unheard. 'Professor MacDonald is correct. We'll become expendable. I conclude that our only hope of survival is to get out of here now, as soon as possible, taking with us all the calculations we have made and all of the supporting data. We'll buy time. Perhaps others are working to build atom bombs. Probably the Russians. But that will take time – time when something, anything, might happen to frustrate the Germans. I know that an expression of what may be described as faith might sound strange coming from a scientist. But it's all I have, and these are most certainly strange times.'

*

'I know this is dangerous for you, and I am sorry. But I think we don't have much time.'

When Alan Grant opened the front door of the MacDonalds' house at the top of Hepburn Gardens, he invited in not only an apologetic Jamie Griffith-Smith but also his wife, Miriam, and their children. Moments later I found myself listening to Miriam's account of what she had discovered about the disappearance of her parents. Obviously deeply distraught, wide-eyed with desperation and in the company of people she did not know, I felt sorry for her, and Jenny sat close on the sofa, taking her hand. From her husband, Miriam knew of the Eichmann memoranda, but the only scrap of information she had on the whereabouts of her parents was the phrase 'resettlement in Perthshire'.

'I think I might, just might, know where the Germans have taken them,' I said, in as measured a way as I could muster. 'When Jewish communities in Hungary were rounded up and deported, they were taken to labour camps. In Perthshire, there's only one large camp and, given the fact that it isn't even three months since the surrender, there's been no time for them to have a new one built. I think the Germans might have taken your parents to the Black Camp at Comrie.'

After a little rummaging in a hall cupboard, Robert MacDonald found a leather-bound copy of *Newnes Motorists' Touring Map of Britain* and he pointed out Comrie to Miriam, deep in Highland Perthshire.

'Why so far away, so remote?' she asked.

Alan Grant and I looked at each other. 'I suspect they chose that site because it will be difficult for anyone to escape, especially in the winter.' And because the Germans do not want what they are doing to become well known or observed in any way – that was the other reason, I thought, but Mrs Griffith-Smith was distressed enough as it was.

After listening to others speak, saying little himself and comforting his wife, it seemed to me that Griffith-Smith had become galvanised, anxious to act, to take risks. Gone was the languid, public schoolboy manner of our first meeting at Crail harbour. Around the MacDonalds' kitchen table we discussed what was possible, what were necessary risks and came up with a plan. Full of assumptions and needing an outrageous amount of luck, I thought our chances of success were no better than fifty-fifty.

Better odds than we had ever had.

3 January 1945

After morning roll-call and another hour standing stock still in the bitter Highland weather, the Levinsons and their neighbours were ordered to form up and follow the soldier in charge. From a store, they were given shovels, picks and two barrows. Beyond the perimeter of the camp, a stream ran through a deep declivity fringed with willows and hawthorns. Close to its edge, the group was ordered to stop.

'From here,' shouted the German, 'for forty metres in that direction, you will dig a pit two metres in depth.'

This was the kind of manual work that none of the prisoners had done for many years, or indeed ever. The ground was frozen hard and snow had drifted against the treeline by the stream.

'Begin!' shouted the soldier. 'The harder you work, the warmer you will be.'

Rafael Levinson swung his pick and the tine bounced off the rock-hard earth. He tried again and this time moved a solid clod of frozen earth, like breaking a piece off a rock cake.

The others took his lead and in that flat, fertile field surrounded by the sheltering mountains of the Grampian massif, a group of old friends began digging their grave.

As darkness fell, Colonel Kritzinger read and re-read his revised orders. Sitting in his office at College Gate, at a desk opposite the windows and their view up and down North Street, he blew out his cheeks and shook his head slowly. Berlin was insisting on an acceleration of the timetable and the imposition of a new and much more severe regime with the American scientists. If progress was not made more quickly, then action needed to be taken against their families. Examples should be made, and his superiors left that to Kritzinger's discretion. But would punishment beatings, or worse, really be effective? Would constant anxiety hinder the scientists' work?

When the colonel looked up from the pool of light on his desk to weigh that consideration, a thunderous blast roared in the street outside. The panes of his office windows were shattered, and shards of glass flew like shrapnel, cutting Kritzinger's face and tearing a huge rent in the sleeve of his uniform.

*

'Small bombs we can make quickly,' said Professor Feldman to Griffith-Smith. At a meeting that morning at the Bute, the scientists had all listened carefully to what was proposed, knowing that the young man in the Vigilante uniform who spoke to them was taking an enormous risk. Who was to say that one amongst their number might be prepared to talk to the Germans, perhaps forced to by circumstances the others knew nothing about. Blackmail? Perhaps a hostage held elsewhere? But after a few questions about their destination, there was unanimous agreement from the team. They would leave, gather up their families, such possessions as could easily be carried, and flee, run for their lives. Several had watched John Campbell die – and his body was still hanging from St Salvator's

193

Tower – and that image, one of them said, would go with him to his grave.

After a little more discussion, the scientists split into two teams and, with materials already at hand, they made eight explosive devices all fitted with a timer. Each was set to go off five minutes after the other and Griffith-Smith distributed the small packages widely at key points in the town. Designed to be noisy and bright but not spray shrapnel, they were hidden in dustbins, post boxes and one behind an evergreen hedge in St Salvator's quadrangle. Only the bomb placed opposite Kritzinger's office was powerful.

Within moments, whistles blew and a squad of patrolling soldiers came running down North Street. Minutes later, another device detonated in South Street and soldiers were being pulled off patrol along the perimeter and into the centre of the town to repel whatever or whoever seemed to be attacking St Andrews.

When Robert MacDonald heard the first explosion, he checked his watch and, with Jenny and Eileen in the back and Alan next to him, pushed the ignition button of his old Humber, nosed it out of the driveway and turned it west, towards the mountains and the Atlantic shore. Taking back roads through Fife and Perthshire, he reckoned they would reach Darroch House in four or five hours.

At the same time, Jamie Griffith-Smith cut the engine of the truck he had driven up from the depot on the Largo road. Having parked out of sight on the track behind the football ground, leaving Miriam and the children in the cab, he walked quickly to the bridge over the Kinnessburn. Only one sentry had been left and while Jamie asked him, in halting German, what the commotion was in the town, Isaac Feldman led his wife, his colleagues and their families under the bridge. At any moment, the sentry could have walked to the other parapet and seen them, and if he did, Griffith-Smith had thumbed off the safety catch on his Webley revolver. Following instructions, they waited in the shadow of riverbank trees until all were through and then walked in a group to the nearby football ground and the truck. Miriam helped them into the back and waited what seemed like an age for her husband to return.

Bombs were still going off but they needed to move quickly.

*

Walking through the early dark, with enough light in the western sky to give the landscape definition, brought back memories for Katie and me. As we made our way across the playing fields of University Park and though the screen of trees at the far end of the rugby pitch, the dark sheen of the Eden estuary opened up before us. Beyond it was the mouth of the Firth of Tay and the Angus coast. To the north-west, the lights of Broughty Ferry, Monifieth and Carnoustie twinkled. Below us we could see the low, sandy headland that had made St Andrews world-famous, the site of the Old Course, the best-known golf course on the planet.

Most of the academic year took place in the winter months and we often ended the day by walking along the West Sands, below the golf course, taking our time, enjoying the salt air, the call of the gulls and the eye-blearing wind off the sea.

But that night, there was no time to dawdle and pick up shells. We each carried a rucksack and a gun slip. Even though we had only one box of cartridges for our shotguns, the lead shot was heavier than I remembered. Once we reached the main road, we crossed and found the railway line. It skirted the Eden estuary and would take us directly and unobtrusively to where we needed to be. Although the line ran across open country and there were no cuttings to hide us, there were no patrols either. The Germans seemed to have concentrated such manpower as they had in St Andrews, and the countryside around the town was only very lightly policed.

After half an hour, Guardbridge station came into view, its buildings visible against the western sky. We checked the time, looked down the track towards St Andrews, gratefully unshouldered our heavy rucksacks and I changed my clothes.

*

Once everyone was safely aboard and the back tarpaulin secured, Griffith-Smith guided the lorry out of the lane by the football ground. As he turned south, the last of the little bombs detonated and Miriam reached across to squeeze his arm. They had a chance now, a plan, and they had to make it work. Once on the Largo road, Griffith-Smith had decided to cut across country to Strathkinness, and from there strike north towards the Eden estuary. They had a long journey ahead and complete concentration was essential.

'Darling,' said Miriam, 'if David is right about the camp at Comrie, in the Highlands, how will we get there?'

He turned and with a rare smile, replied, 'We're going to take the train.'

*

In St Andrews, the serial detonations had caused chaos. While Colonel Kritzinger was receiving first aid for the cuts on his face and a shard of window glass was being removed from his bicep, soldiers were knocking on doors, rousing residents, searching for answers.

When a patrol turned down North Castle Street and door-banging produced no responses, despite the fact that the lights were on in all the houses and, in one kitchen, the radio was playing, one of the sergeants began to suspect something. In frustration, soldiers broke into Kilrymond Lodge, the corner house occupied by Professor and Mrs Feldman, but there was no one to be found. A cheerful fire was burning in the grate. A runner sent to the Bute Building returned to report that no one was working in the laboratories.

'None?' asked Kritzinger. 'Are you sure? None of them are to be found anywhere. They must be hiding somewhere. They cannot have simply disappeared. Find Griffith-Smith for me. He knows the town better than we do.'

*

'You will do precisely what we tell you to do. When the train from St Andrews arrives, follow our instructions. Do you understand? Yes or no?'

In heavily German-accented English, wearing Griffith-Smith's dress uniform stripped of its insignia under a black overcoat and a regimental hat he had doctored, I shouted at the stationmaster.

'Now you will telephone the main signal box at Leuchars Junction and instruct them to clear a path for us through to Perth, and then beyond to Crieff and Comrie. Do you understand?' I bellowed again. 'And remember, I understand English. Perfectly.' Perhaps I was overdoing it a little when I added, 'This is an emergency! Business of the Reich, of highest importance.'

Griffith-Smith stood beside me, making sure the stationmaster could see his pistol.

The train from St Andrews to Dundee was due in ten minutes. Only two carriages, it shuttled back and forth between the town and Leuchars Junction, where passengers had to change trains. And this was the last train of the day. Katie had assembled all of the Americans and their families on the platform.

When the stationmaster had finished his call, Griffith-Smith tore the flex out of the wall and I shouted, 'This is a secret mission that must remain secret.' And with that, we tied the poor man's hands with his telephone flex and locked him in his own lavatory. When he started shouting, no one would hear him until the morning.

Once back out on the platform, we heard the train coming from St Andrews before we saw it. Scarcely waiting for it to stop, Jamie and I boarded. 'On behalf of the Department of Public Safety, this train is now commandeered for military use.' Griffith-Smith walked down the corridors of its two carriages, ejecting puzzled passengers to wait on the platform. 'There will be another train along soon,' he could not resist adding.

Meanwhile, with a pistol in my pocket, I spoke to the engine driver and his stoker, explaining what was happening and that they were required to comply with my instructions – immediately and without question.

Once Katie and Griffith-Smith had made sure that all the Americans were on board and that Miriam and her children had found a compartment where they could sleep, the locomotive clanked forward, crossed the River Eden to begin the long journey into the mountains.

XII

'MacCaig?' Robert MacDonald pushed some coins into the slot on the telephone box by the side of the road. 'Are you still able to meet us in Arisaig? I'm in Fort William and should be with you in an hour.' The line crackled but MacDonald heard the old man agree to meet him later at his shop.

On the quayside, where moored boats bobbed on the tide and the clutter of creels, fishing gear and nets were piled against the gable end, Donald MacCaig's establishment was no mere shop but an emporium. A post office, a purveyor of foodstuffs (mostly tinned), a retailer of hardware from lamp wicks to paraffin, a lending library, a specialist in oilskins and water-proof clothing, and, when Mrs MacCaig was in the mood, an excellent bakery, it was the hub of the village, and indeed all of South Morar.

Before he began driving west, Robert MacDonald had explained that, having decided to spend some of the New Year holiday at Darroch House, he had invited so many guests that he would need food, especially Mrs MacCaig's pies, scones and bannocks, and of course plenty to drink. The old man had a key to the house: would he mind delivering and MacDonald would call in later that evening to pay? Famously, Donald MacCaig ran a cash business and was particular about prompt payment. And did he have any second-hand shotguns and cartridges in store, by any chance? Would it be possible to hire them? Some of the New Year guests might want to go out for a little rough shooting over the holiday.

When they at last reached the ocean at Loch nan Uamh, where Prince Charles Edward Stuart had made landfall in July 1745, and where he boarded a French ship a year later after the failure of the rebellion, a brilliant half-moon had risen in a clear winter sky. For a mile or two the road hugged the Atlantic shore, the dark heads of the mountains of Moidart rising to the south, beyond the pale shimmer of the sea loch. It was a sight that salved the soul. For Robert MacDonald, it was a return to his native place, the heartland of the great Lordship of the Isles, where MacDonald chiefs had been hailed as kings, rulers of a vast Atlantic principality that stretched from the Isle of Lewis to the Isle of Man. As he travelled further and further into the west, history seemed to fold him into its heart, leaving the chaos and manifest evil that afflicted the world behind him.

'You all right to drive all the way?' asked Alan Grant, snapping MacDonald back to the present. 'I hear the sound of regular breathing in the back seat. Do you want a nap?'

Robert shook his head, saying he was fine. It was not far now. He turned down the sharp bend under the railway viaduct and plunged the car into the shadows of Druimindarroch, the ridge of the oak trees.

*

Belching plumes of steam, the night train rattled through the Fife farmland, its rhythms lulling most of its exhausted passengers into deep sleep. Katie and Griffith-Smith patrolled the corridor running beside the compartments, reassuring, talking quietly to those still awake, still fearful.

Trying to stay out of the way but grateful for the furnace-like heat from the boiler as the stoker shovelled in coal, I had decided to remain in the cab of the engine. Even though the driver and his mate seemed afraid, even cowed, neither meeting my eye when I spoke to them, I had no reason to trust them. And they knew a great deal more about trains and the railway than I did.

Above the din, I shouted, 'When will we reach Perth station?'

The driver leaned out of the cab and peered into the rushing darkness. 'We'll cross the Earn soon and then the Tay. Ten minutes.' He held up all of his fingers.

Perth station was potentially a choke point. If the signal station at Leuchars had suspected something and wanted to stop us, or the station master at Guardbridge had somehow freed himself, I guessed that would be where the points had not been changed for a through train and we would be forced to pull up.

'Coal,' the driver shouted to me, pointing at the tender behind and above the boiler. 'We'll need to take on coal somewhere.'

That had simply not occurred to me, but before I could ask how much was left, the rhythm of the train changed for a few seconds as we crossed the girders of the bridge over the River Earn. A mile or two to the east, it ran into the Firth of Tay and thirty miles to the west, it wound its way through the village of Comrie.

*

'*Feasgar math dhuit,*' said Donald MacCaig as he unlocked the door of his emporium.

His habitual 'Good evening to you' in Gaelic always sounded more like an accusation than a greeting to Robert. How was it that a MacDonald of Morar, a descendant of the Lords of the Isles, had lost his Gaelic, the ancestral language of power, the language that was dying of disuse, the language of the grey defeats of the past?

As the old man switched on the lights, Robert looked up at the ornate Celtic lettering of a sign above the counter. It read

Siol na h'Alba, the Seed of Scotland. Long ago, when Robert made the mistake of asking what it meant, it turned out that MacCaig was a member of a small nationalist group whose goal was not the independence of Scotland. 'Leave the Lowlanders to the English. They have nothing but disdain for us,' MacCaig had said. The Siol na h'Alba group had a higher ambition than the creation of border posts at Berwick and Carlisle: they wanted to usher in a new golden age for the Highlands, with nothing less than the revival of the Lordship of the Isles. Harmless, but passionate, thought Robert.

'How many guns will you be wanting to hire?' asked MacCaig. 'I have four.' From under his counter, he lifted out the gun slips and, one by one, untied them. He carefully unwrapped the freshly cleaned and oiled shotguns from their soft cloths. Elegant, their stocks intricately tooled and with gleaming wooden butts of richly coloured woods, they were objects of great and lethal beauty. 'The Midland and the Joseph Lang should suit those of our guests not used to doing much shooting. Or they could be shot by a lady. They're light and the kick is not terrible.'

Small and rotund, speaking slowly with the characteristic sibilant 's' of the Highlander, MacCaig was a good salesman and as he showed the shotguns to MacDonald, he was also doing mental arithmetic, working out how much money he could get away with charging. A lot, he thought. MacCaig picked up a gun that seemed more sleek and streamlined, older than the others. 'This is Spanish, an AYA. I've shot it myself on the moor. Lovely swing and it is an ejector.' The old man smiled. 'You have to remember that when you break the gun, you should stay out of the way when the spent cartridges come flying out.' And finally, saving and savouring the best for last, he untied the last slip. 'This is my own. A Purdey. I'll lend it to you, Mr MacDonald, but only if you shoot it yourself.'

With a dozen boxes of twelve-bore cartridges, Robert laid the gun slips carefully in the boot of the Humber.

Ever curious, and with no reticence whatever, MacCaig emerged from the shop £150 richer than he had been minutes before. He peered into the car windows, waving and trying to place the people that had come west with the MacDonalds. He had seen them before, he was certain.

*

I jumped when the driver pulled the cord for the train's whistle as he slowed under the glare of the bright lights of Perth station. The signallers seemed to have directed the train into a central through track, the middle one of three that passed between platforms.

'We do not stop here. You understand?' I said to the driver. We were going much more slowly than I would have liked but I could see no movement in the station, no soldiers waiting to board us. I had asked Katie and Griffith-Smith to make sure everyone was lying on the floor to give the impression of an empty train. But no one seemed to be about. Staying in character, I shouted, '*Schnell! Schnell!* Faster! Faster! We need to make progress.'

Only a few seconds later we had left the lights of the station behind and were gathering speed as we moved through the western suburbs of Perth and into the darkness of a Highland night.

*

With its white façade rising up like a huge tombstone, Darroch House looked ghostly in the moonlight. Three storeys high, very imposing, it looked down on a long, wide paddock that ran down to the loch shore. And beyond, twinkled the distant lights of Arisaig. Behind and around the sides of the house, stands of Scots pines and ancient oaks sheltered it from the Atlantic storms and the winds that swept off the moorland to the south. To keep out the hungry hill sheep, a drystane dyke with a ditch below it curved around behind the trees and then stretched like open arms on either side of the paddock that led the eye down to Loch nan Ceall and its white, sandy beach. Robert MacDonald sometimes thought of his house turning its back on the wind, with the collar of its coat pulled up.

The Humber rattled over the cattle grid, waking up Eileen and Jenny, and came to a halt in the close between the back door and the outbuildings. Robert had asked MacCaig to light the Aga stove and take the chill off the house, but when Jenny opened the sitting room door, the room was icy cold.

'Alan and I will get logs from the store, if you can get a start with that kindling,' said Robert.

Fires, their lighting, how to arrange logs and create the most warming blaze . . . all of these things delighted Jenny MacDonald. With some old newspaper she made minister's sticks by rolling up a few pages into a long tube, flattening it and then twisting and folding the result into a plait. Laying three of these cross-wise in the grate, she then snapped twigs into short lengths and stooked them like miniature sheaves of corn into a wigwam shape. Only then did she light the fire. Everything was so dry, having been in the kindling basket since the summer before, that it caught and crackled immediately.

In the hallway, Alan Grant was waiting by the telephone. He had asked the operator to connect him with a Borders number, his father's hospitable friend, Ian Landles. When the phone rang he picked up and spoke clearly and quickly. 'Ian, will you please tell your guest all is well and that he should continue to lie low. Thank you. Goodbye.'

Goodness knows who might have been listening, but his father had to know that he and especially his beloved granddaughter, Katie, were OK. John Grant was sensible and would sit tight.

The butter was rock-hard but Mrs MacCaig's bannocks were soft and fluffy. Still wearing their overcoats, the Grants and the MacDonalds sat close to the blaze, sipping watery whiskies and eating tinned ham sandwiches. It was late but the long day was not yet over. Robert set an alarm clock for 6 a.m. and settled back into his favourite armchair, one with a high back, long seat and high arm rests, while the others trooped upstairs to bed.

*

'I am Major Klaus Saxl from the Department of Public Safety. And where is your salute, Private?'

When the train drew into Comrie station, I jumped down from the cab onto the platform, only to be challenged by a sentry. In harsh, parade-ground German, I told him that my colleague and I needed to see the camp commandant immediately. We did not care if he was asleep. We had urgent business, a matter of the greatest importance to the Reich.

In the office, I watched the commandant read the orders I had typed at the MacDonalds' house earlier that day. He looked up, handed the sheet of paper back to me and shrugged his shoulders. 'It makes no difference to me. Two fewer old Jews to dispose of. Saves me two bullets after roll call tomorrow.'

When Griffith-Smith and one of the guards reached Hut 21, he unlocked the door, switched on the light and rattled his stick on the corrugated iron. Jamie winced at what he saw. 'Levinson!' he shouted. 'Levinson up!' Their son-in-law pulled his hat as far down his forehead as he could, but when the terrified prisoners saw who it was, Rafael opened his mouth and was about to cry out when Griffith-Smith hit him hard on the side of the head, saying in accented English, 'Silence! Do as you are told! Come quickly, now!'

While Griffith-Smith and I were at the camp, Katie and the stoker found Comrie station's coal store. After shunting backwards a little way, the tender was moved closer but, maddeningly, the coal bins lay on the other side of the second track. Rousing all of the American scientists, Katie organised a chain. 'Only the big lumps,' said the stoker, 'I can break them up.' And so from hand to blackening hand, lit by a torch, coal was loaded onto the locomotive. The engine driver and the stoker watched, wondering who their passengers were.

When Katie saw the headlights of the vehicle returning from the camp, she herded everyone quickly back into the carriages as the stoker fired up the boiler.

'I am sorry I hit you, Dr Levinson,' said Griffith-Smith, 'but I thought you were about to give the game away.'

As the train shuddered, moved off and began to pick up speed, the doctor and his wife sat down in the carriage wide-eyed, dazed, certain they were dreaming as Miriam wrapped them in her arms and Griffith-Smith held up their grandchildren to kiss them. Katie brought blankets and the only food she could find – shortbread and a tin of corned beef.

Jane Levinson turned to her husband and said quietly, 'Perhaps we won't die today.'

Intended only for suburban use or short-haul journeys, the train made slow but steady progress. From the shore of Loch Earn, we turned north through Glen Ogle and then sharply west along the wide strath of Glen Dochart. Even in the small hours, the half-moon sky was bright enough to define the horizon of the high mountains of Breadalbane, Beinn Challuim and Beinn Cheathaich.

When we slowed at the junction at Crianlarich to join the West Highland Line, I saw that the engine driver and the stoker were tiring, and no wonder. 'How much further to Arisaig?'

The driver shrugged. 'Maybe two and half hours. It's a long

time since I was on this line. But after Rannoch Moor, we'll have a slow climb.'

I was still running on adrenalin after the theatre of Comrie Camp, and I watched the driver constantly. Once through the Nevis ranges, down into Glen Spean, we rolled through the Great Glen to Fort William, the Firth of Lorne and the last leg westwards to the ocean and Arisaig.

4 January 1945

Startled awake by an alarm clock bell that sounded more like a fire engine, Robert MacDonald groaned as he levered himself up out of his armchair. He removed all of the luggage, the tinned food, the four shotguns and the boxes of cartridges from the boot of the Humber and rattled across the cattle grid, driving up to Arisaig to meet the train. With only a rough estimate to go on, he did not know when, or indeed if, it would arrive. Robert parked outside the little station and closed his eyes.

There was just enough light in the eastern sky for Donald MacCaig to see who it was that had driven into the village at such an early hour. The morning train down from Mallaig and its boxes of fish and shellfish would not stop at Arisaig and the first train from Fort William was not due for two hours. So what, or who, was Mr MacDonald waiting for?

*

Katie and Jamie roused all of their passengers as the train puffed along the north shore of Loch Eil. When they arrived at their destination in half an hour's time, everyone had to be ready to get off the train and get out of sight as fast as possible. Hopefully, there would be no one about at that early hour. Katie also wanted everyone to be awake as they glided around the elegant curve of the Glenfinnan Viaduct.

A pale pink winter dawn crept over the Nevis ranges. It lit the far shore of Loch Shiel as it wound away south from the little strath and the monument. Standing in the corridor with the American scientists and their families, Katie explained that the tall monument below them commemorated the place and the moment when Prince Charles raised the royal Stuart standard on April 19th 1745. 'It was almost exactly two hundred years ago. The Highlanders were rebelling against what they saw as German tyranny, the Hanoverian monarchy. George I was a German. That's what we're doing too!'

*

'Your journey is over and you may return to St Andrews. But you must never speak to anyone of this. Never. It is a secret matter of the utmost importance to the Reich. I have your names and the addresses you gave me, and I'll know where to find you if I discover you have been talking.'

Deliberately abrupt, and with as much menace as I could summon up, I did what I could to intimidate the driver and the stoker. But I had my doubts about our expedition remaining a secret for much longer.

Making several short round trips, Robert MacDonald took all of the luggage and the four children to Darroch House while Katie walked the mile and a half with all of the adults, except for the Levinsons. By the time everybody and everything reached the house, it was mid-morning on a clear, crystal, sunny West Highland day.

In the cavernous kitchen, Jenny and Eileen were frying eggs and bacon, slicing bannocks and scones, heating pies in the Aga, filling dishes with jam and watching it all disappear as fast as it was put on the long kitchen table. Katie was counting. There were twenty-nine mouths to feed, twenty-five adults and four children. It was many more than I had first bargained for and the logistics of keeping them safe, fed and watered at Darroch House would not be easy.

*

Donald MacCaig had not been able to make out every passenger who alighted from the train but he knew that this was no New Year holiday party. He had remembered the Grants from summer holidays before the war, but the others who rushed out of the station that morning were a mystery. They did not look Scottish, or English. Was it their clothes, their haircuts, even their way of walking? They seemed to be foreigners, but he had not heard anything of what they were saying to each other. One way or another, he would find out.

Also, there were only eight bedrooms in the big house. Something strange was going on. Why had Mr MacDonald lied to him, and what did he want with those shotguns? At least one thing was clear, and it cheered the shopkeeper: they would need feeding, and he went into the kitchen to encourage Mrs MacCaig to do some more baking. Perhaps he himself would take a turn out to Taigh Darroch to see how they were fixed.

*

'Mommy! Mom!' The only American child clattered into the kitchen, panting for breath, pointing behind her. 'There are monsters out there!'

The child seemed genuinely distressed and for a moment I wondered if we had been followed in some way. But when I went out of the porch, I saw the monsters about fifty yards away. Grazing quietly in the paddock were two red deer, one of them a magnificent twelve-pointer stag. Not many of them in New York.

'What do we do now, Katie?' After a lunch of game pie and tinned soup and a delicious nap, we had wrapped up warm for a walk around the policies of the house. 'It's nothing short of a miracle that we're all here. But I think that somehow they'll eventually find us. Maybe sooner rather than later. Too many loose ends along the way. So we must move quickly.'

The constant warmth of the Gulf Stream meant that snow rarely lay around the shores of Loch nan Ceall. When we reached the brilliant white sands of the beach, a flat calm sea looked green while, beyond it, the mountains of Morar glowed a cold blue.

'The people of this place, Gaelic speakers, see colours differently,' said Katie after a long moment gazing north over the loch. 'They talk of the sea being *uaine*, or green, and the land as *gorm,* blue.'

That was the point, I thought. It was our land we were fighting for, our history, our people, their decency and their freedom to love the place where the mountains were blue and the sea was green.

As we walked back up the paddock, and the two monsters lifted their heads from the grass to look at us, Katie put her arm through mine. 'This is not just your fight, David, not just your responsibility. There are some very clever and resourceful people here. Let's talk to them.'

*

'They'll be frantic,' Feldman said. 'By now it will be clear to Colonel Kritzinger that we have all gone and unless he can find us quickly, his superiors will be furious.' It was a prospect that clearly amused the little professor.

In the kitchen, more than twenty of us had squeezed around the large table or were perched on window seats or sitting on the floor.

I agreed. 'They'll comb the countryside looking for us and sooner or later will realise that we hijacked a train. So even though we seem to have put a lot of distance between us and them, the odds are that they'll eventually find us.'

With Feldman introducing them, his colleagues began to contribute. Dr Bradley Kaye made an obvious point, so obvious that it had not occurred to me. 'If they attack us here, that will be confirmation that they have no more bombs. We are "it". The only game in town. Nobody else can possibly be working on this to such an advanced level.' He paused, looking around the room with a raised eyebrow, letting the thought settle. 'And the other thing, something that might be a comfort, is that if there really are no other bombs, then they can't risk killing us.'

Having to raise my voice a little as discussion ranged back and forth around the room, I said, 'I think we have to concentrate on two things.'

Like an orchestra conductor, Professor Feldman raised his hands to quell the hubbub.

'First of all, we have to be able to defend ourselves if we are attacked. Bradley is right. All of you scientists are not likely to be shot at, although accidents often happen. It's everyone else, including and especially your families, who are in mortal danger. So please allow two soldiers to assess our situation methodically.'

Griffith-Smith itemised our meagre arsenal. In addition to his pistol, we had seven shotguns and twenty boxes of cartridges with twenty-five shells in each. And that was it. 'Shotguns are only lethal at short range,' added Griffith-Smith, 'and I have only one box of ammunition for my pistol.'

Around the room, I could detect one or two shudders. This sort of military directness naturally scared people, even academics who had been working on the most fearsome weapon ever seen.

Jamie went on to say that, apart from himself, me, Katie, Alan Grant and Robert MacDonald, no one else had any experience with shotguns.

'Hey. Over here.' The wife of one of the American scientists raised her hand. 'Hi, I'm Rita Curtis. I shot skeet when I was a kid. I was pretty good, better than my brothers.'

Everyone laughed. Perhaps we could become a band of brothers and sisters.

'From what you said,' added Bradley Kaye, 'you have a heck of a lot of cartridges, five hundred? We can make something out of them. I guess there's some bleach and maybe paraffin round here?'

Robert MacDonald nodded. 'We have both. And I think there are other ways to discourage the Germans from getting close to the house that don't involve weapons.'

As gloaming fell, our discussions were slowly refined into practical plans that would begin to be put in train at first light in the morning. With no idea how much time we had, there had to be some urgency. We needed to get busy.

5 January 1945

'I think you understand what is required.' A tall, straight-backed soldier, Oberführer Stengel towered over Colonel Kritzinger's desk at College Gate in St Andrews.

Along with a unit of sixty Waffen SS commandos, Stengel had driven up that morning from Army Command North at York. Without any warning, he had stormed into the building and made straight for the commandant's office. After a thorough briefing, some of which he had the colonel repeat, Stengel was satisfied that he understood precisely what had happened. How it happened was another matter. Incompetence, criminal incompetence and an unwillingness to use harsh methods in pursuit of an outcome vital to the Reich – those were the reasons why this disaster had been allowed to happen.

Stengel opened the holster of his Luger, inserted a single

bullet in the chamber and laid it on Kritzinger's desk. 'I will leave you now.'

While he waited in the outer office to hear the shot ring out, Stengel issued orders to the clerks. There was to be an immediate meeting of all the NCOs and junior officers in the garrison, and the senior officers from the Department of Public Safety would be required to attend. Immediately. And all of the files on the American scientists were to be reviewed. Did any of them have links, friendships in the local community? Someone must have seen something.

After five minutes, Colonel Stengel had heard nothing from Kritzinger's office. Having waited long enough for him to behave with honour, Stengel strode back into Kritzinger's office to find him staring fixedly at the pistol on the desk.

Without any hesitation, Stengel picked it up and shot Kritzinger in the head at point-blank range.

*

'Fertilizer!' exclaimed Brad Kaye as he, Robert and I rummaged around the garden store behind the house, looking for spades, shovels, picks and barrows. 'I can use that.' He pointed to a stack of hessian bags. 'The ammonium nitrate can be made into an explosive. And in the right casing, it can create shrapnel.'

I smiled at Robert. We had an asset. Some of the scientists had been reticent, said little or nothing at the meeting, but Brad Kaye seemed in his element. And out in the paddock, there was another asset. Without wasting cartridges, Rita Curtis and Alan Grant were showing two of the Americans how a shotgun worked, how to shoot it and allow for the recoil so that it did not bruise their shoulders.

At first light, Jamie Griffith-Smith, Robert and I had walked what we thought might make a defensive perimeter around Darroch House. Behind the wood at the back ran the drystane dyke with the ditch below it. If all of the winter's detritus could be cleared out of it and it was deepened, it could become an effective barrier. Uphill, I had come across an ancient military deterrent that would make it formidable: blackthorn. It carried vicious spikes. Sometimes six inches long, they were needle-sharp and each twig and branch carried many thorns. I asked Katie to organise a party to cut it all and fill the ditches with it. Anyone who blundered into one would quickly come back out.

Realising that the perimeter was much too long to defend with only eight weapons and six people who knew how to use them, Jamie and I became convinced that we had to force whoever came after us to attack where we wanted them to, funnel them into a narrow approach. If Brad Kaye was right, the Germans would not risk bombarding the house – a dead scientist was a disaster. If we made most of the perimeter behind and at the sides of the house as secure as possible, then the only direction they could come at us was at the front, up the paddock from the loch. The effective range of a shotgun, choked down to concentrate the shot as much as possible, was about fifty yards. And so that was where we began to dig a ditch.

Rafael and Jane Levinson watched from the windows as we cut the turf and carefully laid it to one side. 'Perhaps this ditch will keep us alive,' Jane said.

*

'So,' shouted Stengel, standing in the office of the Department of Public Safety, 'you have not seen your commanding officer for two days? Where does he live?'

With four of his Waffen SS commandos, the colonel was led the short distance to the Griffith-Smiths' house in South Street. When Stengel saw a group of framed photographs on the mantelpiece, he turned to the officer who had brought them. 'Is this him?' When he took the photograph out of its frame, he read the names on the back. 'Miriam? This is his wife? That is a Jew name.'

More searching, spilling the contents of drawers on the floor, revealed the Griffith-Smiths' marriage certificate. 'Levinson. That too is a Jew name. From Glasgow, I see.'

Stengel shouted to one of the soldiers to find the nearest office of the Department of Internal Affairs. 'They have begun the resettlement programme, no?'

*

'That's a lovely one, my dear, big and purple. I think it fell from a chestnut tree.'

Dr Levinson carried a large sack in the woods behind Darroch House. With their mothers, the four children had been assigned to the vital task of collecting as many sacks of last summer's leaves as possible. This was their third, and Rafael Levinson had decided that an educational dimension might keep them at it before boredom set in.

'What is this one?' He held up a windblown branch of brittle copper beech. 'And these are oak leaves. Look what a beautiful shape they are.'

By lunchtime, when the famished children ran into the kitchen, the Levinsons and their little workers had picked up half a dozen sacks of fallen leaves. After he had set them in the garden store, the doctor thanked me for a delightful task and asked what the leaves were for.

'Disguise, Rafael, disguise.'

*

In the years immediately before the war, when Jenny and he had spent more time at Darroch House and regularly met guests off the Arisaig train, Robert had a games room built next to the garden store. There were, after all, plenty of days when the rain sheeted off the Atlantic. He had installed a table-tennis table and a full-size snooker table.

The great attraction of the latter for Bradley Kaye was the long, bright rectangular light above it. Having covered the green baize surface with a protective cloth and laid wooden boards on top, he began to set up his bomb factory. On the door of the games room, he hung a sign with a drawing of a skull and crossbones at the top, and underneath: *Danger. Keep Out*. All manner of unlikely items joined the bags of fertilizer, the cartridges, bleach and paraffin.

'Why do you need tennis balls?' asked Robert MacDonald as he handed over a net bag full of old, bald ones. 'And a pressure cooker?'

The American smiled, winked, clicked his tongue twice and shut the door. And then opened it again. 'Demonstrations later. Not close to the house. Or people.'

Meanwhile, I found a cupboard full of fishing gear and, with Katie's help, spooled out a reel of line. Having cut a six-foot length, I found it impossible to break. 'I saw some fence posts stacked at the edge of the wood. Do you think you could find a couple of kindling axes?'

The ditch across the paddock was almost deep enough and I asked two of the Americans working in it to come with me. By the wood store there was a chopping block and, with an axe, I showed them how to get a very sharp point on the end of a post.

'When you finish these, look around in the woods for any straight-ish fallen branches – not too brittle, and about as thick as your forearm. We need as many of these sharp stakes as you can make.'

*

216

When Jenny parked the Humber at the quayside in Arisaig and she and Eileen walked over to MacCaig's shop, they paused to turn and look over Loch nan Ceall to the white façade of Darroch House. A low winter sun was throwing shadows, but in the clear air it seemed that every detail of the landscape was graphic, in sharp focus.

'*Ciamar a tha sibh?*'

Both women jumped. Neither had heard Donald MacCaig steal up behind them to ask how they were. But Eileen amazed him by replying, '*Tha gu math, tapadh leibh.*' She and Katie had begun to learn Gaelic at evening classes before the war and enough of it had stuck for her to say that she and Jenny were well, thank you.

MacCaig looked discomfited, as though he had just had his pocket picked. Pointedly, he replied in English.

Having navigated his considerable girth behind the counter of his shop, with its jangling till, weighing scales and their stack of black weights and a wide chopping board, MacCaig put on his white grocer's apron, ready to do business. Yes, Mrs MacCaig had indeed been baking. If Mrs MacDonald could say how long they were all staying, perhaps a daily order of bannocks and scones and any other items could be delivered? And how many were they catering for?

Jenny MacDonald politely ignored this inquisition and the two women set down their wicker shopping baskets on the counter and began working through their list.

From the back shop, the beaming, rotund Mrs MacCaig appeared, an excellent advertisement for her talents. She carried a wooden baker's tray piled with good things, some of them still warm from the oven. 'MacCaig has a flitch of bacon and some salmon he has cured.' Referring to her husband in the traditional, formal style, she also shot him a withering look. 'And I'm sure you will not be needing any help to slice them.'

217

On the short journey back to Darroch House around the head of Loch nan Ceall, Katie and Jenny passed under the ancient shadows of the oak woodland of the Strath of Arisaig.

'He's such a busybody, that man,' said Jenny. 'I never feel comfortable in his company and I dislike the way he looks you up and down. I feel I'm being sized up, not a thought I enjoy. How Mrs MacCaig has put up with him all these years, I can't imagine.'

He did keep decent whisky, though, and they had managed to prise two bottles of Islay malt out of him.

*

'Hut 21 is empty.' The camp commandant at Comrie had leapt to his feet when Colonel Stengel barged into his office. 'We liquidated all the old Jews this morning.'

A wasted journey, thought Stengel. But then something occurred to him. 'All of them? You shot all the old Jews?'

For a second or two, the commandant weighed his options. 'Ah, no, not all of them,' he finally replied.

'Now, let me guess,' said the colonel. 'What happened to Dr and Mrs Levinson? Are they still here?'

As the pit of his stomach churned, the commandant could see that nothing good would come of this and so he related the events of January 3rd.

'What do you mean, you do not know where the train went? Did you not ask? Did you not go with them to the station? So far as I understand it, there are only two possible directions, east or west. And you do not know which!' Stengel opened the door of the office and shouted to the staff sergeant, 'Bring me a map. Now!'

*

'The atom bomb was devastating in another sense,' I said, as we sat down in front of Jenny's blazing log fire in the sitting room at Darroch House. 'It not only destroyed London and devastated the south-east, it also left us leaderless. The death of the king and the royal family, the prime minister and the government has hollowed us out. There's no one in Britain we can turn to.'

Alan Grant was pouring glasses of Bruichladdich and insisting that the Americans added a little water. 'And that means the US government holds the key to all of this,' he said.

Robert MacDonald picked up the thread of our thinking. 'If we can convince them that the Germans have no more bombs, then everything changes. And then add to that the possibility that Professor Feldman and his team can supply them the data that will allow a prototype bomb to be produced quickly . . .'

He was interrupted by a fit of coughing. 'Wow!' said Rita Curtis. 'This stuff is firewater!' And then she took another sip of the peaty Islay malt. 'I'd say it's a hell of a bluff to call,' she went on, 'and before we left, or were kidnapped, I heard that President Roosevelt was sick, real sick. He has to use a wheelchair.'

From a long discussion of options, it became clear that we would need solid documentary evidence, as we could not prove, beyond doubt, that there were no more bombs.

'But the story is compelling,' said Katie, looking at me. 'You've kept notes in your precious journal that you think I don't know about. If you could flesh those out, it might be even more compelling, more convincing.'

Professor Feldman interjected. 'Yes, forgive me, but I think you need more than that. I propose that I draft a scientific analysis, detailing all that we've done since we came to Scotland and giving a detailed estimate of how long it will take to make a viable bomb, with others using the work we have done. I can add to that an account of my continued but fruitless requests to be put in contact with the German scientists who built the first bomb. And there's also the question of the high volume of heavy water shipments we've received from Norway. Before the war, I had some understanding of their output and I think we were receiving all of it. Such a document, signed by all of us, combined with Mr Erskine's journal would, I think, be persuasive. It might prompt investigation, at least.'

The western sky sparkled with stars, Sirius shining brightest and the upended Plough climbed above the Morar mountains. Tired of talking, tired of planning, Katie and I went out into the paddock after supper in search of stillness. The tide was high, the waves shushing, lapping on the white sand as we walked slowly along its wrack-strewn fringes. Swaddled in scarves and heavy overcoats, we said nothing to each other, enjoying the silence. But on that starlit night, I felt we had never been closer. Hidden until then by the headland at Morroch, the kindly lights of Arisaig reflected on the water and the beach began to run into rock pools and a scatter of ragged boulders. We stopped, ready to turn back to the house.

I took off my glove and, gently touching Katie's cheek, I said, 'I have never loved you more than I do now.'

*

Stengel's instincts told him they had gone west. Even though the idiot commandant, who would soon be cleaning the Jews' latrines, could tell him very little, it was clear that Griffith-Smith had somehow extracted his parents-in-law from the camp. But he had a train, and you don't need a train for three people. There must, thought the colonel, be a link with the disappearance of the scientists. Leaving his men in their vehicles, he walked into the little railway station. The track led east or west. Why would they go back the way they had come? It was much more likely they had gone into the mountains.

Looking closely at the map spread on the commandant's desk, Stengel had found himself daunted. It was a vast area of glens, sea lochs, islands, moorland and mountains. They could be anywhere. Or, anywhere that a railway train would take them. Tracing it with his finger, he followed the black line out of Comrie on the map. From the junction at Crianlarich, it led south towards Glasgow and since that was where the Levinsons had come from, he rejected that option. His convoy of three trucks, an armoured car and his staff car would turn north and head for Fort William. It seemed like a hub for the West Highlands. He could not follow the railway line across Rannoch Moor or up over the foothills of the Nevis ranges; there was no road, but the map suggested that was desolate country, in any case. Griffith-Smith had his family and twenty Americans to hide, feed and look after. He would need to be near a village or a town.

6 January 1945

My concentration was broken by a very faint knocking at the door. I had found some space and peace to fill out the notes in my journal in an upstairs sitting room at Darroch House. Over the last day or so, I had been told a great deal of what had happened elsewhere and to others, things I had not seen for myself, and I wanted to record it all.

'Come in, please come in.'

A small, mouse-like face appeared round the side of the door. 'Hi. I'm real sorry to disturb you. My name's Millie Harbison and I don't want to speak out of turn.'

Her words were tumbling out in what was clearly a rehearsed speech. 'When I listened to all the talk about the US government, I had an idea. It might not work, and I don't want to get anyone's hopes up, but my brother, Averill Thomson, is a diplomat who's currently posted to the US consulate in Edinburgh. At least, I think he is. He was the last time I spoke to him, when we were still in the US. Since we got to St Andrews, we haven't been allowed to use the phone. So he might have been posted someplace else. I just don't know. But I still have his private number. But he did say that his calls were listened to. I don't know. Anyway. There it is. Sorry to disturb you.'

'Please, sit down, Millie – may I call you Millie?'

*

'Hello. Yes, hello. Is that the Department of Public Safety? Yes. Good. It is Donald MacCaig who is speaking.'

Using the telephone box outside the railway station rather than the handset in his hallway, where Mrs MacCaig might overhear him, the shopkeeper went on. 'I represent Siol na h'Alba. In fact I am the *ceannard,* the president.'

There was a pause.

'Siol na h'Alba. S-I-O-L, N-A, H, apostrophe, A-L-B-A. Surely you must have heard of us?'

Another pause.

'Yes, well, I'm telephoning you to report suspicious behaviour at Darroch House, near Arisaig.'

XIII

Robert carefully loosened the frame of the dormer window so that it could be opened inwards rather than pushed up and down. The sashes were stiff and speed might be important. The smallest bedroom on the top floor of Darroch House had the best view. Not only did its window look north over the loch to Arisaig, anyone sitting on the left-hand side of the shelf-like seat in the dormer could also see to the east and the coast road after it turned towards the house at Morroch Point. Robert set down a pair of binoculars and a whistle he had found amongst the fishing tackle and went off to look for the Levinsons.

Outside, Jamie and I were standing with Bradley Kaye on the shore at the farthest west end of the white sands, at least five hundred yards from the house.

'Okay,' said Brad. 'I only have one sample. I definitely don't want to waste the others. They were damn difficult to make.' He held up the frame of an old tennis racquet with the strings replaced by a loosely fitted oval of canvas tacked onto the frame. 'You heard of an atlatl? A spear-chucker? This is my equivalent. I need to get something in the air quickly and as far away from me as possible.' He grinned at both of us. 'Jeez, I hope this works.'

Brad carefully took a tennis ball out of a bag. Looking like a cartoon version of a bomb, the ball had a white cotton fuse sticking out of it. Motioning for me and Jamie to move behind him, he placed the ball in the centre of the canvas tennis racquet.

Then he lit the fuse and, as though he was serving for the match, he launched the ball high and far into the sky – where it exploded like a firework. Bradley whooped and danced around like a dervish.

'What's that rattling noise?' I asked.

'It's the lead shot from your cartridges hitting those rocks. Shrapnel from the sky.'

Rafael Levinson felt like applauding. Watching from the dormer window with Jane and Robert, he saw the bomb explode and, far from frightening him, it lifted his spirits. No longer would they be victims. It was good to fight back, good to resist the black tide of evil that seemed to be engulfing Scotland and, indeed, the whole world.

Robert had swung open the window and, having advised the Levinsons to wear every scrap of clothing they could, he pointed out what to look out for. With the binoculars, it was possible to make out people moving on the quayside at Arisaig, MacCaig's shop and the hotel. And where the road to Darroch House turned around the headland, its whole length to the cattle grid near the house could be seen.

'If you spot anything – vehicles, walkers, anything coming our way – blow that whistle and one of us will come up immediately. The toilet is at the top of the stairs.' Robert smiled. 'And in two hours, two others will come to take your place so that you can come down and warm up.'

Elsewhere, Alan and Katie had found six fence rails and a box of six-inch nails. Between two trestles, they were banging them through at two-inch intervals. When they flipped each one over, the nails bristled like the quills of a hedgehog – spikes like these, known as caltrops, had been used to disable charging horses and men since Roman times. The rails would be laid across the road beyond the cattle grid to puncture the tyres of approaching vehicles. But not yet.

First, Jenny MacDonald was going to drive Millie Harbison and me into Arisaig. Millie needed to make a phone call.

*

It was a still day, the low sun bright in a blue sky and no breeze off the ocean to chill the bones. It was a good day for a walk, to get out to smell the clean air, not be cooped up all the time behind walls, not to be told where to go and where not to go.

Bradley Kaye's wife, Marilyn, had hated St Andrews. Even though it was possible to walk around the three streets, there were no open spaces, no greenery, only small patches of lawn. For a girl born in Wyoming, in the suburbs of Laramie, with the Rocky Mountains at her back and the great plains of Nebraska and Dakota to the east, she had been raised in the long vistas and the free air of the wide-open spaces.

When they came to Darroch House, she saw the big skies once more, but almost immediately everything was shut down again. Marilyn knew that a fortress had to be built. Hell, she had been born not far from a US cavalry fort, but just for an hour or two she needed to get away. 'Come on, honey,' she said to their five-year-old daughter. 'Come on, Lisa, let's go hiking!'

From his high vantage point, Dr Levinson saw Marilyn Kaye walk down the paddock to the white sands, her little daughter skipping along beside her, but he was distracted by the ditch diggers. For some reason, they seemed to have filled it in. At least half of its length had been turfed over and Alan and Eileen Grant were emptying the sacks of leaves that he and the children had picked up. All very puzzling.

A loud clank and a shout from the direction of the road attracted his attention. With Robert MacDonald's help, two of the Americans had attached ropes to the cattle grid and managed to pull it up like a drawbridge. And then, bracing themselves, planting their feet in the grass, they lowered the metal grid back down to its original position.

*

'The ambassador is in Edinburgh!' said Millie Harbison when she returned to the car. 'Of course he is. I never thought of that. When London was bombed, our embassy was destroyed and all the poor people there were killed. There's a new ambassador, John Booth, an associate of Harry Hopkins, Roosevelt's man.' Talking, as usual, very quickly, very excitedly, Millie exclaimed, 'And he will see you. Right away. Or as soon as possible. Soon as you can get to Edinburgh!'

Before she went into the phone box by the station, I had given Millie clear instructions on how the British system worked, and when to press Button B. I thought it important she made the call alone. Who knew who was watching? 'Donald MacCaig, certainly,' Jenny MacDonald had said. 'He watches everything.'

And Millie seemed to take an agonisingly long time before I could see her begin to talk. And then she talked, and talked. For at least ten minutes. I hoped she would remember to insert more coins. But when she climbed back into the Humber, breathless and excited with her news, she said several times that her brother, Averill Thomson, had made an important point. When I arrived at the consulate in Edinburgh, I should not only bring all my documents with me but I should get inside, out of sight, as quickly as possible. The building in the centre of Edinburgh, in one of the elegant terraces of the Georgian New Town, now had the status of an embassy and it was therefore sovereign US territory. 'That was the last thing I heard Averill say. I promised to make a particular note of it and to tell you directly.'

But when Millie ended her call there had been a second click as another receiver was put down.

*

226

After walking for only half an hour, Marilyn and Lisa came to the boggy shore of a small lochan on the fringes of a big pine wood, which seemed to stretch uphill like a dark green carpet. All the time they had been climbing up from the shore they could see the roof of Darroch House below them and Loch nan Ceall beyond.

'Mom! Look!' A red squirrel scuttered up one of the Scots pines and Lisa squealed with delight. The track they followed was sheltered, wide and with drainage ditches on either side. As they walked on, the quiet of the forest slowly closed around them. It seemed to become another world, natural, unfettered, free and full of life, even in midwinter. For the first time since she had arrived in Scotland, Marilyn felt her shoulders drop, she felt her limbs loosen as she filled her lungs with clear, clean air.

Katie, meanwhile, was looking for paths. In the woods behind the house, she looked for trails of flattened grass where deer and other animals made their way through the trees. Creatures of habit, they rarely deviated, usually taking the most direct, least obstructed route into cover. And if anyone somehow managed to get through the blackthorn-filled ditches and over the drystane dyke, it would be those paths they would take. With the help of the stake-sharpeners and the fishing line she and I had found in the house, Katie was tying tripwires.

'Three feet beyond them, maybe four, it's hard to judge. That's where we set our short stakes in the ground,' said Katie to the American scientist who was helping her.

Her reasoning was that if a man of average height tripped over the tight and all-but-invisible fishing line, he would fall but his momentum would mean he would hit the ground about four feet further on. 'The soft underbelly,' she said with an uncharacteristic smile, 'is where we want these vicious little stakes to hurt them.'

Later, Katie joined Professor Feldman, Robert, Alan, Jamie, Millie, Bradley and me in the sitting room.

'I have to go to Edinburgh as soon as possible,' I said. 'And we have to work out how it can be done.'

'Don't you worry,' piped up Millie, 'Averill will look after you. My brother is a big, stand-up guy, very smart, very determined. And he loathes the Nazis.'

We discussed simply jumping in the Humber and taking the huge risk of driving all the way there.

'Too many places where you could be stopped,' said Robert. 'And too many single-track roads. What would happen if you met an army vehicle coming the other way?'

'But we cannot waste time,' I said, 'I need to go now.'

Katie interrupted: '*We*, David, *we* need to go now. I'm not letting you out of my sight. We will risk the train. There's no other option.'

In a fishing satchel, I packed my journal and the document Feldman had compiled. Jamie Griffith-Smith gave me his pistol and the ammunition. 'It's now or never,' I said, and for some reason that prompted us all to shake hands.

And then Rafael Levinson blew a loud blast on his whistle.

*

The bell above the shop door jangled. 'I am Colonel Stengel of the Waffen SS. Was it you who telephoned?'

MacCaig nodded, much taken aback at the sudden arrival of an abrupt, aggressive soldier in a black leather greatcoat and the death's head insignia on his cap.

'You will now tell me all that you know.'

At that moment, Mrs MacCaig came though the doorway from her kitchen, wiping her floury hands on her apron.

'Well, yes, it was me,' said MacCaig. 'But I would be wanting just now to discuss with you Siol na h'Alba and how you

228

might be placed to help the cause.'

Stengel leaned across the counter and smiled. 'I know nothing of this and care even less. You will tell me all you know about these people. Now!'

The shopkeeper jumped and, with his wife's stare boring holes into his back, he edged around the counter towards the door. 'I can show you if we go outside.'

*

Through binoculars, I could see the portly figure I took to be Donald MacCaig on the quayside talking to a tall German officer. He was pointing at Darroch House. Behind them I counted three trucks and what looked like two other army vehicles partly hidden behind them.

'The bastard,' said Robert MacDonald, 'the miserable, money-grubbing bastard. MacCaig has betrayed us. I wonder what the Germans are paying him.'

I ran downstairs with Jamie and set quickly in train all of our deterrents and defences. On the road beyond the cattle grid, Alan and Katie laid down their caltrops, the fence rails studded with six-inch nails. After they ran back over the cattle grid, it was pulled up and Rita Curtis distributed shotguns and boxes of cartridges to all who would shoot them.

But I could not find Bradley Kaye anywhere. And then for the second time, Rafael Levinson blew his whistle.

From the dormer window, I could see Brad on the beach and it looked as though he was calling, cupping his hands on either side of his mouth. By the time I reached him, I was panting so hard I could barely get any words out, and he spoke first.

'I can't find Marilyn and Lisa. Looked everywhere,' said Brad.

With great difficulty, I explained what had happened and why he had to come quickly back up to the house, reassuring

229

him that his wife and daughter couldn't have gone far. They would be found or appear. Soon. Just as urgent, I said, was the fact that the Germans had arrived, three trucks, maybe fifty, sixty soldiers and we needed to be ready.

*

'And so you gave them four shotguns and how much ammunition?' asked Stengel. Much taller than the shopkeeper, the colonel had gripped him by the arm, tight.

As the conversation went on, all one way, and MacCaig gave him an estimate of how many people were at Darroch House, he quickly began to wonder if he had acted rashly, made a bad mistake. Just as the Irish Republicans had sought German help in the First World War, so he and Siol na h'Alba were willing to bargain in this war for their independence. He was only following the lessons of history. And wasn't that a central part of what the Nazis believed? That each race should have a right to self-determination, to their own identity and nationhood?

'What is the range of the guns you gave them?' MacCaig heard the German say.

'Well, it is for shooting game birds they are used, you know.'

'Yes, yes, I know what a shotgun is.' Stengel was growing impatient with this little fat shopkeeper.

'Well, it would be fifty yards, perhaps seventy, depending on the choke.'

Stengel nodded, realising that, with his submachine guns and rifles, he would have an immediate advantage. 'Now, Mr MacCaig, I want you to go over to the big house and talk to them.'

*

Bradley Kaye was beside himself with worry. And I had the callous, calculating duty to keep him from leaving the perimeter to search for Marilyn and Lisa. 'Look, Brad, if they have gone walking and got lost, they can't have gone far. This is a small peninsula.' That did not remotely convince me, far less him. Looking out of the dormer window, he once again picked up the binoculars and scanned the horizon.

Around the house, there seemed to be a strange sense of calm. In the kitchen, the sitting rooms, no one had much to say. Outside, walking up and down the gravel forecourt, Rita Curtis, Katie and Alan Grant had broken but loaded shotguns folded over their arms, and they simply looked north to the loch and over to Arisaig. Cloud had blown in off the ocean and gloaming was gathering quickly.

'David, David,' Katie called to me. 'There's someone here to talk to you.'

On the far side of the cattle grid, I could see Robert MacDonald talking animatedly to a small, portly individual.

'This is MacCaig,' Robert told me, 'the man who is speaking to the Germans. A man who is frankly a disgrace to his country and to himself. And the Germans have asked him to speak to us.'

Without once meeting my eye, he told me that if we gave up all the American scientists and their families, then the rest of us would be left in peace.

'Do you believe that, MacCaig?' said Robert.

For the first time, he raised his head and looked directly at us both. 'No, no, I do not think I believe it.' And with that, he turned and began to walk slowly back to Arisaig.

*

'I don't think they'll attack us during the night,' I said. 'The risk of injuring or killing one or more of the scientists is too great.'

Jamie, Robert and I agreed that a rota of watches ought to be set and that all had to be in readiness in case I was wrong.

Bradley Kaye had sat in silence in the sitting room but just as we began to sort out a list, he began speaking quietly. 'Why should we sit here and wait for them to come to us? So that I can find my wife and my baby, I need every last one of these bastards dead. Every one. And only when they are, can we all go find Marilyn and Lisa. We should go over there, late, when they're asleep and kill them all. All of them.'

*

Deep in the darkness of the pine forest, Marilyn had long ago lost her way. Perhaps she had even been going around in circles. Lisa was exhausted. It was cold but the great trees meant that there was at least shelter. And for some reason, she felt they were benign, guarding them both.

'I'm thirsty, Mom,' said a small voice.

In her overcoat pocket, Marilyn had found part of an old bar of chocolate, but she had nothing for them to drink. The darkness, the blanket of the night was so dense that she did not want to go blundering around looking for a stream. 'Suck this slowly, honey. You'll feel better. And don't worry. We'll have this little adventure and tell Daddy all about it in the morning.'

They had sat down in the bole of an old Scots pine and made a bed of all the shed needles from the larches around it. Opening her overcoat, she folded Lisa close inside it and hoped that at least her baby girl would find a little sleep.

*

With the box of incendiaries cradled on Brad's lap in the passenger seat of the Humber, and Katie, Rita and me squashed in the back, Robert drove very slowly, with no headlights, along the coast road to Arisaig. I had told Jamie and Alan to be ready for an attack at first light if we did not return. The best thing was for them to go up to the dormer, the lookout post, and keep their eyes fixed on the village.

'MacCaig! MacCaig! Get up!'

Having broken in through the back door of his shop, Robert and I were by the shopkeeper's bedside, surprised that Mrs MacCaig was not beside him.

'They are in the village hall, most of them,' he said. 'And some in the hotel. But I don't know how many.'

Robert and I took some pleasure in tying him to the bed and wrapping a gag around his mouth. 'Maybe this will teach you to keep your mouth shut,' said Robert through gritted teeth.

Brad, Katie and Rita had found the German trucks, staff car and armoured car parked opposite the hotel. The village had no street lights but nevertheless they hugged the shadows of the fishing sheds. When they were certain no sentries had been posted, they flitted like bats across the street to the nearest truck.

But then Katie stopped suddenly and pointed at the cab of one of the trucks. The passenger window had been wound halfway down and what looked like cigarette smoke was drifting out of it. There were sentries, but they had taken refuge from the cold night. Putting her finger to her lips, Katie motioned for Brad to do what he had to do while she and Rita clicked their loaded shotguns closed in case any of the cab doors opened.

Brad unscrewed the petrol cap from the tank behind the cab and very carefully and gently he pushed a tennis ball bomb into the cylindrical spout, making sure its white fuse was showing. When he had done the same with all the vehicles, Katie and Rita retreated into the shadows of the houses and returned to the Humber where Robert and I were waiting.

'That's the village hall.' Robert pointed to a concrete building with a corrugated iron roof that stood a little way back from the street line.

Moments later, Brad came racing back from the hotel car

233

park and pulled me, Katie, Robert and Rita down behind the car.

The explosion was tremendous, yellow flames roared into the night sky and large parts of the trucks lifted into the air before crashing on the road. Debris fell around us and clattered onto the corrugated iron roof of the hall. And perhaps six German soldiers had died in the blast. We ran towards the double doors.

'Wait,' I hissed, 'wait until at least ten of them get through the door before you shoot.'

And then death came rushing quickly.

We stood close, could not miss.

The Germans were lifted up and thrown backwards like rag dolls by the barrage of shotgun fire. Brad Kaye was screaming at them. Robert calmly reloading. Rita held her gun at waist level, like it was a pistol. Within thirty or forty seconds, we killed or maimed many men, so many that the others in the hall realised that through the doorway certain death waited. Brad ran forward and threw three more tennis ball bombs inside the hall and would have followed their blasts if I had not dragged him back by the collar. From the direction of the hotel, we heard shouts and the sound of shots. We ran for the Humber and, as Robert gunned the engine, bullets tinged off the bodywork.

'How many?' said Brad, breathless, his chest heaving. 'How many of those bastards did we get?'

Once Robert had driven out of range, he slowed on the narrow road around the headland, his headlights swinging across the old woods, knowing that they had no vehicles to pursue us.

'I'm not sure,' I said. 'Maybe twenty. They just kept coming. It was crazy.'

Rita looked wild-eyed. 'I shot eight cartridges. One barrel at a time. And I didn't miss.'

Robert rattled us across the cattle grid. By the fire in the sitting room, everyone was waiting, anxious for news, desperate to see us all return unharmed. Looking across the loch, they had seen and heard the explosions. Jenny MacDonald poured stiff drinks and, as calmly as I could, I set a rota for the night watch. At first light, they would come. Whatever was left of them.

'I can't go to bed. I won't sleep.' Katie was shaking, holding her whisky glass with both hands.

'Let's go up to the lookout and take the first watch.'

With blankets around our shoulders and a candle flickering in a glass windshield, we looked down across the moonlit loch. The shells of the trucks were glowing red, smouldering and the village hall was ablaze.

*

'Why were there no sentries on patrol? Why did they sit in the trucks?' screamed Colonel Stengel at an NCO. Shattering glass had injured him but he paid no attention to the bleeding cuts on his neck and face. 'Bring me a report on the number of dead and wounded and a count of what weapons and ammunition we have left.'

Stengel walked quickly down to the quay and looked across the loch at Darroch House. The building was in darkness except for a scintilla of light in a top-floor window. Pushing at the door of MacCaig's shop, he was surprised to find it open.

Spreadeagled on his bed, his wrists and ankles tied to the four corners of his brass bedstead, the shopkeeper heard footsteps stamping up the stairs. And he pissed himself.

When Stengel tore off the gag and pushed his bleeding face close, MacCaig whimpered with terror at what seemed like a hellish apparition, a nightmare.

'What were their names?' the German demanded.

He knew only Robert MacDonald, not the other man.

'After they asked you where my men were billeted, did they say anything else to you? Anything that might be of use to me?'

When MacCaig shook his head from side to side, Stengel grabbed his jaw tightly, pushing his jowls together, opening his mouth. Pulling his Luger from its holster, he shoved the barrel into it and pulled the trigger.

*

When I looked at my watch, it showed 2 a.m. and Katie was sound asleep on the mattress next to the dormer window. The candle shed a warm light, and in repose her face looked peaceful.

Hearing movement outside the door, still very jumpy after the events of the night, I instinctively reached for the shotgun leaning against the wall.

Bradley Kaye came in. 'Can't sleep neither,' he said. 'You want some company?'

More than once I had been told that the night is coldest just before the dawn, but as we looked over the loch, waiting for the dark sky to turn grey and the Morar mountains to become a horizon, neither of us shivered. There was too much whirling around our heads.

'In the morning, we'll kill the rest of them,' Brad said quietly, looking out of the window. 'We'll kill them all and then we'll find Marilyn and Lisa. Okay?'

Once again, we talked over the detail of what we had planned and how it had to change since the raid on Arisaig.

'They now know several things,' I said. 'First and most important is that they cannot risk killing Feldman, you or any of the other scientists. And, from St Andrews, they know what you all look like. The rest of us are expendable. Extracting you and the others is a very difficult thing to achieve and while we've made it harder for them, that's their objective. They won't care about anything else.'

7 January 1945

Stengel had lost thirty-two men, either killed or so badly wounded by blast burns or shrapnel that they could not walk. Leaving behind a detail of two men to guard and care for the living and get help to bury the dead meant he had a force of twenty-six, including himself. And having lost all of his vehicles, they would have to attack on foot. At least their weapons and ammunition were largely intact. Stengel knew that while the shotguns had been devastating at short range, he and his men could approach close to the house without risk. The range of their own weapons was much longer.

In the hotel dining room, the colonel mustered all of his men fit for duty. It was 5.30 a.m., still very dark, but he had calculated that dawn would break when they reached their objective. That was the time to attack, before defenders were fully awake and aware.

'We will seek to set up the MG 42 machine guns directly in front of the house. Before we begin firing, Sergeant Fischer will take two men behind the house to see if they can break in from that direction.' Having pinned a map to the wall, he went over his plans for a second time. 'Remember, you now know that these people will fight. They are dangerous and they took us by surprise. But we are Waffen SS and vengeance will be ours. *Heil Hitler!*'

*

As a clear day began to dawn, the dark heads of the Morar mountains would be lit soon. Rafael and Jane Levinson joined us at the dormer window to take over the watch. They brought welcome mugs of tea and hunks of bannock and jam.

'This is the day, is it not?' said the old doctor, clapping his hand on Bradley's shoulder. 'Young man, I was told that you fought like a lion last night. We're proud of you. Can you do that again today, do you think?' Levinson smiled. 'But whatever happens, Jane and I want to thank you both. In the last few days we've seen the worst and then the best of our fellow human beings. What greater privilege is there than to be with men and women who risk their lives for you?'

On the edge of the gravel forecourt, we set up three firing positions behind a turf rampart revetted with fence posts. Behind them there were two more positions, in first-floor bedroom windows that could be lifted out when the time came. Between the close behind the house and the pine wood, there was no field of fire and so Katie and Jamie had no option but to patrol the fringes of the trees in case the perimeter was breached and any Germans got beyond the trip wires and the stakes. Brad and I walked quickly down to where the ditch had been dug across the paddock, about fifty yards from the house. The day before, the sods of preserved turf had been laid over the latticework of a series of old trellises, and any evidence of ground disturbance had been hidden by scatters of fallen leaves.

At each end of the ditch, Bradley had set up two large porcelain teapots filled with very volatile explosive and, as we primed them, we heard Rafael Levinson blow his whistle.

On the road rounding Morroch Point, Stengel marched at the head of what was little more than a platoon. It was difficult at such a distance but I thought I could count about twenty men. All of them were carrying not only weapons but also wooden boxes of ammunition. I shouted down from the dormer that everyone should take up their positions, and for Miriam

Griffith-Smith to take the children into a back bedroom, and on no account should they go near the windows.

By the time I joined Alan Grant and Brad in the firing positions on the forecourt, I did not need binoculars to watch the Germans approach. I felt the fear rising in my throat, like bile. Perhaps it was the waiting. Better to react than wait.

'They're pulling down the dyke at the side of the paddock,' shouted Robert MacDonald from an upstairs window. 'They're throwing down stones on the thorns in the ditch.'

And so we waited. And we watched. On the higher ground of Keppoch Moor across the loch, a winter's day was dawning. I could see the yellow light edging over the peat hags and the willow scrub by the shore. In the churn of emotions, concentrating and drifting, I kept seeing movements all around, but it was impossible to tell if it was the enemy, or birds, or my own imagination.

Once all of the German platoon, and what they were carrying, were across the tumbled dyke, the tall officer I had seen talking to MacCaig led them directly towards us, making no attempt to spread out, walking erect and not crouching like advancing infantry.

'They know we have only shotguns,' I shouted. 'They'll come close to us. Hold your positions.'

My God, I thought, what the hell do we do now? We can't touch them, even if they are only a hundred yards away.

*

Marilyn woke as the sun touched the tops of the pine trees. She must have slept, at least a little, and Lisa shifted, warm, snuggling closer, grunting as her eyes opened.

'Mom, my nose is cold.'

Marilyn looked around and sighed when she saw a stream glint in the shafts of sunlight only twenty yards away. As she cupped her hands to let Lisa drink, she realised that the sweet, peaty water would help them find their way back. The stream will flow downhill, she thought, and we will find the shore, eventually. But as she pushed Lisa's fair hair behind her ears and adjusted her Alice band to keep it in place, Marilyn looked up suddenly.

In the distance, she could hear an extraordinary sound. Like ripping cloth, it was the sound of gunfire, machine gun fire.

*

Capable of twelve hundred rounds a minute, only pausing to change the belt of bullets fed into its chamber, the MG 42 was a devastating weapon. Stengel had his men set up both machine guns, and they were pouring fire at the white façade of the house, shattering windows, ripping out the frames, riddling the porch with bullets, pockmarking the walls as the white harling flew off like shrapnel. The sound was deafening and in the back bedroom, the children were screaming, half-crazed with fear. Miriam tried to cover their ears, pulling them to her breast. It seemed that the old house shook as this withering fusillade hit it without cease for five eternal minutes.

As I kept my head down behind my turf and wood barrier, I remembered Sergeant Taylor, the landing craft and the first few terrifying minutes on Queen Beach.

When the machine gun fire at last stopped, the momentary silence seemed far away as our ears rang, but it was suddenly split by a roar from Robert from the first-floor window.

I looked up. The Germans were running at us, bayonets fixed, charging, like the clans at Culloden.

'Brad!' I screamed.

Both of us took aim at the teapots planted at either end of the hidden ditch. The Germans were picking up speed, but not firing at us. They were trying to storm the house.

'Wait!' I shouted to Brad. 'Wait!' And then, 'Now!'

We fired. The pots exploded, the first Germans reached the

fringe of fallen leaves, their boots went through the turf and a wall of fire leapt up and engulfed them. Explosives planted at the bottom of the ditch sent earth flying through the flames as most of Stengel's men fell in, screamed, clawing at the turf to get out of the inferno they had run headlong into. Human fireballs, coated in burning paraffin, four of them twisted and writhed as they reached the near side. Through the flames, I could see that the officer had managed to stop in time, with three or four of his men. I heard the sharp report of his pistol as he put those screaming in the hellish pit out of their misery.

*

The sound of machine gun fire had stopped but Marilyn had followed the stream out of the pine wood and now, at last, she could see the loch in the distance and, below where she and Lisa stood, a plume of blue smoke rose from the paddock in front of Darroch House. About one hundred and fifty yards further, and their path would reach the drystane dyke that skirted the sheltering wood.

'Stop! Do not move!'

Marilyn turned around to see a German soldier pointing his rifle at her chest. Two others ran up the hill to join them.

*

I stood up out of the firing position to look at a landscape from hell.

The paraffin incendiaries, and the fertilizer-fuelled explosives Brad had made, had been fearfully effective. The fire in the ditch raged on and the stink of burning flesh filled the air. Blackened bodies lay on either side. With the remnants of his platoon, the officer had retreated to the edge of the paddock where they had broken down the dyke, abandoning their machine guns.

'All of them. All of them,' shouted Bradley. 'We need to kill all of them!' His face streaked with mud, his hair wild, he seemed demented, a rage burning inside him.

Katie came running around the side of the house to see what had happened, and was horror-struck at how effective our defences had been.

I felt it was safe to pull back to the house, for the moment. Suddenly I felt parched and in the kitchen, its floor strewn with shards of shattered glass and wood from the window frame, we gulped water, looking all the time out at the paddock. The Germans had charged the house because they could not risk killing the American scientists. Now their numbers were reduced to only three and they had no more options open to them, except retreat. But Brad was right, although his motives were his own. We had to capture or kill the officer and his two men. If they made it back to Arisaig, they would call for reinforcements.

When I found Professor Feldman and his wife, both of them white with shock after the machine-gunning of the house, I told him that whatever happened, Katie and I had to get away soon. I asked him to keep my fishing bag safe with its contents: my journal and his document. Robert joined us to say that the Humber was ready. Our plan was to race out of the policies and cut off the Germans' retreat at Morroch Point.

But it turned out that they were not about to retreat.

The officer and five of his men were marching up the paddock towards the house. When I came out of the porch, I saw Alan and Jamie holding Bradley Kaye by his arms as he struggled and kicked at them. When the officer halted his men, only twenty yards from us, I saw that they had Marilyn and Lisa with them. Their hands had been tied behind their backs and the Germans had put nooses around their necks.

The little girl was sobbing, whispering, 'Mommy, Daddy,' over and over.

XIV

'Go! Go now,' hissed Robert MacDonald. 'There's a rowing boat moored just beyond the headland. Go! Both of you.'

While all eyes were on Marilyn, Lisa and an enraged Bradley Kaye, Katie and I slipped back into the house, found the fishing bag and left by the back door into the close. I still had Jamie's revolver and pouch of ammunition.

'Where is the boat, Katie?' She pointed west towards the ocean, to a scatter of rocky islets in Loch nan Ceall.

And we ran.

'Don't look back,' I said. Katie sat in the stern of the rowing boat while I pulled on the oars towards Arisaig quay. 'Just look at me. Or look at where we're going.' In truth, as I looked over her shoulder, I could make out little of what was happening in front of Darroch House. Inevitably our people would be forced to surrender, but perhaps one or two, like us, had escaped. Maybe more, maybe none. But I could not dwell on that. For any of it to mean anything, Katie and I had to get safely to Edinburgh, to the US consulate and to Averill Thomson and his ambassador.

I hoped against hope that he was indeed a stand-up guy.

As we came alongside the quay, I reached out to grab one of the mooring lines strung out along the side and pulled us close. The village was in chaos. Debris from the explosions lay everywhere and the hall was a smoking ruin. What came as a surprise – and a relief – was that no one was about to watch our passing. At least, no one I noticed.

Such as it was, our plan was to walk the coast road to Mallaig and hope we could catch the ferry to Oban. From there a train could take us to Glasgow and on to Edinburgh. Anything and everything could go wrong, but it seemed to me that we had no other option. It was a desperate gamble, a last throw, but to go in the opposite direction, take a train to Fort William, was much more likely to meet difficulties if the Germans called on reinforcements, as they surely would.

We walked in silence up the hill out of Arisaig and on past the moorland at Keppoch. Drifting once more, lulled by the hypnotic, metronomic rhythm of putting one foot in front of another, I thought of days long ago, of the first time I had seen this place. For me, the road to Mallaig winds along the most beautiful coastline in the world. At school, we were blessed to be taught by a classics master who instilled in me not only a love of language but also a love of the West Highlands. One Easter, he brought six of us to Morar to stay at a youth hostel at Garramor, not far from where Katie and I were walking. The landscape captured my young heart, the road turning and rising up to show me long vistas across the ocean to the islands of Rum, Eigg and Muck and to the grandeur of the Cuillin ridge on Skye. But the detail, close to, of the little coves, the white-sand beaches, the undulating dunes and all the colour of their flora meant that this place was not just cold, majestic spectacle, like Glencoe or the Torridon mountains. It had gentleness, softness and everywhere were the benign, light touches of human hands. All those sunlit years ago, I felt that God had taken my hand and I walked with him in the Garden.

As we made our way past Bunacaimb, Portnaluchaig, the glorious beach at Camusdarach and reached the bridge over the River Morar, I realised that, lost in my reverie, I had said nothing to Katie for an hour.

She was weeping, silent tears running down her cheeks.

The light was beginning to fade in the west. When we turned a corner, past the ribs of a wrecked fishing boat, there was a bench. Having no words, having no idea what was happening to her parents or her aunt and uncle, all I could do was hold her close and hold her tight as she began to sob, to let it out. Intent on Katie, waiting for the tears to run their course, I gazed at the islands on the edge of the ocean, the islands of the evening.

On the *Lochiel*, the Oban mailboat and ferry, we drank stewed tea with sugar as though it was nectar and ate scones, which were not young, with cheese and sticky jam. And felt better.

'I'll see if they have blankets so that we can sleep on the benches on the deck.' Anxious about my fishing bag and its contents, I wanted to be apart from other passengers. Near the stern, behind the funnels, we found a good place where the breeze was not strong.

Only one other passenger joined us on deck. A tall man in a long dark overcoat, wearing a trilby hat, he stood at the rail as the ferry swung out of Mallaig harbour and turned south past Eigg and Muck on its way to the Sound of Mull and the Firth of Lorne. After a few minutes, he went below.

In the cafeteria, I bought some cigarettes and, not having had tobacco for some time, we relished them. It seemed that luck was at last with us. Oban railway station is only a step, less than a hundred yards from the ferry terminal, and by a miracle, with only moments to spare, we caught the last train to Glasgow Queen Street.

*

Under the yellow light of a telephone box, the man in the trilby hat was dialling an Edinburgh number. 'Hi, Averill. Yes. It's Leonard here. Yes, Leonard Gregory. He's on his way, with his girl, and I don't think he spotted me. And no one else is following them.'

After Gregory and Averill Thomson replaced their receivers there was a second click on the line.

POSTSCRIPT

As we walked wearily up the steep steps out of Waverley station, David stopped and turned to me. On an impulse, it seemed, he asked me to carry the fishing bag with his journal and the vital document drawn up by Professor Feldman inside it.

'Let me go alone,' he said. 'I just want to be sure that nothing can go wrong. I don't know these people, the Americans.'

It was early in the morning of January 8th 1945 when David walked across Princes Street. To allow him to get ahead of me, I waited for a moment or two on the deserted pavement. Through the pale, dawning light, I looked west along the length of the empty street. The city seemed vast, ghostly, a faded memory of itself. When he reached Heriot Row, where the US consulate was, David was about a hundred yards in front of me. While he crossed the street to walk up the steps and ring the bell, I waited with the fishing bag under the shadows of the trees of the gardens opposite.

And then he died.

Everything happened at high speed. A car swerved around the corner. A man got out. Shot my David dead. Then, after opening David's coat, searching his clothing, the gunman got back in the car and it raced off.

I ran, ran for my life. I ran home.

EPILOGUE

Dawn, 17 June 1945

Inside the dovecote, the man shivered. For hours, almost exhausting the batteries of his torch, he had been reading, flicking back and forth through David Erskine's remarkable account. It was as John Grant, the old soldier, had said: an entirely different version of recent history, and its conclusions upended what had become accepted as the new world order. At last, it seemed, there was hope.

But Feldman's deception – the estimate of six months before a viable bomb could be produced – that concerned him greatly. Had the professor been able to sustain that? What would the Germans have threatened? Their wives, their families? Very likely.

But Professor Feldman's paper also encouraged him, even though he understood little of the detail. Clearly the scientists' work had been held back by the extraordinary events of Christmas 1944 and the first few days of January 1945. Nevertheless, they claimed that they were close to building a viable bomb, and here was all of the evidence, all of the calculations needed. Time was short. Perhaps it had already run out. But at last he had the hard, documentary evidence he desperately wanted and now he could move quickly. He wrapped the precious journal and the scientific paper carefully inside its protective oilskin.

When the man pulled open the wooden door of the dovecote and made to walk out into the early morning light, he felt the cold steel of the barrel of a gun press on his temple.

'Do not move,' said a voice. 'Stay exactly where you are. Keep looking straight ahead.'

The man felt a hand take the oilskin package out of his.

'Now, take one step forward and put your hands behind your back.'

Around his wrists, one at a time, handcuffs were clicked shut. He felt a hand push him hard in the back.

'Start walking towards Abbey House. Quickly! Move! If you turn around, the barrel of my gun will be the last thing you see.'

A slow, pink dawn was rising behind the trees along the riverbank and, one by one, the stars disappeared as a summer sun warmed the morning chill. When they reached the car parked outside the empty house with its windows boarded up, a rear passenger door was opened and the man was bundled in. The engine sputtered into life and they moved off.

'Tell me your name,' said the driver. 'Your real name, not the alias you've been using.'

The man could see the driver's eyes in the rear-view mirror. 'I'm Averill Thomson, from the US consulate. And is that Jamie Griffith-Smith's pistol you have, Katie?'

As she drove up the steep hill out of Dryburgh, Katie's tone did not soften. 'You may or may not be who you say you are. Bitter experience has taught me to trust no one.' She paused. 'And someone I loved died outside the American consulate.'

Once over the Tweed at Mertoun Bridge, she followed the winding road into St Boswells and, at the junction at the Green, where the gallows still stood, stark against the horizon, Katie turned north on the Edinburgh road.

'When I saw you hide from the Vigilantes who came to the hotel last night, I decided it was worth taking a chance. It took you much longer than I thought to solve it, but you persisted with the puzzle. And that encouraged me.'

The man shifted uncomfortably in the back seat. 'Katie, if you could take off these damn handcuffs, I could give you a card with my name on it.'

She looked in the mirror, said nothing and drove on into the hills.

'It was the dogtag, Katie,' said Thomson. 'I know this is painful for you to think about, but when we found David's body on our doorstep, we were able to identify him because he was still wearing his army dogtag.'

They had begun the long climb up Lauderdale into the green folds and steep-sided valleys of the Lammermuirs. Flocks of grazing ewes moved slowly across the flanks of the hills, summering out on the high pasture.

'And that's what brought me down to the Borders. That's how I was able to make contact with John Grant, your grandfather. I didn't know what you looked like, and when you introduced us at that talk on Roman antiquities a few months ago, you didn't give your name. And I never saw you again. Were you watching me all that time? I had no idea.'

Katie fought back the tears as she drove up to the long summit, the hill at Soutra. She could make no response, say nothing. The stone, the weight in her heart, would not shift and it stopped up her mouth. On the long, straight road across the watershed plateau, she tried and failed to begin a sentence, to ask a question. Since David's death, she had never felt more alone, more desolate in all her life. Glancing in the rear-view mirror, she saw Thomson smile a tight smile.

'Why don't you pull over?' he said. 'It's a beautiful morning. Perhaps we could sit and talk for a while?'

It seemed that all Scotland lay before them. From the roadside they looked down over the Lothians to the spires of Edinburgh and the castle rock, beyond to the Firth of Forth and across to Fife, and along the farthest horizon, the sentinel mountains of the Highland Line rose up through the morning mist. Scotland seemed unchanged, as it always was.

'Thank you,' said Thomson as Katie unlocked the handcuffs. But she kept her distance as they sat at either end of a crumbling old concrete bench much cracked by frost. And she kept the revolver in her hand.

'I ran home,' said Katie after a time, tears on the edge of her voice. 'All I could think was to come home to the Borders, and all I had left was my grandfather, John Grant.' She stopped and swallowed hard. 'And I don't have him now.' She paused once more. 'I made a copy of David's journal. It was a way of keeping him with me a little longer. I added a good deal, things I knew or realised had happened, or would make things clearer. I shall never forget what the Levinsons told me of the camp at Comrie. And then I hid the journal in the dovecote.'

Thomson held up his hand. 'Why didn't you simply just give it and Feldman's paper to your grandfather for safe-keeping?'

Katie shook her head and explained that she had seen what had happened to the people she loved and she could not put him in danger. So she told him a little, and set a puzzle. 'You had come down to the Borders by that time, and I wanted to set a test. I knew that my grandfather liked you. He knew he was dying and I was certain he would pass all he had on to you. But I never asked him if he trusted you. Death always comes suddenly, even when you expect it. So, for the last few weeks, I have followed you and watched you going to Dryburgh Abbey all those times, watched you making calls from telephone boxes.' Katie had never let go of Jamie's revolver, simply laying it on her lap. 'And I still don't know if I can trust you. You may have been talking to the Germans, making calls to them. Everyone else seems to have given up, given in.'

The sun had begun to climb high in the summer sky and Thomson shaded his eyes with his hand. 'All right, Katie. To show our bona fides, I'm going to tell you everything I know, and break several federal laws in the process. Although we didn't get the journal or the scientists' paper – the Germans were clearly following both of you on that morning in January – we were able to corroborate one or two elements of the story. The hangings at Berwick, St Boswells and St Andrews became common knowledge. We knew Jews were being rounded up and, from Millie's telephone call, we understood what was going on at St Andrews. But we needed to know much, much more of what happened.'

As Thomson rubbed his welted wrists, he blew out his cheeks and sighed loudly. 'Okay. What I'm going to tell you now is highly classified. You may not trust me, but I'm going to trust you. After my sister called me, the ambassador spoke directly with President Roosevelt. Our assessment was and remains that the Germans' military dominance is much more apparent than real. Leaving the atomic bomb that destroyed London to one side, their army is actually in very poor shape. Although they have appropriated a great deal of our equipment and supplies, their armed forces were much more depleted than we thought, badly led after all of those purges, and exhausted. We believe that they can be defeated using conventional weapons. We'll attempt to build a bomb with Feldman's findings, but its use would, I'm certain, be a very last resort. And there is one other vital element. We still have eyes and ears in Germany, and it became clear that the laboratory at Oranienburg, where we think the London bomb was made, was completely destroyed by the RAF.'

Thomson paused, took a deep breath. 'More than that – and this really is most sensitive – we're certain that the Nazi leadership is in turmoil. Hitler may be sick. Who knows, but his decision-making appears to have simply ceased. We understand that he has become even more delusional, refusing to leave the

251

bunker in Berlin, refusing to believe that the Russians have surrendered. Goebbels is running things. He does everything in Hitler's name and seems able to manipulate him to sign all and any directives. We think that the Germans may indeed be bluffing about the existence of more bombs and David's journal adds a great deal to that assessment. It's a strategy with Goebbels' fingerprints all over it. It's the biggest of his Big Lies.'

Katie had been able to gather herself a little. 'But you need the journal and Professor Feldman's paper to convince the White House to act?'

Thomson nodded. 'It's the missing piece. But we also had a difficult hiatus. With President Roosevelt's death two months ago, we could not be sure that President Truman would see things in the same way. But in our last exchange, he put forward a simple view. Somehow, we had to find a way to resist. The world would continue to plunge into an abyss of evil, or darkness, if we did not act. And I think that when the president sees the journal, or a digest of it, along with the scientific paper, he'll act, decisively.'

Looking out over the vast panorama, over Scotland in the fresh, summer sunshine, Katie stared for a long time, breathing the clear air. 'I need to know two things.' And at this, her voice wavered. 'What happened to my parents?'

She gasped and put her hand to her mouth, her breath shuddering, fighting for control, as she heard Thomson say, 'We cannot be sure, but we think they're alive, imprisoned with the MacDonalds and the Griffith-Smiths at the camp at Comrie. There may be a link with the work going on at St Andrews. It may be that Professor Feldman has struck some sort of bargain – maybe accelerated progress in return for their lives. Something like that. Or the Germans may want to put them on trial once they have the bomb. We simply don't know. And please, Katie, this is not meant to sound like a condition, or some kind of bargaining chip . . . but if you feel you can let us have the journal and Professor Feldman's paper, President Truman would be prepared to authorise a special forces raid on the camp to free them. We still have the capability to do that.'

Katie could keep back the tears no longer and she wept bitterly for what had been lost, and for what might be redeemed.

Letting her be for a few minutes, Thomson bided his time, and then asked, 'What's the second thing?'

She looked up at him, fixing him directly and steadily, silent tears running down her face. 'Where is David buried?'

*

'Hi. Jack? Yes, it's Averill Thomson here.' He was in a telephone box in St Andrew Square in Edinburgh. 'At exactly 11 a.m., I'll walk up the steps to the consulate carrying a package of the utmost importance. To reassure my contact, will you please look out for me at exactly that time and open the door without me ringing the bell?'

When they parked in Heriot Row, where David Erskine had died five months before, Katie looked along the street in both directions but could see nothing suspicious. At last, she gave Averill the package. Speaking calmly, fighting down the tears, Katie said, 'This is all I have of him. Please take it to your ambassador and make the best use of it you can.'

And with that, she walked up the cobbled street to St Cuthbert's Cemetery to look for David.

29 June 1945

Seventy-Ninth Congress of the United States of America;

At the First Session,

Begun and held at the City of Washington on Friday,
the twenty-ninth day of June, 1945.

JOINT RESOLUTION

Declaring That a State of War Exists Between the Government
of Germany and the Government and the People of the United
States and Making Provision To Prosecute the Same.

Resolved by the Senate and House of Representatives of the United States of America in Congress assembled. That the state of war between the United States and the Government of Germany which has thus been thrust upon the United States is hereby formally declared; and the President is hereby authorized and directed to employ the entire naval and military forces of the United States and the resources of the Government to carry on war against the Government of Germany; and, to bring the conflict to a successful termination, all of the resources of the country are hereby pledged by the Congress of the United States.

(Signed) Sam Rayburn, Speaker of the House of Representatives.
(Signed) Kenneth D. McKellar, President of the Senate.
Approved June 29th, 1945, 3:05 PM E.S.T.
(Signed) Harry S. Truman, President of the United States.

Acknowledgements

This novel began life in March 2020 as Britain was locking down in the face of the Covid pandemic. The idea was to supply some online diversion, what I hoped might be a ripping yarn to be serialised on my publisher's website. A bit of fun, certainly for me, and maybe for a few readers. But when the story took on a life of its own and began to move faster and faster, I could barely keep up and completed it far in advance of any deadline.

Jan Rutherford at Birlinn encouraged me enormously in writing what was my first novel, and Hugh Andrew and Andrew Simmons added their enthusiasm and great expertise. When the manuscript was sent to Craig Hillsley to be edited, it improved once more and I learned a great deal as versions travelled back and forth on the ether. I have written a lot of non-fiction, mainly history, but I quickly discovered that novels are very different and Craig introduced me to a new set of necessary sensibilities and I am very grateful to him.

I am blessed to have a group of long-suffering friends who read and fact-check my non-fiction, and when I sent them this manuscript, many helpful suggestions came back. I thank them all for their kindness.

I'm grateful to everyone who helped me improve *The Night Before Morning* and I had so much fun writing it, making stuff up.

Alistair Moffat
Selkirk
June 2021